TEMPERING

THE ROSE

Other Books by Dionne Lister

The Circle of Talia YA Fantasy Series

Shadows of the Realm
A time of Darkness
Realm of Blood and Fire

Short story collection

Dark Spaces

Women's Fiction under Eloise March

Close Call (A Doris & Jemma Vadgeventure)

TEMPERING THE ROSE

Book 1

The Rose of Nerine Fantasy Series

Dionne Lister

First Published 2016
First Paperback Edition
ISBN: 978-0-9946025-0-3

Cataloguing-in-Publication details are available from the National Library of Australia **www.librariesaustralia.nla.gov**

Published by
Dionne Lister
Sydney, Australia

About the Author

Dionne Lister is a Sydneysider with a degree in creative writing, two Siamese cats, and is a member of the SFWA. Daydreaming has always been her passion, so writing was a natural progression from staring out the window in primary school, and being an author was a dream she held since childhood.

Unfortunately, writing was only a hobby while Dionne worked as a property valuer in Sydney, until her mid-thirties when she returned to study and completed her creative writing degree. Since then, she has indulged her passion for writing while raising two children with her husband. Her books have attracted praise from Apple iBooks and have reached #1 on Amazon and iBooks charts worldwide, frequently occupying top 100 lists in fantasy.

Dionne has worked as an editor, has published a YA epic fantasy series called The Circle of Talia, and is currently writing The Rose of Nerine fantasy series. You can find Dionne on her website www.dionnelisterwriter and other social media.

Dedication

To all those who struggle against injustices every day, I dedicate this book to you. Know that you are truly special and worthy of everything good in this world, and that although the universe has worked against you, it is not because you are inadequate. The universe has a lot to answer for.

Chapter One

Addy crouched on the roof and stared over the parapet to the cobbled street below. A royal seeker stood watchful at the whorehouse door across the street. The dim light from a wall lantern threw his angular features into shadow. The threat of his scowl and the sword hanging from his hip would be enough to keep most people away. But not Addy. Not tonight.

The crisp air burned in her throat. Her thumb caressed the smooth timber of her bow. Back and forth. Back and forth. The rhythm did little to soothe her nerves, and she bit her bottom lip. The sting of it occupied her mind, keeping negative thoughts from sending her into retreat. In her other hand, she gripped a cold arrow shaft so hard her nails dug deep half-moon indentations into her palm.

She had dreamed of this moment for the past seven years. Once her arrow pierced her father's heart, she could get on with her life. At twenty-one, she was young enough to have a future — one far from the city of Pyren, no doubt — but it was more than she had been brave enough to believe in before escaping her mother's indifference and father's abuse five years earlier.

What if my mission goes wrong? The searing image of a long-suppressed memory ignited, like a flash of lightning. Her thumb ceased stroking. She missed a breath. Nervous energy spread from her chest into her throat, and Addy inhaled slowly to calm herself. She blinked, trying to clear her mind, then refocused on the closed door.

She would never go back. Death was preferable to ending up where she had started — under the *care* and control of High Seeker Radnok and her addict mother.

Addy tilted her head to one side then the other, stretching her neck. Her gaze never left the whorehouse door. If she missed this opportunity, there would be no other. She would be on the run, or dead.

The seeker stepped quickly to the side as the door opened. Harp notes cascaded out with the haze of smoke and two more seekers; the men beckoned to a horse-drawn carriage waiting nearby. The horses moved forward, the strike of hooves on stone breaking through Addy's focus, making her start.

She stood.

Relaxing one hand took great effort. Addy swiftly nocked an arrow. String taut, she rested her icy hand against her face, the comforting pressure of the bowstring against her cheek helping her focus. *Any moment now. You can do this, Addy.*

High Seeker Radnok stepped through the gloom. His footfalls matched the clack of hoof on stone as he moved into the light, into range. He was as she remembered — tall, broad-shouldered, arrogance in the tilt of his head, dark beard framing a sneering mouth.

Addy inhaled deeply then held her breath, trying to temper her racing heart. The carriage moved closer. It would soon block her shot.

No more time.

Radnok lifted his gaze from the approaching carriage and looked right at her, his eyes widening.

Her hands shook. Another flash of memory. Blinded again.

Never going back.

The clop of hooves.

Shouts.

Never going back.

Radnok's face relaxed, his surprise disappearing.

She reached deep inside for the burning fire in her belly. The cocooning molasses of calm the fire brought slowed the world. Harp notes vibrated longer and became deeper. Her vision intensified — things far away seemed closer. Radnok's hateful face was so clear. She could even see the smirk line next to his mouth.

Despite the world moving slower for her, Addy's heart galloped with fear. She saw the triumph in Radnok's eyes, saw it turn into something worse. He thought he had won.

Between one heartbeat and the next, she released.

Chapter Two

Music that reminded him of spring and another life filtered into the large, warm kitchen. He daydreamed of his wife's face … well, ex-wife. He had abandoned Mayna and his three children the day he'd deserted his post. It was the day his dreams and hope had died. His chest constricted with pain — he longed to hold his family in his arms again.

'Kerwyn the Coward' and 'Kerwyn the Deserter' his former comrades had named him that day. Those men had been his friends — how easily they'd shut him out. But they were right; he had deserted them when he decided he was done with Radnok's vileness. He clenched his fist as anger heated his cheeks. Because of Radnok, Kerwyn had lost his pride, his livelihood, and his family.

When Lyssa appeared in the doorway, his heart beat faster, and he almost believed it was Mayna. But the large expanse of lily-white bosom pushing out of her lusciously tight dress, and the tickle in his nose of her rose-petal perfume, soon brought him back to where he really was — a brothel. He licked his lips.

Lyssa's brow was creased, her words low and hastily spoken. "High Seeker Radnok is here! You have to go."

Kerwyn narrowed his eyes and clenched his jaw. Would he ever be free? Running was not his preference, but it seemed to have become a habit. He longed to stand up to Radnok, to hold him accountable for the evil he had done, but today was not the day. Acid rose in Kerwyn's throat. *You are the coward they named you. Go on, coward, run, like you always do.*

Lyssa reached him as he gulped the last mouthful of mulled wine to wash down the aftertaste of failure. Kerwyn stood. Lyssa gave him a brief hug; then he strode to the back door of Love 'n Ale Whorehouse. His dirty fingers fumbled as he clumsily turned the knob. With no time to brace for the cold outside, he nodded a hasty thanks to Lyssa and stepped out.

He shut the door and forced himself to walk quickly rather than run down the alley. Noticing the forgotten mug clutched in his hand, he hated himself more. Kerwyn threw it with all the force he could muster, and it smashed loudly on the cobbled ground, scattering pieces of porcelain about the laneway.

Kerwyn the Coward. Well fucking deserved. The one sanctuary you have, but when he turns up, you scurry like a cockroach surprised by the light.

When Kerwyn reached the end of the dark thoroughfare, he turned left. Another laneway brought him to the better-lit main street. With a glance at the seeker guarding the doorway — Farbyn was his name — he put his head down and crossed the road. He heard coarse throat clearing, then Farbyn spat. Kerwyn clenched his fists but kept going.

Fucking murderers. I'll make you all pay one day. Their laughter echoed in his head as he remembered their reaction when he had uttered those words. They had seen him sink even lower than their opinion of him — destitute, begging. Why was he even alive? The gods knew he had nothing to offer the world. Too much of a coward to be a seeker, then too much of a coward to do what he knew was right.

A horse whinnied. Radnok's conveyance, waiting for its master — the leader of the king's Royal Seeker Network. What Kerwyn wouldn't give to be able to escape the cold and lie inside the carriage for just a short while, but that would be too risky.

A rosy hue disturbed the corner of his vision. He jerked up his head. A faint pink glow shone from atop one of the roofs overlooking the street. He blinked, not quite believing. "Holy Ephrestine, it can't be," Kerwyn whispered. He had never thought he'd see this in his lifetime: legend in the flesh. The shelon wasn't strong yet — the aura was too translucent, but the colour....

"Var's balls." A puff of white accompanied his whispered curse. He turned his head away then looked up again, just to be sure. What was The Rose of Nerine doing here? She was a being of prophecy, the one Ephrestine's disciples had been waiting for.

He glanced at the seeker guarding the door. "Pig shit." If Farbyn saw her, she'd be captured, tortured, and killed. Luckily, Farbyn was one of Radnok's less experienced seekers, his gift of *sight* weak. Yet still, he needed to warn her. But how? The past four years of living rough, in particular the past month in the cold, had slowed his once-agile body. At thirty-five, he was no longer a lad who could perform physical feats on a whim.

Shouting to the shelon on the roof would only draw the seeker's attention. Did he have the strength to knock Farbyn out and yell at her to run? Did she even know what she was, who she was? If she did, she wouldn't have come at night when her aura was like a beacon to any seeker worth his place in the network. He tried not to look at her again, in case Farbyn followed his lead.

The only way to warn her was to join her on the roof, and since the building would be locked, reaching her would involve Kerwyn scaling the exterior. He shook his head, disappointed. That was never going to happen. He nervously rubbed his fingertips together, anticipating her discovery. It was like watching a galloping horse throw a rider — you knew it was going to be bad, but there was nothing you could do.

So, what was she doing here, in a country that hated her kind?

The whorehouse door opened. Two seekers emerged and cast dismissive glances at Kerwyn before calling Radnok's driver.

The horses moved forward. Each sharp hoof strike pulled the tension in his body tighter.

High Seeker Radnok appeared, silhouetted in the smoke and light that beckoned from the brothel's seductive interior. There had been a time when Kerwyn had thought Radnok a kindly man, taking in a bastard teenager to work for the king, to be a seeker no less. That time was long gone. Fear warred with Kerwyn's desire to do the right thing, and he hesitated.

Don't look up, Radnok. For the gods' sakes, don't look up. I need to warn her. His legs wouldn't move. The scars on his back itched — inflicted by Radnok the day Kerwyn had deserted his post. Kerwyn stood unmoving, as if thick ropes threaded through his feet and anchored him to the ground.

Radnok swivelled his head around and looked up. His mouth twitched, triumphant, smug, just before he dove forward, rolled and stood, in one smooth motion.

Lyssa, who lingered just outside the door to bid her client farewell, stiffened. Her mouth drew in a surprised breath, and she looked down, to the shaft protruding from her heart. She tried to grip the door frame, but her delicate hand slid futilely down the wood as she slumped to her knees.

No! His beautiful friend. *Why? This can't be happening. Not Lyssa.*

Kerwyn couldn't let her die alone. It was a small thing to give, but it was all he had. "Lyssa!" Kerwyn ran to her, despair dulling his desire for self-preservation. Whatever Radnok would do to him was worth the risk of holding his friend one last time.

When he reached the ring of light cast by the wall lamp, one of the young seekers, who had followed Radnok out, punched Kerwyn in the sternum. Searing pain exploded in the middle of his chest, stealing his breath. Kerwyn clutched his chest as he fell. He slammed onto his back, the air driven from him once again. He gasped, needing a breath. Nothing happened for a few moments, panic rising inside him, but then it came — sweet, blessed air. He ravenously gulped as much as he could.

Radnok's excited voice sounded clear over Kerwyn's rasping inhalations, the whinnying horses, cursing seekers, and cries of the prostitutes who had seen their sister fall. "Leave him until later. Get the shelon. Hurry!"

Dragging in another breath, Kerwyn stared at his friend, her body slumped on the pavement. Her closed eyes would never again meet his in a flirtatious exchange; her sweet words, honest words that had kept him clinging to the gossamer hope of staying alive long enough to see his family again, be worthy of them, would never again be spoken. He shut his eyes tightly, wringing a tear from one. Against the freezing air, the tear scalded his skin as it carved a path down the side of his face. It reached his jawline, hanging for a moment before losing its precarious hold and falling to the ground. Hope and love fell through the abyss with it.

The brothel mistress appeared. She observed Lyssa then gazed around, her hands on her hips, the displeasure in her voice evident. "Who did this? Someone will have to pay. She was one of my best workers. Girls, get inside. You have work to do. I will not have my paying customers inconvenienced." She ushered them inside before addressing the bereft girl kneeling next to Lyssa. "Ellen, you may remain. Your next client is not for another twenty minutes." The mistress shook her head at Kerwyn and stretched a cold smile across her face for Radnok before she returned inside, back to work.

Radnok stared down at Kerwyn with dark eyes, his gold earrings glinting in the light. The seeker drew his foot back then slammed his boot into Kerwyn's stomach. Grunting, Kerwyn curled into a ball, sharp pain tearing through his stomach to his back. He tried to breathe then winced, waiting for the next blow.

Radnok's voice receded as he returned inside. "Farbyn, I won't use the carriage right now. Bring the girl to me when she's caught. I have need of more entertainment this night."

The door slammed shut. Kerwyn shivered on the icy ground, his cheeks, nose, and fingers already numbing. Ellen sobbed quietly over Lyssa's lifeless form.

Kerwyn prayed the shelon had escaped, but it wouldn't be thanks to him. He didn't even have the strength to look up to see if she had gone. The coward in him had won again. Recounting his many other failures, and afraid for his estranged family's safety should Radnok want to punish him further, he shut his eyes and willed death to take him before morning.

Chapter Three

Radnok jumped out of the way, and her arrow embedded into the whore's chest. Bile rose in Addy's throat. *Oh, gods. Oh, gods! I'm so sorry. This wasn't supposed to happen.* How had Radnok known she was there? Her heart hammered; she had killed an innocent person, and Radnok was still alive. *Please forgive me, Telouse.* Regret and dread darkened her thoughts.

Radnok's loud, confident orders for his men to catch her easily reached her perch three floors above the street.

Addy ran to the other side of the roof, tucking her arm into her bow so it rested securely on her shoulder. She burrowed her hands into her long coat sleeves and gripped the rope she had tied in place earlier. Using her sleeves to stop the rope burning her palms, she stood on the parapet, turned to face the roof, and descended.

She landed in a crouch, sprinted across the laneway, and scaled the brick fence of a darkened terrace house. Across the grassed yard she ran, but there was no way out between buildings. It was either go up and over the roof, or break in and go through.

Quiet footfalls sounded from the other side of the fence. Addy froze and listened without making a sound, but the footsteps stilled. Hands appeared at the top of the wall.

Addy forced down panic. Silence no longer necessary, she grabbed her dagger and smashed it hilt-first into a window then used her covered elbow to bat the debris out of the way before climbing in. The window wasn't wide, and she had to twist her shoulders to fit, her hips touching the edges of the window frame as she slid through.

"Who's there?" a man called.

"Sorry, just passing through." Unable to see in the dark, Addy crawled along the floor, ignoring the need to jump up and run as fast as she could.

"Lassie, you be trespassing. Get out of my house, now!" A man appeared in front of her. Dingy light scarcely illuminated her surroundings when the man removed the shutter from his lamp to reveal a small flame.

"If you'd show me the way, I'll gladly leave." She stepped towards him.

"Who's gonna pay for the broken window?"

Addy reached the man as one seeker, grunting and wheezing, squeezed through the opening.

"Sorry," she said as she pushed past the man and felt her way down the hallway.

A seeker's voice came from the gloom, only feet away. "That stupid shelon is glowing brighter than a funeral pyre after a plague. Thanks for lighting our way, bitch."

Addy couldn't stop to puzzle out what the seeker meant. With the lamplight not reaching the hall, she stretched her arms out in front to check for obstacles. Addy walked as quickly as she could down what she hoped was the hallway leading to the front door.

Sweat dampened her brow, and she had a strong urge to ditch her coat. Heavy footfalls sounded, coming from behind her, which meant both seekers were inside, and they were close.

The home's resident called out, "Hey, you can't go in there. Who are y—" His voice stopped, followed by a thud.

Addy's back tingled with awareness and dread, and she fought the need to run, expecting the seeker's hands on her at any moment. The seeker must be right behind her, ready to strike.

"There you are."

Eyes wild, Addy turned, dagger held in front. Swallowing her fear, she said, "Come near me, and I'll slice you more times than a barbecued pig on feast day."

He laughed. "You may be shelon, but if you had any real power, you would have used it by now. That aura of yours is as weak as coward's piss."

She took a tentative step back, then another. The air in the hall was cool, foreboding. The seeker's hulking mass was just out of reach, and Addy's skin crawled at his nearness. He was almost touching her. She shuddered.

"What have I missed?" It was the other seeker, forced to stand behind his friend in the narrow interior.

"Nothing. Disappointingly, this will be one of the easiest retrievals we've ever made. High Seeker Radnok will be pleased." Addy could hear the smile in his voice, his shadowed face too dark to read.

She stepped back again, and again. Her bow clacked as it bumped a solid object, and she started. Dagger poised in front, she felt for a bar behind her with the other hand. *Please be a door. Please.* And there it was — nothing had ever felt as good beneath her fingers as that timber edge.

The seekers' breaths were audible in the small space, their shallow inhalations becoming faster, louder.

Addy reached for the heat in her belly before focusing on her arm. The why of it escaped her, but she was stronger when she concentrated on and guided the force within. The bar lifted easily, and she pulled it forward. As soon as she released it, she jumped to her left. Her shoulder struck the wall, but there was enough of a gap for the door to scrape past her.

The seeker lunged. Addy pulled the door all the way open, slamming it into him.

"Whore!"

Satisfied, she leapt through the space and ran.

Frigid air slapped her face as she vaulted the low perimeter fence. She had scoped out the area earlier, and if she continued down this street, there would be another, and another — a dead end would mean the end of her. Terror at what Radnok would do to her gifted her speed, and she desperately drew in one grating breath after another. Why had those seekers called her "shelon"? She wasn't a heathen magic user — surely her Treloahn heritage was proof of that.

Footfalls thudded on the street behind her.

The city park was only two blocks away. If she could reach it, she would have more of a chance. She could release more arrows and skewer those bastards before she disappeared.

Addy reached the end of the street, almost slipping on the icy surface as she sped around the corner ... straight into someone running the other way. The impact slammed the air from her, and she hit the ground hard. Pain shot from her shoulder down her arm. Dark-clothed legs quickly surrounded her, arms reaching down.

Aggressive hands pulled Addy to her feet and ripped her bow from her arm. Her throbbing shoulder made her wince. Not wanting them to see her weakness, she did her best to scowl, which was easier than she would have thought. She met her captors' gazes one by one; maybe this could be turned around. If she could get close to that piece-of-shit Radnok, she would have another chance to finish what she had started.

As they followed two other seekers, Addy squirmed and twisted against the hold of the two men who dragged her the short distance to the whorehouse. The man on her right almost lost his hold. "Var's balls! She's a feisty one, eh, Tanner?"

The other seeker, Tanner — a tall, wiry man — pulled hard on Addy's upper arm. "Stupid bitch. Want me to break it?" Sharp pain speared to her shoulder.

Addy kicked out, connecting with the side of his shin. The seeker grunted and stopped before pivoting and facing Addy. His eyes coldly regarded her, and Addy leaned back, fearing the violence promised in his gaze. Radnok's eyes had always darkened with the same craziness before he had inflicted pain on her, and she fought to keep her eyes from revealing her terror; she knew this seeker would gain power from her distress. His strong fingers tightened around her arm while he pushed the hood off her head with his other hand.

Her thoughts raced as she desperately attempted to figure a way out of his hold. He tangled his fingers in her hair and grabbed a thick section. Wrenching her head back, he exposed her throat. Pain radiated from the base of her neck. Was he going to kill her? Hopelessness threatened to overwhelm her, and her heartbeat pulsed in her throat. She had a sudden need to piss. There was no escaping this time. *Don't give up, Addy. Don't you dare give up.*

He leant over her, his face an inch from hers, the stink of rotting meat emanating from his mouth. She breathed faster, shallower, panic gripping her as surely as the seeker did. She couldn't turn from his fetid breath because of his hold on her, and she coughed, trying to rid her body of his disgusting, exhaled air. She stared at the dark sky. *Please, mighty Telouse, help me. I don't want to die.* Addy had never heard of their god intervening to help a mortal, but it didn't stop her from hoping.

Tanner's breath rolled over her face as he spoke in a low, terse voice. "Master Radnok wants you alive, or he would have told us to kill you, but that doesn't mean accidents can't happen." He yanked her head back again, the underside of her jaw aching as everything stretched. That was useful information. None of Radnok's seekers would dare contravene his orders. It didn't mean she was safe, far from it if this seeker was taking her to Radnok, but she had time to escape. That's all she needed — just a bit more time. Her breath came more evenly, and her thoughts slowed.

"One more fucking twitch and we'll do much more than break your arm. Understand?"

Addy stared upwards, stubbornness and the desire to show no fear staying her lips. The seeker released her arm and soon had something sharp at her throat. Despite the frigid air that partly numbed her exposed flesh, Addy felt the tip of what she assumed was a dagger pushing into her skin. The thump of her heart drummed in her ears.

The seeker leant over further to stare through his straight, blonde fringe into her eyes. "Do. You. Understand?" The knife pressure increased.

She wanted to spit in the bastard's face, but she hadn't suffered through this life to let Radnok win. "Yes," she answered through gritted teeth. The pressure disappeared, and the seeker dropped her tresses, not bothering to replace her hood. Both seekers secured her arms again, and as they walked, Addy resented each placid step. *Son of an Ephrestine-worshipping heathen. By the time I escape, you'll be dead too.*

To distract herself, she reflected on her apparent "aura". Only Nerinians with two shelon parents had auras, and she wasn't one. She had been born in Treloah. Her parents could not be descended from shelon; it would mean forfeiting their right to live in Treloah, and it would lead to their torture and death. Her fa— the man who had fathered her, Radnok, could not have Nerinian heritage. That would be the irony of the century — the man who hunted and abused his own kind. No, that was unbelievable. So how?

The stone walls of Love 'n Ale came into view. The corpse of the unfortunate woman she'd killed lay to the side of the door. Addy swallowed, and tears of guilt moistened her eyes. *What evil have I done? Holy Telouse, I'm more like Radnok than I thought. She's dead because of me. Dead. I'm so sorry.* She hung her head, ashamed and appalled. By killing Radnok, she would save many from harm, there was no doubt, but she didn't want to kill faultless bystanders in her quest for justice.

A dark shape that appeared to be a pile of rags lay next to the corpse. As they neared, the shape shivered. Addy was suspicious of most people, avoided them if truth be told, but seeing these two pathetic figures, knowing she could easily be one of them, allowed tears to leak through her carefully constructed barrier.

Muffled music greeted them when they reached the whorehouse. The tall seeker pushed Addy in the back, forcing her down. Her knees slammed into the cobblestones. "Fuck!" The pain doubled her over, and she hugged herself, rocking back and forth trying to ride out the excruciating pain that speared from her knees down to her shins.

Someone ripped her quiver from her back, snapping the leather strap. *Not my arrows, no!* Pain like fire burned through her injured shoulder as her hands were bound behind her back, but she resisted as best she could, twisting one way and then the other, at least making it more difficult for her captors. Her bonds secured, the pain from her shoulder pulsed down her arm, the ache making her wince. She needed something else to focus on. Choosing the pile of rags rather than the red-stained body, Addy searched for the person's face among the fabric debris. His bearded chin and dirt-smeared cheeks formed out of the gloom, but his eyes were closed.

Who had he been before this? From what heights had he fallen? Would they both be dead by morning, united by the basest of occurrences?

Louder. The music was louder. Addy looked up to see Radnok, the man who had no right to call her daughter. Pushing all the years of festering hate into her eyes, she matched his steely gaze and ignored the urge to run, to cry, to close her eyes and curl into a ball on the icy ground. Whatever was to come, she would not look away. She would die with her pride in place. She would not let him control how she saw herself. Never again. Let him remember her defiance, not her weaknesses.

"Good work, my seekers." He bent slightly, removing his glove. Addy refused to break eye contact, but she remembered those hands well and swallowed — the softness of his skin proclaiming a man who had never undertaken hard labour in his life, the long, elegant fingers, strong fingers that had no boundaries. Fingers that had brought her pain and pleasure she wanted to forget. She had often dreamed of chopping those fingers off, one by one, before slicing off his hands and watching him bleed to death.

He struck her cheek, forcing her head to the right, the slap a percussive embellishment to the harp that still played. There was no soothing the stinging, with both hands secured behind her back, but then his fingers were there, and he gently drew them across her painfully tingling skin. Addy jerked her head away, trying to avoid his vile touch. She blinked away tears and saw the vagrant staring at her, sadness and apology in his eyes. *Even the lowest of the low pity me. Why was I even born? Telouse, please help me.* Her god had never answered her prayers before. She hoped this time would be different.

"I see you've lost your necklace." His finger trailed from one side of her throat to the other. Disgust turned her stomach. Addy willed Radnok to move his finger nearer her mouth so she could bite it off.

As much as she loathed Radnok, she also hated her weakness, knowing she hadn't lost her parents' gift — the necklace. When her mother had given Addy the platinum chain with the rose pendant to her on her eleventh birthday, she had told Addy she loved her, and that she should never take it off. The necklace was supposed to be a symbol of her mother's love. Addy had finally admitted to herself that her mother didn't love her four years after she had escaped; it was then she had taken it off. She was ashamed to admit she still carried it, in a hidden pocket sewn into her boot.

Radnok bent down and spoke quietly, so only Addy could hear his smooth voice that pulsed with the promise of violence and his barely contained pleasure. "It's about time you returned. I have plans for you ... plans that will change our world. I'm sure your mother will be pleased to see you. You have worried her with your childish behaviour. But no more.

You will be punished accordingly." He pinched her chin hard between thumb and index finger. Radnok looked from her to one of the seekers, a portly man with greasy dark hair gathered with leather cord at the back of his neck. "Bring her to the questioner's cell. We'll have some fun."

One man at each arm, she was hauled to her feet. *No, no, no, no!* She looked at Radnok, her eyes threatening. *I'll fucking kill myself before I let you touch me again.* She tried, unsuccessfully, to twist out of the seekers' hold, their fingers gouging harder.

"No!" A voice, low, gravelly. The air stretched with tension, like a taut bow in the moment before the arrow flies. Everyone stopped, except the vagrant, who rose stiffly.

Addy blinked, and hope grew within her. Could this broken man help her escape, or would she be responsible for yet another innocent life lost?

Radnok turned, stared at the man as if he wanted him dead. "You dare to interrupt the work of the seekers?"

The man straightened and rolled back his shoulders, as though preparing for battle. His laugh was wry. "You call that work? Being part of your *work* sickened me. I've lost everything because of it. I'm ready to die, but before I do, I will do something I should have long ago. I will do what is right." The vagrant smiled, and Addy sensed he was truly happy. He launched himself at Radnok, the glint of a small dagger blinking against the darkness of his rags.

Addy, not wanting to miss her chance, however small, kicked, landing a blow into Radnok's balls. She screamed an incoherent battle cry and writhed violently, trying to loosen the hold of the men who gripped so hard their fingers dug painfully into her arms. She drew from the cauldron in her belly. With a burst of strength, she threw herself to the ground, jerking the seekers off balance to fall with her. In her briefly altered state, her action seemed like sinking through water rather than falling, but she hit the ground hard enough. Unfortunately, the slowness was only in her head.

Their hands slipped off, and while they tried to stand, Addy jumped up to run. Two seekers waited, one she recognised from the earlier chase. Two more seekers held the brave vagrant. He had made little difference to her chances, but at least he had drawn blood. Addy admired him for that and smiled at the thought that Radnok had suffered at least some discomfort. Radnok wiped the cut under his eye, smearing crimson across his cheek before punching her would-be saviour in the face. Blood gushed from his nose, coating his lips and chin.

Addy's satisfaction turned in her stomach. *Smear-of-shit.* She wanted to kill Radnok right now, but she was far outnumbered. Instead, her guilt for abandoning the vagrant not strong enough to stop her, she pivoted and ran. The seekers were on her immediately, tackling her. She had no hands with which to break her fall. *This is going to hurt like a —*

Addy was aware of the thud when her skull met the ground. Needle pricks of pain gouged a path through her head. Though she fought it with everything she had, darkness such as she had never known drew her into its deathly embrace.

Chapter Four

Her first thought as she woke was *how much mead did I drink last night?* Her second thought was Radnok's triumphant sneer. Disappointment and anger emerged when she remembered why she had blacked out. Images came unbidden: the prostitute dead; Radnok standing over her; a homeless man. Jumping back in time, an image of her mother's terrified face appeared — Addy at eleven, Radnok holding her hand to take her away to a seeker stronghold. But more than her face, Addy remembered her mother standing still, her expression indifferent as she watched her daughter dragged to a fate worse than death.

Needing to escape her past, and despite her queasy stomach, she tentatively opened one eye, and then the other. Moving faster than she thought possible in her agonised state, she rolled onto her side and vomited onto a hard-packed dirt floor.

Coughing from above and a muffled voice sent fear skittering through her. "Can you sit?"

Unable to defend herself, Addy closed her eyes to steady her spinning head and prayed no one attacked her. She sat slowly and opened her eyes again, looking up as she did, hoping not to see a seeker.

The vagrant stood over her. His dirty hand, fingernails bitten down as far as was possible, covered his mouth. *He's alive! Thank Telouse.* A small smile curved Addy's lips, but then his sour odour reached her. She wrinkled her nose at his matted shoulder-length brown hair, expecting something to come crawling out at any moment.

She narrowed her eyes at him. *Why is he covering his mouth? He's the one that smells.*

He shrugged. In a muffled voice, he said, "I can't stand the smell of vomit. No sense in both of us throwing up." He studied her face, and the tension around his eyes relaxed. Five steps took him to the other side of the small, stone-walled square room where he sat cross-legged and watched her.

Addy clenched her teeth and lay back on her side while a wave of nausea tossed her insides about. The sensation soon passed. She gingerly placed fingertips on the side of her head. *Shit, there's a bloody dragon egg on my skull.* She felt her inside coat pocket and her boot. Both daggers were gone. *Of course they are.* This time she didn't sit, the hardness of the floor preferable to throwing up again. "Thanks for trying to help me before."

He barked a short laugh. "I wasn't much help in the end. Sorry."

"At least you tried. So, who are you?"

The man tilted his head to the side, appearing to think, but didn't answer.

"Okay, then, I'll be more specific. What's your name?"

He lowered his gaze. "Kerwyn the Deserter."

"The deserter of what?"

Keeping his head bowed, he shook it. Apparently, Addy was not going to have her questions answered anytime soon. She supposed it didn't really matter, not when they were both so close to death. With her head pounding and her stomach heaving like flotsam in a storm, she didn't have the energy to dig deeper. She pushed herself away from her vomit, inching across the dirt floor until her feet hit the bars of her cell, half a body length from where she had started.

Outside the cell was a shadowed hallway. The stone blocks of the wall glistened with trickles of water under the flicker of light from a torch that hung just out of sight. Addy eyed the cell door. *Would I be so lucky?* Addy kicked half-heartedly at the door, to see if there was any give. *Nope, of course not.*

"Shhh! Don't draw their attention. If they know you're awake, they'll come."

Radnok's seekers wouldn't be taking her somewhere pleasant to play with ponies. She carefully put her leg back on the ground. "Well, how do we get out?"

When he didn't answer, she stared at him. The slightest shrug told her everything she needed to know, but what did she expect from a man with worse than nothing? He had nothing *plus* the benefit of dried blood crusted on his short beard and around the bent appendage that used to be a fully functioning nose. Lifelong imprisonment or death were the two choices remaining to him — and chances were, he wouldn't be the one choosing.

Sitting up again and resting her back against the bars, Addy drew in a sharp breath, regretting it as her nose filled with the caustic stench of vomit and mustiness. Her shoulder hurt almost as much as her head.

What a disaster the previous night had been. How had it all gone to horse manure so quickly? Addy pinned Kerwyn with her gaze. Who was this man that he had stood up for her against Radnok? Maybe he knew something that could help her. "Do you know about the auras?"

Kerwyn looked at her and seemed to be weighing something up, but whatever it was, he kept it to himself.

"Ah, so you do know something. How is it that I supposedly have an aura if I'm not shelon?"

Kerwyn licked his lips. "Are you sure you're not?"

"I think I know what I am, and unless you want to accuse my father, Radnok, of being one of those evildoers, there's no way I can be." Addy almost laughed at the man's bug-eyed expression. "I wouldn't worry about making slanderous accusations — we can hardly be in anymore trouble."

"I used to be one … one of them, the seekers. Are you Adrastine?"

Addy nodded. He had obviously been a seeker for a long time if he knew her name.

Kerwyn watched her carefully and scratched his arm. "Rumours were that he isn't your father."

No one escaped being a seeker, so how had this man done so? And why would he be telling her this? Was he even telling the truth? If he could be believed, he was not a hapless vagrant — he would have fighting skills and knowledge way beyond Addy's. But why would he help her? Maybe he had seen the truth of who Radnok really was.

Nevertheless, he was calling her parentage into question, and even though she would like to think she was not spawned by the world's most vile person, Kerwyn was wrong. "Let's just forget my parentage for a minute, seeker, or deserter, whoever you are. If you were a seeker, that means you have the sight." She snorted her disdain. "Do you see an aura when you look at me?" Addy waited for his "life-altering" verdict. She almost laughed at the thought. *Yeah right. What a load of pig shit.*

The ex-seeker squeezed the knuckles on his right hand with his left hand, the cracks making Addy wince. Kerwyn said, "Yes. And it's … it's a colour that shouldn't be."

Addy groaned and lifted her hand to cover her eyes. With her middle finger and thumb, she massaged her temples. Treloahns hated Shelons. Following the Telousian doctrines, their god, Telouse, warned that shelons were spawns of the devil, Var. "Then why aren't you scared of me, seeker? If I have an aura, I surely have strong powers. For all the hells' sakes, I'm sick of asking questions. Just tell me what in Telouse's name is going on?" She hated herself for even considering buying into the whole shelon thing. Her father had made a living from capturing and imprisoning suspected shelons, but Addy was not one. And only once had she seen something magical or unexplainable. She was present when a shelon had resisted arrest. He had been a slightly built man with otherworldly strength. He had picked up one of her father's biggest seekers and thrown him over twelve feet. It had taken eight of Radnok's armed me to kill him, three of them being killed in the process. As a child, it had frightened her and given her the impression all shelons were violent, but now she realised she would have done the same in his situation.

Her father had managed to play on people's fear of the unknown, convincing King Orlon to create his now-famous seeker network, with Radnok at its head. She ignored the murmuring of her conscience, which taunted that the energy she possessed when she concentrated could be related to shelon power. She shook her head. *No, that would make me an evil heathen. Telouse would surely condemn me to hell. And Lilliana told me it was just a skill passed down through her family. I can't actually do anything with it like throw someone twelve feet or conjure fireballs. It's definitely not magic.*

Kerwyn fixed his gaze on her, a knowing look filled with calm. Sitting straight, he breathed in a single deep breath then recited:

"And even times one autumn night

A rose of river and desert

Replacing moonlight.

Fire fiercer than a shooting star

Will burn a path

Through the tar

Of treachery.

But if the star should fall before Venturan is cleansed

Peace, and this world, will find an end."

Addy blinked, hoping her best not-impressed expression graced her face. His words were blasphemous. "How in the hells does that answer my question? My head hurts too much to try to decipher some ancient horse manure. Not only that, but it sounds as if you're quoting prohibited scripture."

Kerwyn laughed. "And that's going to get me into even more trouble? It's past time to worry about repercussions. To answer your question, your aura is the colour of a rose. To be specific, the colour of the deep-pink desert rose of Nerine, and it's shot through with gold, like the valuable gold dust coating the riverbeds of Nerine. I wasn't sure the prophecy was true, but now...."

"Prophecy?" Stabbing pain smacked her between the eyes. She closed them and swallowed another lump of vomit that tried to escape. "You're talking about Var's work now. I'm not some evil heathen. How can you accuse me of such? If I knew magic, I'd use it to get out of here." Addy opened her eyes again and glared at Kerwyn. "No wonder you didn't make it as a seeker. You're the enemy."

Kerwyn shook his head. "I'm not the enemy. You've been fed lies about the shelon for too long. I wasn't sure the prophecy was right, but seeing you makes it clear to me. Evil does live among us, but it isn't the shel—"

Squeaking hinges silenced Kerwyn, and a door banged against a wall. Addy shared a frantic look with Kerwyn. The ex-seeker motioned to her to lie down and shut her eyes. Maybe if they thought she was still unconscious, it would give them time to think of a way to escape, although how she was getting out of a locked cell without outside assistance, she had no idea.

From the footsteps, Addy thought there must be three seekers. She hoped none of them was her father. A key clanked in a lock, and a man asked, "What's that fucking horrid smell?" The door swung open, hitting Addy in the knee. She couldn't stop the small groan that came out and prayed it sounded like a reaction made in unconsciousness.

A different voice came out of the gloom, gruff and impatient. "Has she woken at all?"

"Not that I've noticed." Kerwyn's voice was quiet, submissive.

"You'll have a brief audience with High Seeker Radnok before having time with the First Questioner, after which you will be taken to the cleansing room. And you can carry her — the high seeker wishes to see her too."

What the hell was the cleansing room? She hadn't heard of that one when she had lived with her parents. Addy didn't imagine it was somewhere a person went to bathe and relax. If they didn't do something soon....

Kerwyn's arms slid under Addy. To her surprise, he lifted her with little effort. She tried not to cough or cover her nose — the vagrant stench was not her favourite smell, even after living with vomit. Addy felt guilty she couldn't help Kerwyn by at least putting her arms around his neck and hanging on — what if he dropped her?

Her limbs bounced as they went through corridors and up stairs, cool air feathering her face. The light on the other side of her closed lids grew brighter, and the damp dungeon smell faded before being replaced with fresh, outdoor scents, probably from special candles and fragrance sticks in fireplaces — sticks soaked in floral oils and oils extracted from the leaves of the pern tree, which gave off a lemony odour.

They had ascended two levels, if her estimates were correct, and they travelled another corridor until they halted. Fear buzzed through her body, and it took all Addy's determination not to jump out of Kerwyn's arms and run.

"Wait here."

Kerwyn asked, "Is High Seeker Radnok in that room?"

"Shut up." A slap followed the command, and Kerwyn jolted forward. Addy tensed, expecting to fall until Kerwyn regained his footing.

Knowing Kerwyn was not one for making meaningless conversation, Addy realised he must be trying to give her information. Any was better than none, but she didn't hold out much hope of escape. Her hand-to-hand combat skills weren't bad, her self-found foster parents had seen to that, but there was no way she could take on three or four seekers when she had a useless shoulder and sore head, unless she could vomit on them. *Hmm, that might be a good tactic to pair with running. You idiot, this is no time for jokes. Think of something, damn you.*

Whatever she tried, she prayed Kerwyn would go along with. He may be a shelon sympathiser, but he had already helped her once; she had faith he would again.

Muffled footsteps and then they were moving.

The room they entered was warmer than the corridor. The subtle fragrance of sweet, warm tea with osco — Radnok's favourite winter drink — greeted them. Involuntary shivers seized her, and she held her breath. *If he can't hear me, maybe he'll think I'm not here.* The thoughts of a petrified eleven-year-old came unbidden. How many times had she discovered a new hiding place, only to be found? Sometimes she would be coaxed out by the sound of Radnok beating her mother, and sometimes the woman earned the beating, in Addy's opinion, by finding her for him, pretending she was there to help, although Addy hadn't fallen for that one too many times. Her. Own. Mother.

They were dead to her.

Her cheeks heated. She forced a breath in, then out, another in. She could do this. She would die before he dominated her again. Control of her life was hers, had been ever since she had escaped, and if she could do it once, as a know-nothing fifteen-year-old, she could do it now.

Opening her eyes, she looked at Kerwyn and almost stuttered. "Where am I?"

"We're—"

Radnok moved quickly to stand next to them, and his velvety yet authoritative tone made her shiver. "You are in my private reception room. Deserter, put the shelon down."

Ephrestine's piss! He's called me a shelon. What in Var's anus? The nausea that had faded returned with even greater potency, and she gagged.

Once her feet touched the floor, her legs buckled. Radnok's nearness had injected her with fear she hadn't felt since the night she had run away. And now he was accusing her of being a dirty, evil shelon? The skin on her scalp prickled. Was Radnok going to kill her?

Calm down. Just focus on escaping. From her vantage point kneeling on a soft, fawn-coloured rug, Addy could take her time, make them think she was weaker than she was. Radnok had no idea where she had been for the past six years, what she had learned. This would be her only advantage.

Sitting back on her heels and wobbling slightly for effect, Addy glanced around, barely noticing the dark wood panelling on the walls and the many portraits hanging there. She made sure she knew where each of the six seekers were.

One seeker stood just behind her, his dagger at Kerwyn's throat. It was the bastard who had threatened to kill her: Tanner. *I'm definitely killing him before I leave.* Her scrutiny jumped from him to two men guarding the door. Both looked to be in their thirties, clean-shaven and alert. Then there was one seeker who stood next to Addy, and two on either side of Radnok, shadowing him wherever he went. Radnok placed a hand on Addy's shoulder, and she shrank back, trying to fight the panic that seized her. His dark eyes stared into hers. The wrinkles she remembered at the corners of his eyes had gone, and although she was probably imagining it, his hair looked darker, thicker than six years ago. The feverish light of madness and cruelty in his eyes had not dimmed; if anything, it shone brighter, illuminating the vileness within him until there was no mistaking it.

To avoid the distress of watching him any longer, she hastily swung her head to the side, and her gaze collided with one of the seekers shadowing him. The man didn't look to be much older than her. His azure eyes stood out, framed by dark, straight hair. His gaze bore straight into hers, making her feel as if he could read her thoughts. The sensation of frenzied butterflies spread through her stomach. *What a waste of such a good-looking man.* Realising she'd been staring, she blinked and looked at the floor. Men were rarely, if ever, to be trusted, and she had no interest in being with one, no matter how attractive or nice he seemed. They were mostly controlling, narcissistic bastards, destroying women's lives.

Radnok's palm on her aching shoulder added to her discomfort and reminded her where she was. His heat seeped through her coat to her skin. His touch felt like poison, shrivelling her from the inside.

He nodded slowly. "We'd best do this quickly. My wife is to arrive shortly, and I would hate to keep her waiting." His fingers dug painfully into her clavicle before he released, turned, and went to his chair, although *chair* was too insignificant a word for it. Raised on a small dais, two steps up, it had thick arms, the back reaching two heads higher than the top of Radnok's head when seated. Gold leaf covered the timber. The onyx-coloured cushions twinkled in the torchlight, and delicate, golden thread crisscrossed the fabric, while lustrous, yellow tassels hung from the front. He sat, settled back, and closed his eyes briefly, a self-satisfied smile forming.

Why had Radnok disowned her, his daughter? Or was he not married to her mother anymore? Normally not a fan of surprises, Addy would have actually appreciated that one. Nevertheless, she didn't want to be here when her mother arrived — more emotional blackmail Radnok could use against her. Although, she had hoped steeling herself against any love that may have remained for the harpy who had birthed her would mean she would feel, at best, indifference, at worst, hate.

Radnok picked up a cup from the small table near his arm. Both his hands coiled around the vessel, like a snake ready to crush and eat its prey. He sipped and brought the goblet to rest on his lap. "Isn't this lovely? Soon you will be punished for your digressions, shelon, but before that, we will see what your hopelessly incapable, would-be saviour has to say for himself."

The high seeker stood and strolled to Kerwyn, picking a stray golden thread off his midnight-blue coat sleeve as he went. The men were of a similar height, but Kerwyn's hunched shoulders made Radnok seem taller. "So, what makes a man throw off his cowardly ways and speak up? Would it be to save a pretty woman? Or would it be to avenge a murdered lover? You do know your 'friend' was killed by this shelon, do you not? It was nothing to do with me."

Addy turned her head so she could better watch the exchange. Kerwyn glanced at her then back at his boots. Fire crackled in the hearth. One of the seekers cleared his throat.

They waited.

Radnok brought the cup to his lips and finished his beverage in one large gulp. He held the cup behind him. "More."

A robed servant appeared from the far side of the room. Addy cursed herself for not noticing the woman sooner. She looked around again, just to make sure there weren't any seekers hiding in the darkened area near from where the woman had just come. The woman held a shiny, silver jug. Supporting the bottom of it with a gloved hand, she poured steaming liquid into the high seeker's cup before retreating hastily to inconspicuousness next to the wall.

"I will repeat my question. Why did you help the shelon?"

Still looking down, Kerwyn rubbed the fingers of one hand against his thumb. His voice was quiet, and Addy strained to hear. "I wanted to do the right thing for once. Something I should have done long ago."

Radnok laughed. His seekers smiled, all except for one — the one with the striking blue eyes.

"Deserting dog! And helping a filthy Ephrestine worshipper. May Var take your soul," the seeker with the knife at Kerwyn's neck said before spitting in Kerwyn's face. Addy shook with the restraint it took not to run over and snap Tanner's neck.

Radnok gazed into his cup before turning a calculating eye on Kerwyn. "You have poor judgment. Very poor. There are so many ways you could pay. We'll see how many we can administer before you die."

The high seeker drew back his arm then shot it forward, pitching the scalding contents of the cup towards Kerwyn's face. Addy jumped up and shoulder barged her father out of the way. Radnok lost balance and fell, but the beverage was in the air.

Kerwyn jerked his head to the side, and the blistering liquid hit Tanner in the face, hot drops splashing onto Kerwyn. Tanner screamed, and Addy smiled at this small piece of justice.

Kerwyn, who had elbowed his scalded captor in the ribs, ran for the door.

They weren't going to get a better opportunity to escape than this. Addy scrambled to her feet, but her father grabbed her legs. *No, damn you.* She pushed down the horror of being trapped in his arms and bent to dig her fingernails into his hands.

A man shouted, "Stop him!"

Looking up, Addy saw the seekers at the door rush to subdue Kerwyn.

Radnok's fingers dug harder into her shins as he tried to pull her legs out from under her, her nail assault having little effect. She twisted, gripped his hair with one hand, and pulled. Even though she felt like a little girl in a ridiculous fight, pulling his hair was the only thing she could think of in this position. Stiffening the fingers of her other hand, she tried to poke his eyes out, making him release one leg so he could use his hand to protect himself.

One leg free, she brought her knee up swiftly and struck his chin while pushing his head down with the hand that held his hair. Then she did it again before looking around, expecting a blade in her back at any moment.

"No!" someone shouted. Swearing and grunts accompanied the spit and pop of the fire.

One of Radnok's personal guards lay lifeless on the floor, blood spreading across the hand-woven rug beneath him. Tanner was also on the floor, face down and still.

Death looked unreal. Three deaths she had witnessed in less than one rotation of Venturan, when she had never witnessed violent death before. It smelled different to when Radnok's mother had died in her sleep. She could almost taste the earthy tang of death. The thick, masculine, and metallic odour smothered the earlier fragrance of Radnok's alcohol-laden tea. It reminded her of a summertime visit to the docks as a child. Radnok had some business and had made her wait for him. Locked in a room above the beach and the ready-made latrine for the dockworkers, she had waited for hours in the steamy heat, breathing in the stench of festering seaweed and human waste.

Sword blades clanged, and the hand that gripped Radnok's hair was jerked about as he tried to dislodge it, sending shooting pains from her shoulder into her neck. She gripped harder. Addy momentarily checked behind her when someone shouted from across the room. The blue-eyed seeker fought his comrades, Kerwyn slashing and parrying by his side, apparently with a dead seeker's sword. *What in Telouse's name?*

The high seeker stopped trying to protect his face. "You will regret this, Rose of Nerine."

Addy froze at the name. There was something she should remember but couldn't. That name meant danger, but she didn't know why. Radnok had encouraged her ignorance of any other religion but Treloahn, and she had happily remained uneducated on the finer points of Ephrestine and the prophecy, like most of her countrymen.

"Fool girl, you have stolen my choices." He reached into his coat, and his hand emerged, gripping a dagger. He plunged it into her thigh as he stood.

Acute pain rent a path through her whole body, and she screamed.

Radnok yanked the dagger from her flesh, choosing where to strike next, like an angry wasp. She hopped backwards, clutching the wound to stem the flow of blood. "You pig-fucking son of a demented whore." She reached for the knife in her boot, but, of course, it wasn't there.

Radnok slashed the blade towards her face. Addy fell backwards and twisted, landing on her good arm. She rolled twice, trying to put distance between herself and Radnok. Grimacing, she attempted to stand, but she couldn't push past the burning in her shoulder and the furnace in her thigh.

She dug deep into herself, reached for the fire that didn't hurt, the cauldron in her belly. Shouting punctuated the air around her, but she sank deeper, drew energy into her blood stream. The pain lessened with every breath, until it was bearable, until she felt almost invincible.

Before she stood, Radnok had closed the distance between them. She looked up, met his gaze, halting him. His surprised face made her want to laugh despite the fear coursing through her body. Was this how it felt to be on the edge of madness?

An urgent voice from behind Addy came slowly, out of the coagulated atmosphere around her. There was something different about the voice that she couldn't place. "We have to get out of here now, before reinforcements come. One of the seekers has escaped. Shelon, let's go."

Addy turned. It wasn't Kerwyn, but the young seeker with the blue eyes. He stood tensed, ready to run, his sword trained on Radnok. She wanted to deny his accusation — she was *not* shelon — but it would have been a waste of breath, and he was her way out, another surprise to be thankful for. But could she leave without killing Radnok?

Radnok straightened his back, lifted his chin. "You betray me, Seeker Jacob?"

The man imitated the high seeker's movements, straightening with an air of control, a close-mouth smile his answer as he gestured for Addy to leave.

"But I have to kill him." Addy stared at the seeker who had just betrayed her father.

Seeker Jacob shook his head before glancing over Radnok's shoulder to the far wall. "There isn't time. Trust me."

"The hall is clear," called Kerwyn from the doorway.

Addy acquiesced, allowing Jacob to push her along while she hastily limped towards the door, stepping around bodies. Seeker Jacob remained at her back, keeping the high seeker at a distance. She didn't want to be retreating, though. She wanted to stay and finish what she'd started.

Regret at leaving Radnok alive washed through her, and she looked over her shoulder. "Tell your *wife* I'm sorry we didn't get a chance to catch up." She wished her sarcastic words were knives, all stabbing him at once.

Radnok spoke, his voice steady and smug. "Kerwyn the Deserter, leave and you sign the death warrants of your wife and three children — Meline, Saken, and Jorgan, isn't it?"

Kerwyn paused at the door and looked in, Jacob shoving Addy out of the door past Kerwyn. Desperation blazed from Kerwyn's eyes, indecision marring his features. Addy couldn't let him do it. She knew her father, and he would kill them anyway, now that he had it in his mind. She stopped and grabbed Kerwyn's arm. "Don't listen to him. We have to get out of here. Now."

"You go. I can't."

Addy would not leave this kind man to face the depraved whims of her father alone. "Damn you. I won't leave without you. He'll kill them and then you, just because he can. If we leave now, we have a chance to save them … or we can stay and fight." Why was she letting Seeker Jacob dictate things? She was injured, but she wasn't helpless.

Kerwyn finally looked at her, his decision clear in his determined half nod. "Stay and fight. We can end this now, and my family will be safe."

A door banged open on the other side of the room. Seekers darted out of a door next to Radnok's chair. *Damn!* They had been so close. There was little chance of killing Radnok now. Disappointment swelled within her, drawing tears. Her chance was gone, and Addy didn't want to stay around to find out how many seekers there were. She shook her head and pulled Kerwyn's sleeve.

"Come on." Seeker Jacob pulled Addy along, and, thankfully, Kerwyn followed. They started forward, Kerwyn slamming the door shut.

Addy limped. "Ow! Careful … my leg."

Seeker Jacob stopped and turned. "If you can't walk, I'll carry you."

"Not in this lifetime." Addy gritted her teeth and, holding onto her energy as if it were a rope pulling her out of a pit full of crocodiles, jogged.

Chapter Five

Queen Valtice stood at the edge of the yellowing field, her face set, showing concern, but not too much — she didn't want to incite panic. She hoped the tight-fitting black shirt and trousers she had chosen for today gave her a bold, powerful countenance. When she had woken this morning, the air had buzzed with uncertain tension. The dark umbra of war had settled on her shoulders.

Two of her men-at-arms stood to her left. Her scribe and advisor, Enyak, — writing furiously in his notebook — and the shelon chief of the village stood to her right, with all two-hundred-and-twenty-two villagers forming a tense semicircle behind her. They watched her, their expectations and fear an uncomfortable force at her back, prickling her skin.

She observed the emaciated grain that had been seared by the hotter-than-normal sun. In the midst of dead stalks lay the corpse of a shelon. Skin a husk of drying parchment peeling from whitened bones, the remains defied belief — the shelon was three weeks dead, not months or years.

Valtice had raced to Jarmantin as soon as she had received word from the village chief. Hope that this was not what it appeared to be had survived until this morning. The thrum of wrongness, of energy flow out of balance, had greeted her on waking. There was only one way to confirm the chief's verdict. No monarch had ever had to do what she was about to, and she feared crossing that line.

Her gaze was drawn to the shell of a person like moisture into parched desert earth, but the sight gave her no relief.

The shelon chief cleared his throat, a reminder to Valtice of their recent conversation. He had assured her he still had access to his power and had just been tired for a few days after stepping into the dying field. If he were wrong, if she lost her powers, she would no longer be ruler of Nerine; that honour would pass to her sister, Sara, the second most powerful shelon next to the queen. The thought terrified her — her sister was not fit to rule; she was egotistical, selfish, and manipulative.

Valtice looked to the ground in front of her and stepped forward, her black boot stopping at the border of healthy green and shrivelling death. At the western edge of her country, where fertile land met rocky shore and sea, energy was being siphoned from the land, and any shelon who entered the affected area would be drained. If it continued, Nerine would turn to dust, as that desiccated body was well on the way to doing. Once Nerine was gone, Treloah, the country across the sea, would follow.

Maybe this disaster wasn't really the beginning of the end of their world. Maybe poisoned soil or diseased grain was the cause of what lay before her. *My mother accused me of always being the optimist.* She laughed. Nervous titters and mutters came from the crowd. *Be the queen they need.*

Queen Valtice knelt in the thick grass. Staring at the sick husks inches away, she brought up her hand, touched her index and pointer fingers to the space between her eyebrows, then brought them down to touch her belly, in a gesture to Ephrestine — the goddess of fertility, health, and power. Inhaling deeply through her mouth, she exhaled through her nose, centring herself. Preparing for the unknown.

She leaned over. One hand came down and rested in the spongy, cool grass. Palm down, fingers spread, she lowered her other hand onto crunchy husks. They crumbled beneath her palm, the first touch sending hundreds of needle pricks through her palm. The pain travelled up her arm then back down through her body. Her palm hit the ground, causing a puff of dust to swirl around it. Her reaction was to pull away, but her hand was almost stuck, and she had to linger and have patience to know what she was dealing with.

The invading hooks of energy embedded into her stomach — the centre of power for a shelon. Valtice doubled over and groaned, cramps assailing her as her life force was drawn from her through the ground. Black and grey mist swirled in her vision.

With effort, she tore her hand from the parasitic ground. The momentum propelled her backwards. She landed on her back, blinking to clear her sight.

Enyak, his concerned brown face hovering over her, offered his hand. She caught her breath then took it and stood on shaky legs.

There was no denying it. The age Nerinians had feared for many generations was upon them. A great war was coming, and if they lost, all of Venturan would die.

Only one person could save them, but she or he was nowhere to be found. They may not even have been born yet, for all anyone knew. She wouldn't give up. The affected area was small, maybe half a mile wide, and ran parallel to the power ley lines flowing through the centre of Nerine. Valtice feared the story would be the same on their eastern border, where the land met the Blue Sea.

She turned to Chief Salwyn, dropping Enyak's supporting hand. "I've seen enough." Consumed by exhaustion, she willed herself to stand on her own. A queen should never show weakness, especially not when her country faced the biggest threat in its history. Her people needed her fortitude.

Chief Salwyn bowed his balding head, his shimmering pearlescent robes of office fluttering around his legs in the warm breeze.

Queen Valtice turned and walked through the quickly opening path through the villagers. *Thank Ephrestine I humoured Chief Salwyn and travelled in a carriage rather than on horseback.* How quickly her energy had been drained. At that rate, the entire country would be ravaged in a year or two. Time was running out, and where would the people go? Shelons would die in a count of two hundred in an affected area. Non-shelons would last longer, but they would grow older quicker, if starvation didn't kill them first.

The carriage driver opened the door and helped her inside. Enyak and Chief Salwyn followed Queen Valtice; her advisor sat next to her, the chief settling opposite. Chief Salwyn watched her with an assessing eye.

"Yah!" A whip crack stung the air. The carriage jerked into motion.

Selwyn place both hands on his knees. The tendons popping out on the backs of his hands betrayed the tension his voice did not. "We have been measuring the gains of the blight. Since midnight, it has claimed five inches. Yesterday it claimed the same, yet the day prior was two inches, the day before three. The pattern is erratic, Your Majesty."

"When did you first notice?"

"Four weeks ago. We weren't sure what it was at first. Within three days, we were sure, so I sent my riders out."

"They made good time. Our messenger network did well. I commend you on your fast action, Chief Shelon Selwyn."

"Thank you, Your Majesty." A proud smile graced his face.

Valtice stared out the window, at the healthy side. She briefly allowed her eyes to shut. *I need to sleep.* Her head bobbed forward, and she caught herself before head butting the window. They would arrive at her lodgings in a three hundred count. Surely she could stay awake that long?

Watching the green-treed hills in the distance and the dark brown smudges of woolly lamacks grazing in the fields, she said to her advisor, "We'll depart this evening, after dinner. There is much to do and little time to do it, and make sure a message is dispatched to our people in Treloah. Finding The Rose is more critical than ever." The rest of what she needed to say to Enyak would be said in private.

Valtice doubted she could tell him the truth while hiding her fear, and it wouldn't do for Chief Selwyn to see how she felt. Their enemy had knowledge no one outside Nerine and the shelons should have. Her country was in a state of war, but who, or what were they fighting? She rubbed at her temple. It was an effort to keep hope from sinking out of reach.

Yet, the worst news of all, Enyak already knew — they hadn't found The Rose of Nerine.

Without The Rose, they had no means to win.

The Rose was the key to everything.

Chapter Six

A fucking unmitigated disaster. High Seeker Radnok stood half a foot from the other man. He looked into Seeker Damos's eyes as they dulled, awareness fleeing to the netherworlds. Radnok stepped back, pulled his sword out of the seeker's chest, and looked around the bloodied room. The body thudded onto the ground, and he kicked its head in frustration.

He hated mess, and what a big fucking one this had become. He leaned over and wiped most of the blood off his blade using the dead seeker's coat. The night had started with such promise. He shook his head, a wry smile replacing the usual sneer. Five of his seekers dead and one of his best on the run. What had made Jacob help Adrastine? Was he a spy or just an infatuated young man? Whatever he was, because of him, that bitch had escaped *again*. She wouldn't be so lucky next time.

Her arrival had caught him off-guard, but now it was time to put his plan into action. Var had sent her back to him, and he had to prove his worthiness. When Var chose his second-in-command, Radnok wanted it to be him, and not his brother. Smarnus was handsome, and he had charisma — so their father had always said — but Radnok was the more stable, more intelligent one. The high seeker had been called cruel, but he wasn't; people misunderstood him. His brother, on the other hand…. Radnok had suffered at his brother's hand many times as a child, so he knew what the world would endure if Smarnus wielded ultimate power. Yes, the people of Venturan would be much better off with Radnok in charge.

As his daughter fled, reinforcements had arrived in the form of four seekers, three of whom were chasing the escapees. He had skeleton staff for his trip into Marcern; it had been meant to be a few days of drinking, pleasures and relaxation, plus time to speak to the leader of the seeker network in the town. It had turned into … opportunity.

Radnok turned to Armen, a simple but competent man, one of the seekers who hadn't failed him … yet. "Do not speak of this to anyone." Radnok grabbed Armen's arm. "Have the room cleaned, the bodies disposed of."

Armen nodded and promptly left.

Since sighting his daughter, he had kept the seekers who had been with him, those who had seen her, in isolation; no one must know of her, the Rose of Nerine's, existence yet. And no one must ever know she was his daughter; it would undermine him. Then he would have to admit he was her stepfather, which would lead to his wife being executed and himself imprisoned for aiding and abetting a shelon.

To gain ultimate control over Venturan and, more importantly, his brother, Radnok needed Adrastine's power. If his twin brother discovered The Rose existed too early, Radnok could lose everything he had worked so hard for. Var knew he hadn't married Adrastine's mother for her cooking skills or love.

Radnok went to the adjoining bathroom and washed his hands, rinsing his face. By the time his seekers returned, Radnok sat comfortably on his chair, sipping the tepid, wine-laced tea, his servant's body cooling on the floor near his feet. Death didn't bother him, but the woman's staring eyes and open mouth were unpleasant. He surveyed the other bodies scattered across the room and wished he had asked Armen to move them into the hallway before the young man had left.

He had to finish this unsavoury business prior to the clean-up crew's arrival. He tapped his fingers on the arm of his chair. *Where are they? They better have Adrastine with them.*

Footfalls sounded from the hallway, and his fingers drummed quicker as he wondered if it was the cleaners or the hunters. He placed the goblet on the table next to his chair as his men came through the door. His hunters ... without his stepdaughter. Radnok sighed, exasperated.

The three men reached his chair and bowed. Breathing heavily, the youngest met Radnok's gaze. "We gave chase as best we could, but we were unable to catch them, High Seeker. Once they escaped into the woods, they were impossible to track in the dark." The man broke eye contact and stared at the ground. His two companions did the same. Radnok could almost smell their fear.

"Incompetent." Radnok stood and folded his arms. He stepped down and circled behind them, his stride slow and measured. "You had one job ... *one*. She's injured *and* glowing like a fucking bonfire." He dispensed with his calm voice and shouted, more for effect than lack of control. "How the fuck did you not catch her? Are you fucking blind *and* lame?"

His men flinched.

Radnok walked around to the front of the group, one hand to his ear, fiddling with an earring, enjoying the feel of the smooth gold as it slid under his fingertips. He addressed the young man who had had the bravery to speak to him, or maybe the man had drawn the short straw from his fellow seekers since he was the youngest of the three.

"Seeker Brewer, please terminate seekers Joseph and Elad."

Joseph and Elad hastily looked up.

Joseph's eyes and mouth opened wide. Elad flicked his head around to look at the door. *I bet he doesn't have the balls to run.* Radnok smiled.

Seeker Brewer stared at Radnok, uncertainty in his eyes.

Radnok leaned forward and pinned Brewer with his stare, annoyed by his hesitation. "Terminate them, now."

Seeker Brewer looked from Joseph to Elad, probably deciding which one to kill first. Then he stepped behind Joseph and grabbed his chin, drew his dagger, and slashed it across the other man's throat, before cutting deeper, through the spinal cord. The unfortunate seeker's head fell back like a child's rag doll. Blood spurted, landing on the rug. The body fell, scarlet liquid streaming out in such a rush that small bubbles floated on top of the puddle it formed on the floor.

There will be no saving that rug after tonight. What a shame. "Well, what about Elad?" Radnok raised one eyebrow.

Brewer's face drained of all colour, and he tripped on Joseph's arm as he moved to stand behind Elad. When Brewer grabbed Elad's shoulder and forehead, Elad whimpered but didn't run.

Hmm, you have more nerve than I gave you credit for.

Radnok still wouldn't save the man. Incompetence in the future would lessen Radnok's chances of winning, and even surviving. His pact with Var was nothing to be taken lightly, and while he had never met the feared god of war, or the devil as some liked to think of him, Var's powerful, tattooed representatives were not to be laughed at.

Brewer's hand trembled, the knife barely touching Elad's throat.

"Would you like me to finish it for you?" Brewer would surely know the implied threat in those words. Radnok wanted him to think doing this would keep him from suffering the same fate. *As if.* Radnok couldn't help but smile.

The seeker shook his head, small, sharp movements. He shut his eyes and pressed the blade firmly against Elad's throat, then sliced across. His whispered, "Sorry, my friend. Telouse, save me," reached Radnok. Elad emitted a squeak and gurgle as he fell to the floor, and Brewer fell to his knees, obviously horrified at what he had done.

What is wrong with everyone? A baby lamack has a better killing instinct than this moron. Radnok would need improved screening processes next time he recruited.

"Adequate work, Seeker Brewer." He would not give praise where it wasn't due, and his work was only *just* adequate. When Radnok placed his hand on Brewer's shoulder, the man looked up at him, his eyes pleading. He was scared, as well he should be.

"I did as you ordered, High Seeker Radnok."

Ah, yes, this one is smart; he knows what's coming. "Yes, you did, and for that you should take great comfort."

Radnok unsheathed his sword, again. Was his work never done? He hadn't had the pleasure of beheading a man before and had always been curious about what it would feel like.

He planted his feet wide. With a two-handed grip on his sword, he raised the weapon. He swung the blade down, not finishing the striking arc until the sword was above his shoulder. Brewer's head thudded onto the floor, and Radnok jumped back to avoid the blood that sprayed across the rug as the torso fell to the ground. It had taken more force than he expected, and he was a tad disappointed that the head didn't actually roll; it had merely dropped and stopped, but all in all, it had been enjoyable. Some may say he was bloodthirsty, but he had not made them suffer. His justice had been swift, and who could criticise him for protecting himself?

No one, except the simpleton Armen knew about The Rose of Nerine's existence, so his brother was unlikely to hear of it. He would have to keep it that way. There were a few seekers in his personal guard he would entrust to hunt her down, but that was all. It was likely she would be back to try to kill him again, so he would wait and be ready.

Radnok wiped his blade on the back of the only clean coat remaining in the profusion of red fabric then exited the room and nodded to the clean-up crew — formed of his most loyal men — in the hall.

Now to proceed with caution. King Orlon, the soft, simpering excuse for a king that he was, must not find out what had happened. If Radnok didn't do this right, control would disappear faster than a woman's modesty in a whorehouse. Only his most trusted staff would be capable of getting him what he wanted: that traitor, Jacob, and his daughter — controlling her was vital to achieving everything he had worked towards for the past twenty years.

He had to do it without alerting his brother, who didn't need to know *all* Radnok's plans. He had promised Radnok his share of authority in the new world he and Var were creating, but if he thought Radnok might become more powerful than him, he would never help him, and The Rose would certainly give him power.

Radnok didn't trust his brother and knew the feeling was mutual. Except right now, his brother needed him, and he would just have to make sure that didn't change until he was ready.

First things first, it was time to visit the king to ensure he only found out what Radnok wanted him to. King Orlon would have to announce his successor soon, because of his failing health. By the time Radnok was done, he would not only have his seekers to command, but an entire army.

He supervised, arms folded, as his assistant packed his bag. They just had to collect his useless wife, and they could leave. He called in a seeker. "Please fetch High Lady Lilliana from her cell." To be fair, it was a bedroom, but Radnok had it locked from the outside. "I'll meet you at the carriage."

It was time to make his move on the capital. When he was finished, Treloah would be his.

Chapter Seven

Three miles out of town and the moon had made a brief appearance, showing they were at halfnight. Dawn was a cold, long way off, the darkness lingering well into morning chores this time of year.

Addy limped over uneven ground, gritting her teeth. She had remained silent about the constant pain in her thigh. Insidious in its assault from the inside out, the agony of her wound clawed at her flesh, bringing her to the verge of tears several times. There was no point admitting to it — they were travelling too slowly as it was. Kerwyn, in front, stopped and spoke the first words any of them had since fleeing the compound. "This is as far as I go. Will you be okay, Addy and Jacob?"

Jacob shook Kerwyn's hand. "Yes, and thanks for your help. Your family?"

"I can't leave without trying to get them to safety. What if he's already killed them?" Kerwyn's voice wavered.

Addy sat carefully on the cold ground and let out a relieved sigh, the sensation in her limb morphing into a pulsing ache rather than stabbing torture for a moment. "You can't think about that. Go and do what you can."

"I'll return if I'm able. I know somewhere I can take them, if they'll come. It will take a few days."

"Don't worry about us." Addy looked up at his face, which she couldn't really see in the dark. "You've done so much already. You should be with your family. Protect them from that cruel deviant. Do you want our help?" That this man truly loved his family gave her back a small piece of her long-destroyed belief that men could do good, were good. What she would've given to have a father like that.

"I'm sorry, Kerwyn, but we don't have time to help. I have to get Addy to safety." *Get me to safety? Why is a seeker helping me?*

Kerwyn approached Addy and crouched to face her. "I'll be fine without you two. My family will be okay where I will take them. How about I return to help you?"

Addy drew breath to speak, and Kerwyn put up his hand to stop her. "I have had dreams, for many years. I don't know why, but I know what will happen if you don't succeed."

"Succeed at what?"

Jacob interrupted. "Kerwyn, do you believe?"

"Yes."

Addy rolled her eyes, knowing they couldn't see her. "Believe in what? You're not talking about that heathen prophecy? Don't tell me you're both disbelievers in the one true god?"

The older man laid a hand on her forearm. "No one is saying Telouse doesn't exist. Addy, there are things none of us understand, but I know, deep inside, that you will need my help. War is coming. Our world could be gone in a year or two if we don't heed Ephrestine's prophecy. Something has changed. Can't you feel it?"

"Don't waste your time, Kerwyn. I'll sort her out. You just get to your family." Jacob clapped him on the back as Kerwyn stood.

"You'll *sort me out*? I've got news for you, seeker. Try anything and I'll snap your neck like a twig." Addy felt vulnerable sitting on the ground with a wounded leg and sore shoulder, but she didn't let any of that project in her voice. She couldn't trust anyone, and needed to get away from him as soon as possible, especially with Kerwyn gone. As soon as Jacob slept, she would leave.

"You have nothing to fear from me, Little Rose. If I had wanted to harm you, why save you in the first place?"

Goose bumps pricked along her arms at the mention of the name, and she shuddered. She still didn't know what it was, but the heaviness of something lurking in the dark set her on edge. "I don't know, and don't call me Little Rose. Men and their perverted ways are beyond the ability of my brain to decipher. Why you lot do all those horrible things, I have no idea."

"What do you mean? Have I done anything horrible since you've met me? And what's so horrible about calling you Little Rose?" The incredulity in his tone had Addy shaking her head. Who was he trying to fool?

"Look, you two need to stick together. Addy, you can trust him. I know people, and he can help you. I have to go, but if I can return, I will."

"Twelve miles west of here is Anderson's Grove. Do you know it?" Jacob asked Kerwyn.

"Yes."

"Can you be there in, say, four days?"

"I'll do my best."

"Meet us there, on the south eastern corner, as the sun is dipping below the horizon. May Ephrestine protect you and light your way. Oh, and let me fix that." Jacob and Kerwyn stood close together, but Addy couldn't make out what was going on until a blue light flared, before immediately disappearing. A small tingle in her belly appeared and disappeared just as quickly, and she rubbed her tummy at the uncomfortable sensation.

Kerwyn grunted — at least she thought it was Kerwyn.

His voice floated out of the gloom. "Thank you, Jacob. I can't believe how straight it is. It might be even better than it was before." Kerwyn barked a short laugh. "Bye, Addy. Take care." Kerwyn turned and jogged off in a north-easterly direction.

"Can you walk?" Jacob asked.

"Of course I can." Addy stood and gripped the wound, carefully placing weight on her injured leg. She winced as talons of pain clutched her thigh, the warm ooze of blood seeping onto her cold fingers. *I could appreciate having warm fingers if it didn't hurt so fucking much.* She tried to concentrate on anything but her wound. "What is straighter?"

"Kerwyn's nose — it was broken, and I fixed it with Ephrestine's gift."

His admission in his belief of a forbidden religion worried her. Had he kidnapped her, not saved her? Whatever it was, she was not going to show weakness. "Oh, really? If you say so. And what is it with you? You're supposed to kill shelons, not save them. Not that I *am* a shelon." Addy snorted to hide her nervousness. The priests of the scythe warned that dabbling in shelon magic was the sure way to hell, but were they wrong? What if that's what she had unknowingly been doing these last few years?

Jacob sighed. His stern voice cut through the dark. "Let's go. We have much ground to cover."

"How far?" Addy's shoulders sagged. All she wanted was to curl up in a warm bed and sleep. In fact, the freezing ground would probably do. Since she had lost connection with the energy in her belly — the natural inner strength her mother said had always been in her family, not shelon magic — the silky lure of bone-weary exhaustion had cocooned her in its weave, dulling her senses.

"How's your leg?"

"It's just a scratch."

"Well, we'll keep going until first light. We need to put as much distance between us and Radnok and his vultures as possible."

"Do you happen to have somewhere *to* go? Or are we just heading to another empty forest?"

"There is a village, fifteen miles from here. They will help, and they have the means to fix your injuries."

"Why are you helping me?"

"I'll explain later. Right now, we need to move." Jacob turned.

Addy was about to repeat her question when a yellow-tinged glow pulsed from Jacob's hand, lighting up a one-metre radius around him.

"What in all the hells?" Addy limped after him, happy to be able to see where she was going. But how had he done it? She grunted in pain and limped faster, trying to see what, if anything, he held. How could his hand glow like that? It was impossible, unless he had dipped it in some new concoction that gave off light, but when would he have done that? She waited, but he didn't answer. She wasn't going to beg and give him the pleasure of being superior if he wasn't going to offer the information. Well, who cared how he did it, as long as she wasn't tripping over rocks and roots and bumping into trees.

After they travelled a while, the ground developed an incline. Addy's leg still ached, but her feet were numb. Every wide, flat rock and nook at the base of a tree tempted her with an offer of a place to rest. Her fatigue didn't care about the frost that sheathed the ground or the light dusting of snow covering the rocks and bushes. She stopped. "Um, I just have to … you know." She jerked her head towards the trunks behind her.

"Okay."

She put a few trees between herself and Jacob and then crouched behind a bush. The air bit into her bare bottom, and her legs shook as she squatted. Fighting to not tip backwards, she finished and stood, dizziness hitting her. She gripped a tree trunk to keep from falling. Maybe she could just lie down for a few minutes. Jacob wouldn't mind, surely. They had covered a fair distance, and there was no sign of anyone pursuing them.

Addy made sure she was nowhere near her piss and sat, resting her back against a large rock, stretching her legs out in front and putting her numb hands under her armpits for warmth. It's not like she hadn't survived sleeping outside during freezing winters before, although she had had blankets. *I'll just close my eyes for a short span. Just one short span.*

"Addy? Have you finished?"

She started. "Huh?" It took her a moment to figure out where she was. "Yes. Just having a break."

Jacob appeared from behind a large trunk. He knelt next to her and put his glowing hand near her face. She blinked. "What in Ephrestine's arse? Get that out of my eyes."

He moved his hand to shine over her leg. "For the love of all that's holy, Addy! Why didn't you say anything?"

So, he had noticed her pants leg soaked in blood. She shrugged and bit her lip to fight off the urge to cry. He sounded like he cared, and it threw her off balance. She wasn't used to anyone showing concern for her welfare. "I'm okay. Leave me alone. I just need to close my eyes for a while, have a rest." She knew she should be worried that he was so close, and normally she would never let a man touch her, but closing her eyes and sleeping seemed far more important. Shutting her eyes, she leaned to the side and laid her head on her bicep.

"I should have seen to this sooner. What in all the hells was I thinking? This is going to make me tired, and we won't get much farther tonight, but we don't have a choice. This might hurt a bit."

"Mmhmm." Her mind tried to send a warning, but Addy was too exhausted. It wouldn't be so bad to die, would it? That was one way of escaping her father.

Her stomach tingled again, and the wound grew warmer from the skin to deep inside, where the dagger had penetrated into muscle. Heat seared her flesh.

She screamed and lashed out, slapping the side of Jacob's head.

The pain and cloying smell of cooked flesh made her retch.

Jacob rubbed his head. "Shit, Addy, I'm sorry. I had to stop the bleeding, and I don't have enough energy to heal it properly while we're out in the open. If I drain myself, I'll have to sleep for one or two rotations of Venturan. We need to get moving." Jacob shone his hand over her leg. "See, it's closed."

Addy sat up slowly and ran her sleeve over her mouth, wiping away any vestiges of fresh vomit. She stared at Jacob. "Sadistic bastard. 'Might hurt a bit' my arse."

He shook his head and clenched his fist, the light coming from his hand narrowing to a smaller beam. "Ungrateful...."

She narrowed her eyes but looked down. The skin had closed. A neat red line, two inches long, ran down her thigh, the edges puckered — another scar to add to her collection. The cloth around it was stiff with half-dried blood, all the way to her knee and around the back of her thigh. "It would have been okay." Her words sounded pathetic, but she didn't know what else to say. How had he healed her? Could it be...? Surely not magic; her stomach clenched. Once, Addy had seen her foster father seal the wound on a pig with a hot iron. He had melted the skin together. Maybe it was something like that? Telouse knew it felt like he had cooked her from the inside out.

"Maybe if we'd stopped walking and I'd bandaged it sooner.... If we had continued, you would have lost too much blood. We're in the freezing cold, and you used your energy at the compound — a bad combination. You're lucky your body hasn't gone into shock. We'll rest here until Little Mother reaches there." He pointed to the sky, a little under where the moon — Little Mother — hung.

Oh, so *he* was giving *her* permission to rest. She growled under her breath. He was watching her; she could feel it.

Lifting her head, she looked into his eyes, wondering why he seemed sad and now angry. She flinched, hating herself for giving him a reaction.

"Don't you ever thank those who help you?"

Oh, that's why he was staring. Addy's cheeks heated. "Thank you for fixing my leg." Damned if she was going to apologise for being slow. She was tired, drained. This day had been one of the most confusing and terrifying of her life. He would have to forgive her for not centring her thoughts on him. He had helped her rather than hurt her, and he hadn't tried to take advantage … yet. It was probably safe to have a quick rest, just shut her eyes for a short while.

She closed her eyes and heard Jacob settle behind her. "I know you won't like it, but we'll have to sleep close together for heat. And trust me, if there was another way to keep warm, I would, but I made a promise to keep you safe."

What did he mean "made a promise keep her safe"? *To whom?* Too tired to think, she shut her eyes and fought the slimy dread of having a man so near. As he slipped his arm around her and snuggled comfortably against her back, she reluctantly forwent any attempt at self-defence and fell into a deep sleep.

Chapter Eight

Late afternoon sun slanted in through stained-glass windows, throwing patches of green, blue, and red across the dark timber floor, brightening the floorboards and the exotic rug that partly covered them. A hundred or so people stood in the high-ceilinged room, tension and expectation silencing them.

Smarnus stood in the centre of the vast, timber-panelled chamber, dark chest hair on display through the low V opening in his red shirt. He felt the gaze of the few women who were in attendance. Over the years, many a woman and man had complemented him on his physique and dark good looks. Smarnus smirked and gazed down at the king of Lachmond.

Lachmond was a largely ignored and forgotten country. Lying south of Treloah, it occupied the southern waters of Venturan and was the smallest of the three countries that made up their world. The king ruled a self-sufficient country and liked to be left alone; he didn't want the superior lineage of his people polluted with foreign blood. Any ships in the oceans off their coastline would be eaten by the frequent tornadoes the Lachmondans had the knowledge to create.

Smarnus's younger twin brother, Radnok, disbelieving of Smarnus's ability to accomplish the task of taking over Lachmond, had once asked Smarnus why he wanted to rule the distant nation. He had smiled to himself as he recalled his answer. *Because, brother o' mine, it has the most skilled army of all Venturan. Plus, I can gather and train my own army in Var's power, while escaping the notice of Treloah and Nerine. Once I'm ready, I will take Lachmond for myself. Then we shall have an easy path to ruling Venturan.*

Smarnus was about to take the first bold step on that path.

Standing in front of King Felson, he hefted his polished sword in both strong hands. Smarnus straightened his broad shoulders and looked King Felson in his watery blue eyes. He nodded to the two xentros holding the monarch. They released his scrawny, blue-silk clad arms and stood back.

"Are you insane? You cannot kill me! I'm the king." He tipped his chin and folded his arms.

Smarnus changed his expression to one of earnest interest. "Will you serve me, Felson?"

The king sputtered, eyes opening wide. He looked to his soldiers, who were being held captive by magic. The xentros, initiates of Var, surrounded the soldiers. The captives' eyes were angry and skittish, but not one of them so much as nodded.

"I'll take that as a no." Smarnus peered around at the room full of soldiers and xentros, some in black livery with his facial likeness stitched in gold over their hearts. The other soldiers would soon wear that livery or be put to death. "I hereby herald a new era for Lachmond. We will prosper as never before. Who is with me?"

His men cheered, pumping eager fists into the air. Felson's soldiers stayed silent, unable to even tremble a lip. Smarnus nodded, and his gaze turned to the king. "My brother didn't believe I could do this, Felson. How wrong he was, don't you think?"

The expectant silence gave Smarnus goose bumps, and he smiled. *Father, you would be so proud of me. I'm about to achieve the greatness I was born for, and this is just the beginning.* He breathed in deeply, puffing out his well-formed chest. Stance wide, he drew the sword back over his shoulder then drove forward, his gaze focused, lips pressed together in determination. The sharp metal bit into the king's neck and slid easily out the other side.

Several spectators gasped.

Felson's surprised head fell to the ground in a fountain of crimson. Could the king see his own body falling to the floor? Smarnus snorted a laugh before he nodded and wiped a splash of blood from his face, admiring it before licking it off his finger. His foolish brother couldn't hear him, but he couldn't resist saying it: "See, Radnok, told you I could do it."

Lachmond was his.

Chapter Nine

Kerwyn's hand slipped on the bark, ripping skin from his palm. He swore under his breath and grabbed again, pushing from his toes. To aid his climb, he had left his coat at the tree's base. When he reached the midway branches of the twenty-foot-tall maple, he stopped and rested on a half-naked branch. He thanked Ephrestine that clouds had almost entirely smothered the moon.

His heartbeat raced, and not just because he had run the whole two-and-a-half miles to his old village after leaving Addy and Jacob. He sat in his neighbour's tree and looked across to the house where his wife and three children lived. He had come here a few times since he had left. His secret visits consisted of glimpsing his family through the tears that never failed to come. Seeing them again, even if they didn't know he was there, was the only thing that had made him cry since he was ten, and it had been the only thing keeping him alive.

His breath caught when he realised he was too late. Three seekers stood in the small backyard. Weakness seized his limbs, and he almost fell. He couldn't let those bastards take his family; he would rather die.

Gulping a deep breath, he prepared to climb down, but one of the seekers yelled and gesticulated at the other two. "He'll have our balls for this! Have one more look around, a good look. Then we'll leave. See if you can find anything that will help track them."

The other seekers answered before re-entering the cottage, their quiet words lost before they reached Kerwyn. Thank ever-loving Ephrestine his family wasn't there, but then where in all the hells were they? They had been here when he had checked on them two weeks ago. Relief and fear warred within him, his head pounding with the battle.

Wherever his family was, he needed to know they were safe. He shivered while he waited for the seekers to finish. After they left, he waited a little longer before climbing down and approaching the back door, which the seekers had left open.

Stepping over the threshold was like going back in time. Tears came unbidden as the smell of smoke from the recently extinguished fire ambushed him, and underneath that, his wife's jaze-blossom perfume. Memories floated across his vision. Mayna walking towards him when he arrived home and throwing her arms around his neck before she kissed him. His children sitting and playing in the middle of the room with dolls and tiny timber-carved horses, but now the house was empty.

He shook his head, trying to snap back to the present; if he weren't careful, he would find himself returned to Radnok's dungeon.

Kerwyn visited each room, stopping at last in the bedroom his two youngest children shared. Sorrow's cruel hand squeezed his heart until he felt as if he couldn't breathe. Meline had been four when he had left; her blonde curls and ready smile always brightened their house. Saken had been six, a serious, thin boy with large green eyes whose generous heart always put others first. So much time he had missed. Sometimes, late at night, he had left food and money at the back door when he managed to get it, but nothing … nothing could replace the lost moments of being with them, of his family knowing he loved them. If he had returned, he would have had to live with shaming his wife in front of their neighbours — Kerwyn the Coward, Kerwyn the Deserter — and who knew when one of Radnok's cronies would show up to hurt his family and grind him into his place.

Sitting on one of the beds, he picked up a pillow and buried his face in it, savouring the lingering essence of his child. *Gods, how I miss them.* Tears burned his eyes. He shut them, but watery grief seeped through his lashes.

He would make this right if it were the last thing he did.

Kerwyn placed the pillow back on the bed. There was Meline's rag doll with its ratty pink dress and brown-rope hair. Kerwyn's mother had made it for her when she was a babe; she had died of the stiffening sickness when Meline was two. He looked to the ceiling as he remembered her.

They had obviously left in a hurry. Meline never went anywhere without her doll. He gathered the doll and gently placed it in his coat pocket then went to the small wardrobe. It looked as if most of the clothes were still in it. A glance in his wife's bedroom told the same story. Taking a torch off the entry wall, he scoured the small cottage for blood. Thank Ephrestine there was none. So, there was a good chance they were still alive, but where had they gone?

Figuring they wouldn't be back any time soon, so wouldn't miss the food, he ate cured meat and bread from the larder and took what food he could fit into his pockets. He returned to his wife's bedroom and pushed the heavy timber bed a few inches to one side to reveal a small square of floorboards that was a slightly different hue to the rest. He pushed down on one side of the square, and the other side flipped up. Smiling and looking to the ceiling in relief, he thanked Ephrestine that their secret stash of coins was there. They had kept it for a time of emergency. He pocketed one handful, leaving another handful of coins, just in case his wife returned, and pushed the bed into its original position.

He snuck away, hopeful he would see his beloved family again, but it wasn't long before despair curled possessively around his heart. With no clues to help find them, were they lost to him forever?

For comfort, he wrapped his hand around Meline's doll. Wherever they were, he *would* find them, and maybe Addy and Jacob could help; Addy was The Rose after all, even if she didn't believe it yet.

Moving faster to warm his blood, he jogged up the hill and disappeared into the forest. He wouldn't rest until he found where they were, and Ephrestine help anyone who had harmed them. The Deserter was ready to face his fears. He would bring his family home and be the husband and father they deserved. Just let Radnok try and stop him. *Mayna, my love, I'm sorry I took so long, but I'm finally coming.* His chest swelled with an emotion he hadn't felt in years: hope.

Chapter Ten

When Jacob had woken Addy, she recognised the grey-hued light that hinted at dawn's approach. It took her another moment to remember where she was and how she had come to be there.

Radnok.

Still tired, but with more energy than she had had before sleeping, Addy rose and followed Jacob, the scar on her leg giving only small complaints. They walked up a steepening incline, which continued until the sun shone weak rays through the trees, the fresh scent of pine trees prickling her nose. The haunting whoop of the white mountain falcon reverberated through the forest, and Addy gazed up into the high branches, hoping to see the shy bird. The falcon eluded her gaze, and she tripped when she caught her toe on a rock. She hastily looked ahead again to where Jacob had increased the distance between them.

Jacob, who was about five inches taller than her, took confident steps, his long stride difficult to match. Addy scrambled to keep up with him, grabbing at trees to improve her balance on the uneven, sloping surface.

Who was he, really, and why had he helped her? Had he committed atrocities working for Radnok? Was this his way of redeeming himself, or was he really a spy, his belief in Ephrestine a giveaway? Distracted again, Addy stumbled and skinned her palm when she landed on a rock. "Pig shit!" White slithers of skin curled up, blood glistening from the stripped lines on her palm. It stung, so she brought the wound to her mouth and sucked it.

Jacob halted and glanced back. "Are you okay?" He came to her, bending to take her hand in his before turning it over to inspect her palm. He caressed the outline of her palm with one finger, avoiding the area of torn skin, his touch sending sweet tingles through her whole body.

She didn't want him to see the effect he had on her and turned her head to look at a particularly interesting bush. "Really, it's fine."

"Does it sting?"

"Yes, but it's f—"

He blew on the graze, causing goose bumps to prickle her arm. She tried to tug her hand out of his grasp. Falling for him was not a good idea; she barely knew him, not to mention that men generally couldn't be trusted. Definitely not a good idea. "Thanks, but can I have my hand back?" She focused her gaze on where they were joined.

He loosened his grip on her hand just enough that she could only slide it out slowly. She felt him staring at her, and, despite her recent advice to herself, mustered the courage to meet his gaze. Bad idea. Light cerulean irises ringed his large pupils, and it was unnerving that his dark lashes framed them to such perfection. The tingles turned to tornadoes, careening through her belly and sex. Very bad idea. She jumped up, breaking their connection.

Addy had been the only person she could rely on for a long time now, and she didn't want to put herself in a vulnerable position. It was best for him to know she didn't need anyone, let alone him. She let her arm fall to her side. "I'm fine, thanks." She plastered a fake smile on her face. She had never gone stupid over a man, like so many unfortunate women she knew had, and she didn't want to start now, even if he had helped her. While his actions had been noble so far, Addy wanted to know his motivations before she formed a definite opinion of him.

Jacob regarded her, his face neutral. "If you insist. Let's go, then." He continued up the hill. They climbed until Addy was so hot she had to push back her hood and wipe the sweat from her forehead. Finally, they neared the crown of the hill. Addy had a sudden ridiculous urge to want to beat Jacob to the top. Breathing too hard to talk, she willed herself to move faster. *Come on, Addy.* Her calves and thighs burned as she accelerated, nearly sprinting. She soon caught up to Jacob, and, pushing harder, the cold air feeling like an ice pick in her throat, she launched off each foot with as much power as she could wring from her tired body. The exertion infused her with a sense of invincibility, of being alive. She relished the fire in her legs as she reached the top, first.

"Woohoo! I won!" She grinned and bent at the waist, resting her palms on her thighs while she tried to regain her breath.

Jacob arrived and stood next to her. "I wasn't aware it was a competition."

She laughed through laboured breaths. "You still lost. Just because you're not aware of something, doesn't mean it doesn't exist."

"You should heed your own advice, Little Rose."

She straightened, about to argue, when she beheld the panorama.

Peace weaved its spell on her, and she felt the tension in her jaw and forehead dissipate. The land fell gently away into a basin of light-green grass and the occasional tree, before rising again and changing to white-capped mountains in the distance. Both white and black falcons wheeled lazily high in the sky, while smaller red-and-black birds darted below them on arrow-shaped wings, sharply changing directions several times, zigzagging to catch insects. A stream meandering through the midst of the valley completed the captivating scene. The early morning sun gifted the land a yellow tint that made Addy feel as if she were walking into somewhere safe.

The tension of the past few weeks, all her planning and worrying about killing Radnok that had kept her awake at night and barely able to eat, melted away. For a moment, she appreciated that the world was bigger than her, that life was bigger than her. She became insignificant and was able to embrace the tranquillity of her surroundings. There would be time enough to bend under the weight of her burdens later. Presently, there was only this magnificent countryside.

The sparse covering of snow at their feet disappeared midway down the hill to be replaced by frost and, at the bottom, dewy grass. Lamacks, their dark heads down, ate their fill. Gazing above the idyllic valley, Addy admired the distant mountains, their elevated, sharp peaks almost lost against the cloudy sky. She could imagine long-extinct dragons wheeling in updrafts above the valleys. What a glorious period that would have been. Addy sighed and wished she could have lived two thousand years ago rather than the present.

Addy turned to face east, shut her eyes and breathed deeply through her nose, savouring the clean, crisp air, the confused fragrance of grass and snow richly entwined in its scent. Straightening her arms, she held them in front and turned her palms to the sun, enjoying the gentle kiss of the rays on her skin. Her insides warmed. It was then she felt Jacob looking at her. Checking to see if she was right, she opened her eyes. She *had* been right! How was it she could tell? The funnier thing was, he still stared — her catching him had made not a jot of difference.

"Why are you staring at me?"

He didn't answer immediately, instead, he watched her with shining eyes, a smile spread across his face. "Your aura. When you shut your eyes with your hands out, the colour became stronger. It's truly stunning. It also means you're recharging. You should feel somewhat better after meditating in the sun, but you'll need longer. I'll join you." Jacob turned towards the east, shut his eyes and tilted his face and palms to the sun.

Addy couldn't help appreciating the angled cut of his jaw, the way the light smoothed over the curve of his cheek, and shadow filled the hollow underneath, but then she imagined the feel of the stubble on his face and tensed; he was a man — an Ephrestine-worshipping one at that.

Addy decided to ignore his beauty — no good could come from him, or any other man. She shushed the little voice inside that told her that wasn't true. Imitating him, she closed her eyes and counted her breaths, ignoring the gurgle of her empty stomach.

As she relaxed into her meditation, Jacob leaned into her, causing their shoulders and arms to touch. Had he meant to do that, or was it an accident? She wasn't sure if she should move away. If she didn't, there was no way she could focus on the warmth of the sun as the heat of his arm held all her attention. Did he know the effect he had on her? She concluded that pretending nothing was amiss was the best course of action. Determined to ignore her growing and unhelpful attraction to Jacob, she started counting. One pig, two pigs, three pigs....

When she reached two hundred, he spoke and leaned away, breaking their contact. "Time to keep moving. We slept longer than I'd planned and are in more danger for it. We can have a drink at the bottom." Jacob nodded to indicate the stream below.

His mention of danger brought the previous day back to her, and her jaw tensed. Damn Radnok and her inability to kill him. Before she could ponder further, Jacob set a faster pace than before, and Addy let gravity pull her down the hill, hidden holes, tufts of grass and rocks trying to fell her as she did. Feet rapidly moving, she watched the ground carefully. The last thing she needed was to twist her ankle or fall and break something. At least this kept her mind from replaying the previous day over and over. Seeing her father had been distressing, and killing that woman…. She had never killed anyone before, but the hate in her heart had given her courage to try; it just had worked out all wrong. Years of training had honed her skills, so how had she shot the wrong person?

The older couple who had taken her in had taught her much. Baccus's peers respected his skill with bow, arrow and dagger. Addy was grateful she had found him. Sadness opened an empty space inside her. She would likely never see Baccus and Marny again. His tutelage had given her hope that she would one day take revenge on the scum who had ruined her life, while Marny's love and care had helped Addy believe in herself again.

That smear-of-shit Radnok still lived, but so did she, and she wouldn't make any mistakes next time.

Reaching the stream, Addy asked, "Now what?"

Jacob indicated the water. "We follow this for the afternoon before we climb again. We should reach our destination by nightfall."

A rabbit, startled by their chatter, jumped down the riverbank. Addy observed it and reached for her bow. Realising it wasn't there, she frowned. "I'm starving." Addy knelt in the grass. She reached into the stream, cupped frigid water in her hands and drank.

Jacob drank too before standing and wiping his hands dry on his trousers. "I can't help you there. Sorry."

"If I had my bow, I could have killed us something." Addy stood and looked at her empty hands, feeling lost without her weapon. During the past five years, she had rarely been without her bow or at least a knife. Not being armed was like being naked in a room full of drunk men. "What about your sword?"

Jacob opened his mouth wide, his brows drawing down in protest as he jutted his head in her direction. His expression spoke of pure horror. "This isn't a sword for hacking at small animals." He ran a hand down the scabbard, caressing it.

She rolled her eyes and folded her arms. *Oh, for Telouse's sake!* It was all right for him; he still had his most-loved possession. "Well then, have you a dagger?"

His looked turned wary. "Why?"

"I'm good with those too. Hand one over. You seekers always carry at least two." She held her palm out, one eyebrow raised.

"Promise you won't try to kill me with it?"

"If you don't deserve killing, I won't kill you. Besides, don't you have special *powers* to protect yourself with?" She waggled her fingers in the air.

Jacob narrowed his eyes. "That's not a definitive answer."

Addy looked to the sky and huffed. "Okay. I promise I won't try to kill you, except if you try and rape me or hurt me in any way. Is that *definite* enough for you?"

Jacob folded his arms and shook his head, his lips pursed. "After all I've done for you, and you think...." He shifted from foot to foot, obviously insulted and uncomfortable, but reached into his boot and pulled out a small silver weapon that he handed to her, hilt first. Addy ran a finger over the smooth, still-warm handle. The initials *JS*, engraved in a swirly flourish, were the only markings on the dagger. She hefted it in her palm to feel its weight and balance.

"Thanks. Wait here." Addy followed the stream for fifty feet before stopping, her arm drawn back. A taupe-coloured rabbit stopped grazing to look at her.

She reached for the warmth in her belly, and time slowed as it always did. A moth flying near the rabbit's ear seemed almost suspended in mid-air. With her clearer sight, she saw veins backlit by the sun in the rabbit's ears. She threw the dagger. It spun once and sailed straight. The rabbit had started its escape jump but was too slow. The dagger struck its neck. It fell, its legs kicking out once, its body twitching.

Addy released the link with the warmth inside, and the world looked normal again. She shut her eyes to stop the sudden dizzy spell while pondering whether she was playing with forbidden magic. It didn't feel like she was dabbling in evil, but she worried nonetheless. *Telouse, if I've sinned, please forgive me.* The dizziness subsided, so she retrieved the dagger and rabbit. "Thanks, rabbit." She knelt near the stream and skinned and gutted the still-warm animal before rinsing her hands and the knife in the icy water.

When she returned to Jacob, her arm rested casually at her side, the rabbit dangling from her hand. "Can you make a fire?"

He raised his chin, bit his lip, and nodded. Addy speared a stick through the rabbit's mouth and out the other side, and then they took turns holding the rabbit over the fire.

Jacob licked his fingers clean after the last mouthful. "I should have given you a dagger sooner." His smile was crooked, sheepish.

She grinned, feeling smug, and her cheeks heated. "If you want something done properly, ask a woman." Addy stood and continued in the direction they had been travelling earlier, her steps imbued with vigour. Without turning her head, she called, "Come on, boy. Let's go." It was a risk, but she permitted the delight from their shared moment to overpower her doubts. This coming night may be filled with nightmares, but this morning she would smile.

Chapter Eleven

The sound of leaves and branches lashing against one another surrounded Addy as they walked. Their well-worn road reached a third of the way up the mountain on the other side of the valley before the path evened out. Night had come more than two miles back, along with a freezing wind that blew in their faces, causing Addy to dip her head and put in more effort than usual to force one foot in front of the other.

The light emanating from Jacob's hand helped them see enough to avoid tripping. Adrastine still hadn't worked out how he did it, but she would before this journey was over. She had asked again this night, when he had first conjured it. He had simply grinned, his teeth coloured yellow from its glow.

His refusal to tell her had made her clench her fists and roll her eyes. Which then made her think of the time she had reacted that way to something Radnok had said. The scar from *that* punishment still striped her back. A blush of shame heated her cheeks.

Argh, why did she let him get to her; she was a grown women, dammit, and what was a seeker doing helping her and believing in Ephrestine? Since when had shelons been seekers? There were other questions she wanted to ask, like to whom had he made the promise to protect her, and how was it that a shelon lived in Treloah when they were banned from the country? Had Radnok ordered him to protect her? If so, then why run? She wasn't ready to ask him yet, as she didn't know what she would do when she had the answers, if he even answered her. Frustratingly, so far he had kept his own counsel on the hows and whys. If he was working for her father, she would kill him.

The glow of lights in the distance beckoned, making Addy's heart rate increase. She briefly imagined heating her frozen extremities in front of a hot fire, and it made her walk faster. "Is that where we're going?"

"Yes. Folkestown. There are people there who will help us. How's the leg?"

"Fine, thank you." Other than the tightness of her skin where he had fused the wound, her injury really was fine. She had forgotten it sometime during the afternoon. More questions poked their ugly heads out of the miasma of her thoughts, and she pushed them back down.

Addy's stomach rumbled — that half rabbit had been digested hours ago. Being hungry made her testy, so that when she walked under the stone archway with its thick lettering proclaiming "Folkestown" and she saw the village's generously spaced street lamps and quaint two-storey cottages with carved timber trimmings and luminescent stone walls, its beauty was lost on her.

As they walked past a circular fountain, a stone cherub with ice sticking out of its mouth the centrepiece, Jacob stopped, smiled, and swept his arm out to indicate their surroundings. "Welcome to Folkestown."

She widened her eyes at his sudden accent — the words smoothed out in a passionate tone, their rhythm almost hypnotic. *What in all the hells?*

Jacob wasn't Treloahn! "Var's balls! Where are you from?" Addy surveyed the village square, making sure no one listened in. He could only be from one of two places — Nerine or Lachmond.

He stared at her, and his expression flickered from regret to determination. "I'm from Nerine."

Of course he is. He's shelon. He really is shelon. Addy smacked her palm against her forehead at her stupidity. He would have hidden his accent because as well as being arrested by the seekers, he would have been tortured for information and killed. So much fuss over someone of a different race. Why shouldn't shelon be allowed to live in Treloah? Apart from their evil magic, they seemed to be much like the people she saw everyday, not that she had actually witnessed Jacob do anything untoward. So far he had only aided her and Kerwyn. Maybe Jacob was different to other shelons, or maybe the Telousian church had an agenda in making the Treloahns hate shelons. But what? Or was he manipulating her right at this moment, coaxing down her guard.

She stared at Jacob, trying to figure out if he actually looked like a shelon. But what did a shelon look like anyway? It's not like they had tentacles instead of arms. As she observed him, warmth radiated from her chest up her throat. She wasn't excited, exactly, but he had given her information she could use against him. Was he trying to gain her trust by admitting he had lied? That was his one mistake, and she really had been beginning to trust him.

"Lost for words, Addy? I never thought I'd see the day."

Lying seemed to be so typical for men. She narrowed her eyes, filled them with all the hate she could muster. Her voice came out as an aggressive whisper. "Liar. Ephrestine worshipper. You've hidden your true self all this time. What are you? A thief or murderer on the run from Nerine? Have you kidnapped me?"

His smile vanished, and he tilted his head to one side and regarded her, his blue eyes sad. "Neither." His Treloahn accent back, he said, "Tell anyone about this and I'll deny it. Besides, I can notify the seeker network any time I want and tell them where you are." He turned abruptly and hurried off, leaving Addy with no choice but to run to catch up.

He was obviously upset, but what was she supposed to think? He was secretive; he never answered her questions. He hardly made conversation, and sometimes he just watched her, whether he knew she was aware of him or not. It was just weird. He was weird. And he was shelon — the enemy.

Would he carry out his threat to inform the seekers of her whereabouts? Just when she thought she may have actually met a man she could put her faith in, one who would really help her. She should know to trust her instincts, and, if not that, experience. Telouse knew she had been abused and taken advantage of by her share of men, both in her own home and on the streets; why would this one be any different? Was it her fault? She had asked herself many times, tried to figure out what she did that made men treat her badly, but the reason eluded her. It wasn't until her foster parents explained it wasn't her fault, that the men had sinned, that she began to think of it from a different perspective, but still, underlying her logic were her fears and insecurities insisting she was leading the men on, needling them, asking for it.

She bit her lip hard and shook her head to stop her unhelpfully spiralling thoughts. *Let him tell the seekers. No one knows where I've been these past six years.* She could go back to her adopted family and bide her time until she figured a way to get at Radnok. Her mind was made up. She would stay here for a day or two, rest her injuries, find a bow and some arrows, some food, and she would be on her way, without Jacob. There was no other reason to let him lead her around the countryside — at least none she would admit to. She forced away the sadness that nudged at her and the hurt that he would so readily betray her. Yes she would miss his dimpled smile and the butterflies he set off inside her, but now it was time to admit she was safer alone.

Jacob stopped at the church and monastery of Telouse, a large yellow-stone building, the blocks straight and orderly. A spire pointed ten feet into the air atop the two-storey structure. Jacob, if that was even his name, knocked on the heavy double wooden doors. Two fast knocks, two slower, then four fast.

Addy pulled the dagger from her boot, keeping a few steps between her and Jacob. He looked around at her and shook his head. *What's that supposed to mean?* She was allowed to be careful, and he had to know she could never trust him.

She could never trust anyone.

Jacob knocked again in the same pattern as before. From inside came the scrape of a heavy bar being removed. Adrastine snuck a quick look behind before watching the door again. The fear that Radnok's men would appear at any moment kept her alert.

The door opened to reveal a short, brown-robed man holding a lantern, the light of which reflected off his bald head. When he saw Jacob, his face registered recognition. He then looked past the seeker to Addy, and his expression turned into a look of wonder. He blinked twice, owlishly, then hurriedly ushered them inside before shutting and re-barring the door.

"Is this *The Rose*, Master Jacob?" the priest asked in awe, his soft voice almost effeminate. The man shook his head like that of a person beholding a miracle as he walked around Addy, observing her from all sides. "Unbelievable. You said you wouldn't return until you had found her."

Shifting her weight from foot to foot, Addy folded her arms, trying to warm her hands under them. "It's rude to stare. If you don't mind?" What was going on? Why did so many people suddenly think she was some mythical being of prophecy? She. Was. Not.

"Deepest apologies, mistress. It's just … I never thought I'd see the day." The priest of Telouse bowed his head and touched his fingers to his forehead in a gesture of respect. Addy turned to Jacob for an explanation. *Mistress?* And again with the never thinking he'd see the day. *What have I gotten myself into?*

"We're tired and rather hungry, Your Holiness. I'm sure my story would be more entertaining if I could tell it with a full belly." Jacob smiled, and the priest clapped him on the back before leading them to the rear of the church, their footsteps echoing in the vaulted-ceilinged room.

They walked down the centre aisle, pews to either side, towards a raised area containing a round wooden table. Two candles on the table bathed the area in light, illuminating a sandy-coloured tile inlayed into the middle of the table. In the heart of that tile was the image of a blood-red rose, its petals open. Adrastine stopped and touched the smooth surface.

"It's beautiful."

The priest stopped and turned to Addy. His voice took on a reverential tone. "Yes, The Rose of Nerine. The giver of life. Ephrestine's vessel and our symbol of hope. It represents the one who will save us." As far as Adrastine had heard, the rose symbolised Ephrestine, not someone who was going to save Venturan from some imagined threat.

Addy shivered. Something dreadful hid beyond the inky veil that obscured some memories from her, memories related to The Rose of Nerine. Every time she heard those words, tension entered her body, and she felt the need to glance around to see who or what was watching. *Why in all the hells can't I remember? What is it about that name?*

"Aren't you a church of Telouse?"

The priest raised an eyebrow and looked at Jacob, worry creasing the small space between his eyes. "Doesn't she know?"

"She knows, but she doesn't believe. She thinks we're heathens and that Telouse is the one and only god. I have warned her not to say anything. If anyone asks, Your Holiness, tell them it represents the beauty the scythe brings."

The scythe was something Addy did know about. It was the symbol of Telouse, reminding the people of the life and abundance the god brought. Wheat could not be used until it was cut down; evil could not exist if the scythe was there to destroy it.

The priest gave her a kindly, if not weary, smile before leading them onto the platform and to a door at the rear. Through the opening was a low-ceilinged corridor with two doors on either side. The second door on the right proved to be a well-equipped kitchen. Flagstone flooring supported a large, rectangular table in the centre of the utilitarian room. A wrought-iron candelabrum upon the table held five candles, three of which were lit.

"Sit," the priest ordered before he disappeared into the larder. He returned with a plate of cured ham, bread, and hard-boiled eggs. "It's not much, but it's all we have on such short notice." He gave them plates, knives, and forks, and they helped themselves.

Nothing had ever tasted so good, except maybe the rabbit they had barbecued earlier. Being hungry was one of her least favourite things, and being cold marginally beat it. She'd had the joy of experiencing both the past few days.

The priest sat opposite Addy, next to Jacob. He leaned towards the young man, and his fingers tapped upon his own knee, every other breath heavy enough to be called a sigh. By the look of his face, if he held back from asking questions much longer, he would explode. His mouth opened and shut twice in the time it took for Jacob to eat half a sandwich. Addy pursed her lips to keep from smiling and wondered why she wasn't more upset at being surrounded by people who shunned the right faith. *Telouse, forgive them for they know not what they do.*

Soon, Jacob washed his second sandwich down with a cup of water, and, while Addy ate, he nodded to the priest. "What would you like to know?"

The priest's questions tumbled over one another, and he stammered in his haste to eject them. Jacob answered them all — when and how he had found The Rose of Nerine, how they had escaped, how they had come here, but he paused when the priest asked where they were headed next.

"That is a question for the morrow. We will stay here for a few days while we plan. I want to procure Addy a new bow and dagger. We need supplies and clothes." Jacob looked at Addy. "Can you ride a horse?"

She straightened her back and lifted her chin. "Of course I can ride a horse. What sort of a fool question is that?"

"Just checking." The seeker grinned … grinned! Then he turned to the priest. "We'll need three horses. We may be meeting someone … The Deserter."

The priest's eyes widened. "Oh, mercy, mother of Ephrestine. The prophecy is true! And you must be The Arcane." The bald man nodded, looking pleased with himself. "Everything will be all right. We are sav—"

"No one is saved yet, and whoever said anything about me being The Arcane? I'm just a servant of Queen Valtice and Ephrestine, may her light guide us. And, unlike The Arcane, I will not be betraying anyone." Jacob swiftly stood, tension in his jaw. "Please show us to our quarters."

Queen Valtice? What in all the hells did she have to do with it? The Rose, The Deserter, The Arcane: who are these people? She needed to get her hands on this prophecy and figure it out for herself. Surely Telouse wouldn't mind her reading it as long as she didn't actually believe in it.

The priest stood and Addy rose, before following the priest out, Jacob behind her. They exited into the hallway and went to a door opposite where one flight of stairs went up and one went down. The priest ascended. On the next level were two rooms. Addy was shown to one, a kind of women's dormitory with eight bunk beds lining the walls. Four were occupied by a sleeping woman and her three children.

"Pick whichever bed you like. You will find a supply of blankets in the cupboard over there." The priest pointed to the far side of the room. Addy thanked him and had almost reached the cupboard when she heard the door click closed. It was pitch black, and now she had to feel her way. It seemed as if she'd be sleeping in the bed closest to the cupboard, then. She grabbed blankets, felt for the bed and sat. The room was cold, so she kept her coat on but removed her footwear, her calf cramping as she used what little strength she had left to wriggle out of one boot.

She lay down and covered herself with three blankets. Clutching the dagger, and finding a semblance of calm, comforted by the sounds of four loudly breathing companions, she slept.

Chapter Twelve

Mid-morning sun intruded through the high window, clinging to the wall opposite Addy's bed. The weak rays were enough to rouse her, and she yawned before opening her eyes. Her legs and shoulder ached, although the bed was comfortable. She desperately wished she could stay snuggled under the warm layers for the rest of the day, but there were things to do if she wanted to get out of here and away from Jacob by nightfall the following day.

Anger chased the rest of her tiredness away. So *close. So damn close, but I failed to kill him.* She sat up, staring around to see if she was alone. All the beds were empty. She must have been tired if she hadn't heard them leave. Her dreams had been filled with blood, death, and Radnok, and she wondered if they would ever be filled with anything else. *I failed.*

Radnok still lived to inflict his depravity on others. How many other children had he abused? How many innocent people had he tortured and killed? Addy was taught shelons were dangerous, but surely they didn't all deserve to die. Telouse warned them of shelons, but Telouse also told them to love others and treat others how you would like to be treated. Addy also knew that not all the seekers' victims were shelon — her father had joked about it with her mother, and Addy had overheard. It was a convenient way of silencing people who proved troublesome to Radnok, the king and other important officials.

How many more innocent people would die, and how many young girls would he abuse between now and the time she killed him? Tears moistened her eyes. Breathing deeply, she silently promised revenge for her abuse and the abuse of others would soon be hers.

She roughly wiped away the tears with the heel of her hand and shook her head to rid herself of an image of Radnok's dark eyes, eyes that seemed to swallow her whole when he looked at her. She shuddered.

Addy forced herself out from under the covers and laced her boots. A washbowl sat on a stand next to the cupboard. After folding her blankets and putting them away, she splashed cold water on her face over and over, to help scrub away the dirt. She washed her hands and wrists then looked at her thigh. The black fabric was torn, the dark rust of dried blood turning it the deepest of reds, but there was nothing to be done about it now. She didn't want to go outside with wet clothes. She didn't smell that great either, but maybe it would help keep people at a distance today.

After leaving the dormitory, she crossed the hall to the kitchen. A plump cook, her grey hair tied in a round bun at the back of her head, bustled around the stove, putting a pinch of something into a pot before picking up a spoon and tasting. Addy couldn't be sure, but whatever was cooking smelled like smoked-fish stew. Two brown-robed monks sat at the table, sipping hot drinks and eating bread, a chunk of butter on a plate between them.

Addy stood at the end of the table and addressed the monks. "Do you mind if I have something to eat?"

Both men, who appeared to be in their fifties, looked up to assess her. One had short white hair, the other greying hair tied in a tail at his nape. It was he who answered, "Of course, my child. Please, sit. You are a little early for the midday meal, but we have some bread and butter if you like." He pushed the plates containing both towards her.

Addy thanked them and took the plate with the bread. Buttering what was there, she ate it all.

While she enjoyed her meal, the monks rose. "Be well, and may Ephrestine's light guide you."

She gave them a half-hearted smile and a nod. "May Telouse's light guide and protect you." Addy nodded at the monks, one of whom raised an eyebrow before they both turned and left.

The cook placed a cup of hot tea on the table. "Here, child. Something to warm you before your busy day."

"Thank you." When the woman turned back to her cooking, Addy dropped her smile. She blew on her drink and took shallow sips. It was hot and tasted of mint and carrowroot — fresh and bitter. Impatient to leave, she took her half-filled cup and empty plate to the washbasin.

"Leave that, dear. I have plenty of time today." The woman's kindly smile elicited a reluctant one from Addy. She wasn't going to turn her back on her god no matter how well they treated her; although, it made it hard to stay cross.

Actually, she found a way to reclaim her anger. "Do you know where I can find Jacob? The young man who arrived here with me last night."

"Oh, yes. What a lovely, polite young man." She smiled, her expression dreamy. "He's on some errands but is returning for the midday meal. He could not have gone far. Everything he wanted to get is in town. You have but to go outside and visit a few shops. He asked me about clothing, weapons, and horses. Hmm, the horses are a little way out of town, actually, but, like I said, he is returning for lunch, so he can't be too far away."

"Thank you." Addy made her way to the front door they had entered the night before. She opened it and peered out. Snow, a hand-span deep, covered the ground, but, unfortunately, a morning's worth of horse hooves, booted feet and carriage wheels had chopped it into dirty mush. Rooftops cradled pure white, which sparkled in the sun against a backdrop of crisp blue. Whatever clouds had brought the snow had blown away, the wind had died down, and happy voices called back and forth across the square — greetings and comments on the weather for the most part.

She looked left and right, deciding the majority of buildings lay to the right. The seekers had taken whatever meagre money she had left home with, probably when she was unconscious. Shit-eating, lamack-fornicating bastards. Anger swelled inside until she thought she might burst from it. Addy yearned to plunge her dagger into their contemptible chests.

"Hey, Addy. You finally got up."

Surprised, Addy looked up. Jacob's eyes matched the sky, his cheeks rosy with cold against his pale skin. A fluttering she recognised from the first time she had seen him warmed her belly. He quickly replaced his friendly demeanour with concern. "Did something happen?"

"No. Everything's fine. I'm just surprised you're talking to me. You seemed a little *put out* last night."

He cocked his head to the side. "You weren't exactly happy either. I'm fine. A good night's sleep has made all the difference. How's the leg? I want to have another look at it when we go back, make sure it's healing properly."

"I'm sure it is. It doesn't hurt at all." She didn't want him looking at her leg, and she damned well didn't want him burning her again.

"It's best to be safe with these things. You don't want to be on the road and have it start hurting again."

She huffed a breath out. "Okay, if you insist, but if you burn me again, so help me, I'll break that pretty nose of yours." *Pretty nose, where in all the hells had that come from?* She reddened at his self-satisfied smirk.

Pretending nothing had embarrassed her, she put her hands on her hips. Her next question sat uncomfortably in her mouth. She wasn't used to asking for help, especially when she wouldn't be able to repay her debts, but she would do what she must to find another chance to kill her father. "I hate to ask, but, as you know, I'm desperate. I need new pants and gloves, also a bow and arrows. Do you have any money I could borrow, please? Well, borrow might be the wrong word. I doubt I can ever repay you." She met his gaze, ignoring the guilt that made her want to look away. *Telouse forgive me.*

He shook his head. "You don't have to borrow it. It's yours. You're my responsibility right now. Anything you need, just ask. I've spent the morning acquiring horses, and after lunch, we'll go and get you measured for some new clothes and a bow. We'll get you a couple of daggers too. I'd love my old one back." He looked at the ground. "It was a gift."

After how rude she was the night before, and knowing she didn't trust him, why was he helping her so readily, arming her? Didn't he fear she might kill him? Her voice was incredulous. "You're really going to do all that for me?"

He shrugged. "Yes, why not?"

"Well, we're not exactly friends. You're ... who you are, and I'm someone who believes in Telouse."

He huffed and looked to the sky before addressing her. "I told you, it's my job to protect you. You may not understand, but please believe me. Why would I risk my own life to save yours if I wasn't here to help you? Set aside the religion stuff for a minute and think. I could have left you to die, more than once."

He didn't blink or turn away, rub his nose or offer any other tell that he was lying.

"Okay, you do have a point. I just...." Addy lowered her voice. "You haven't exactly answered all my questions. And we were always taught to fear Ephrestine and shelons. It's hard for me to suddenly un-believe it."

"It's not exactly easy for me, either. Do you know how hard it is to save someone who hates you?" One corner of his mouth turned up just enough for Addy to realise he wasn't upset.

She smiled in return. Maybe he wasn't such a bad person, even if he was a man. She felt a twinge of regret that she would be leaving and wouldn't discover more of who he really was. "Okay, then, thank you. Can I keep your dagger until I have the other ones?"

"Sure. Do you want to go to the blacksmith now?"

Excitement made her smile, and she resisted the urge to jump up and down. "Yes, please."

Jacob led her down the main street. Single- and two-storey stone buildings lined both sides of the road, and trails of smoke streamed from their chimneys, painting grey smears against the azure sky. Signs fixed to the front of the shops proclaimed "Candles and Wood", "Apothecary", "Grain & Spices". A boy who could not have been more than twelve, red scarf around his neck and bright-yellow woollen hat pulled over his ears, sauntered past calling out, "Hot pork pies. Hot pies baked today! Only one copper piece." A woman and her two children hurried to the boy, taking three pies from his basket. The pies smelled so good, but there was food waiting back at the monastery, and there was no way Addy would ask for one morsel more than she had to from the seeker; he had already been more generous than she could have hoped for.

Some 700 feet later, they arrived at the end of town, demarcated by a return of closely spaced trees bordering the roadway. This was one of two places she most wanted to go — the smithy.

Small metal shavings littered the hard-packed dirt floor, and near the far wall, his back to them while he heated metal in the forge, stood a tall man, his muscles straining out of his dirt-smeared brown shirt. A great number of blackened tools hung on the wall next to the forge, while a steel anvil sat behind the blacksmith.

"Horace!" Jacob called out, and the man slowly turned, smiling when he saw who it was.

"Jacob. Back so soon?"

"I've brought the woman I was telling you about — the one who needs throwing knives and a dagger."

Both men turned their attention to Addy, who stood straighter. She let her recent anger burn in her gaze. It never helped to be too nice or womanly in front of a man, especially when in his domain, unless you wanted to be treated like an easily fooled moron. She gave the blacksmith a nod.

The man turned his focus back to Jacob. "So, what do you want? I have some examples back here." The ignorant man, addressing Jacob and not her. They were buying knives for *her*, not for *him*.

The blacksmith went to a display case. Addy followed. Soot covered the glass, the contents impossible to see. The man had to open it to show them his wares.

Addy placed her hands on her hips. "*I* was looking for the heaviest you have. Plain — no embellishments."

The man turned to her, reluctantly showing her the knives. Addy picked one up after the other, testing their weight and balance. One of the lighter knives had scrollwork and flowers engraved in the handle — *how ridiculous*. She pursed her lips. The knife she eventually held out was plain from hilt to tip, the heaviest of the lot. "I'll take two of these, please. And that dagger." She pointed to a black-handled knife she had tried earlier.

"Are you sure?" The man asked, wiping his hand on his leather apron. "This one is lighter, better for a woman." He held up the floral-engraved knife.

When Addy spoke, her tone was like sinew stretched thin, almost ready to snap. "*Of course* I'm sure." *Idiot. Why do so many men think women are stupid?* Addy had been subjected to men's superior attitudes her whole life, and it grated on every one of her nerves.

The blacksmith clenched his teeth, but Addy stood her ground, arms folded.

"*Fine*. Will that be all?" he asked.

Addy turned to Jacob, who looked somewhat embarrassed, his expression darkening. He shook his head at her. Well, he would just have to get over it. "Do you want anything while we're here?"

"I ordered a couple of things earlier, so no, I'm good."

The blacksmith was back to addressing Jacob. "I'll have everything ready for you tomorrow afternoon."

"Thank you, Horace. I'll see you then." Jacob turned to Addy, his face stern. "Let's go."

Addy narrowed her eyes at Jacob. What made men think they owned her, or that her opinion was worth less than shit? She stalked out of the shop, past Jacob, who was obviously waiting for her in fear she'd do something destructive if he wasn't around to stop her.

As soon as they were out of the shop, she spoke, her voice low and tense. "Who do you think you are, treating me like that?"

He had the nerve to look angry. "Treat you like what? What did *I* do?"

"Firstly, you ignored the way that oaf treated me. Secondly, you had the hide to look like *I* embarrassed *you*. That man was rude to me. He thinks I'm an idiot because I'm a woman, and you're no better for going along with it. Is that what you think of me, that I'm stupid?" She stopped, fury taking up all the space inside her before she let it out in a breath. "I appreciate you helping me, I really do, but I can't do this. I thought I could, but I can't." Without giving him a chance to answer, Addy strode back to the monastery.

Shutting the door after entering the church, she realised she had just killed her chance to get new weapons. There was no way the seeker would honour his promise of getting her whatever she needed since she wasn't going to do what he wanted. Damn her stupid temper for goading her to act before she thought. Normally she was more patient than this, less emotional. Why did being near Jacob affect her so? She wanted her old self back, the self who could ignore how people spoke to her, the self who didn't desire the good opinion of others, well the good opinion of one particular other. It was definitely time she resumed her solitary path.

She sought the priest who had first let them in. After asking another monk, who had been sweeping out a formal dining room into which she had wandered, she was directed to a study come library on the second floor, near the men's dormitory. What it lacked in size, it made up for in welcome.

Bookshelves lined all available walls, a patterned red rug covered the floor, and three smaller tables held lamps, while a rectangular table in the centre of the room held a smattering of books, with a chandelier hanging above. She breathed in the mustiness of those tomes, remembering how she'd lost herself in many a story as a child trying to escape the aftermath of Radnok's abuse.

A small fireplace warmed the area, and two monks — one reading, the other writing in a large codex, ink stains on his fingers — sat opposite each other at the table.

The man she only knew as "Your Holiness" looked up. His voice, as usual, held a light, kindly tone. "Ah, The Rose of Nerine. What can I do for you?"

"Can you maybe just call me Addy, please?"

He smiled. "If you wish, but there will come a time when you must acknowledge the truth, Addy."

"Truth is subjective." She shrugged. Stubborn man. Ignoring his words seemed like the best course of action if she wanted to get out of there sometime during the next few days. As usual, she couldn't hold her tongue. "I have a favour to ask." He nodded for her to continue. "I don't like asking, but I wonder if you had pants and a warm shirt you could spare. Mine are in need of washing, as am I. I was hoping to have a bath and clean clothes before I leave tomorrow."

"But of course, Ro— Addy." He placed his pen down carefully and stood. "We'll see Mistress Karyn, and she'll draw you a bath. As for the clothes, I thought Master Jacob was attending to that." He led her out of the room and down the stairs.

"He might have been, but not anymore. You see, I'm not going with him when I leave. I'll be returning ... home."

He raised both eyebrows. "Home? Have you told him?"

"Yes."

"I see." His voice held the patronising tone of one who believed they knew better.

She didn't have the energy to argue. Right now, she just wanted a bath. She was leaving by herself, whatever he believed.

Addy's anger didn't subside until she was submerged in a large tub of hot water. The steam caressed her face as it rose to the ceiling. She held her breath, closed her eyes and slid down, the water enveloping her in its sultry embrace. When her face emerged again, she kept her eyes closed and just *was*. It was tempting to stay cocooned like this forever.

But there was no such thing as forever.

Soon images of Jacob intruded on her meditation, and she recalled the jolt of arousal that teased her every time they touched. She imagined what it would be like to kiss him, their lips gently meeting for the first time, before she slid her tongue over his lips, tasting him then dipping into his welcoming mouth. She opened her eyes. *Not helpful, Addy. You want to leave him, not be with him.* Not to mention her fear of being intimate with a man. Her experiences to date had all been against her wishes, except for one time when she was sixteen, and the boy was clumsy and selfish. She had yet to see how sex could be pleasurable, but Jacob made her think it might be, in the right circumstances. Still, what if it wasn't, even with him? She sighed. *Love is just not for you. Telouse has other plans for your life, like saving innocent people from Radnok. So get your arse out of this tub and get started.*

She reluctantly exited the tub, dried, and dressed in undergarments that must have been donated by local families, judging by the faded fabric. She donned a grey dress that left her ankles and dirty boots bare, the hilt of Jacob's knife peeking out of the top of one boot. Whoever was supposed to wear this dress was a head shorter than Addy. White lace trailed up her neck, stopping just below her chin. It felt as if someone was choking her, and she kept putting her fingers inside the fabric, trying to stretch it away from her skin. Maybe the monk had given this to her in the hope she'd beg Jacob for new clothes after all. Even so, she was grateful for the gift.

She relished the feeling of clean, dry woollen socks and wiggled her toes. They had managed to find two pairs for her. She would have one spare for the road. Considering how this excited her, Addy acknowledged that her life was not going how she had envisaged when she first set out to kill Radnok.

Hungry, she headed for the kitchen. The cook from this morning was still there. *Did she ever rest?* "Hello, ma'am. Would I be able to have something to eat?"

"Hello, dear. Yes, of course, but you can't eat here. You're supposed to be taking lunch with Master Jacob and His Holiness in the dining hall."

"I'd prefer to eat here, if that's okay. Wouldn't you like some company? I could help with the washing up." She gave her best sad-eyes pleading look.

"I'm afraid not. As much as I'd love you to sit here with me, His Holiness has requested your presence. If you don't attend him, he will think I've been remiss in my duties." The cook's best pleading expression had the added advantage of a trembling lower lip and was heart wrenching, much better than Addy's. The cook had won; begging was obviously not Addy's forte. She turned, not wanting to be the reason the cook was punished. Sighing, Addy left.

The dining room was just large enough to fit a long rectangular table with seats for fourteen people. At present, only three of those were taken. The bald monk sat at the head of the table, with Jacob to his right and the monk from his study sitting to his left, chewing and still reading.

They all looked up when she entered. Addy stopped at the far end of the table and nervously held onto a chair back, running her thumb back and forth over the timber and missing her bow. Jacob stared at her, his gaze sliding from her face to her boots and back again. His closed-mouth smile did nothing for her temper.

"Welcome, Addy. Please join us." The priest stood and indicated the seat next to Jacob.

She inhaled, fortifying herself for the torture of having to be polite to Jacob. She sat and adjusted her seat so it was as far away from him as possible, which unfortunately wasn't very far.

He leaned over and whispered, "Nice dress. The faded blue-grey is almost the same shade as your eyes."

Was that a compliment or an insult? Addy glared with such hatred she wondered that he didn't die. *If only I had smiting powers.* "It is a nice dress, and I'm thankful for it. Thank you, Your Holiness."

"Our pleasure, Adrastine. It is our duty to look after all those who seek the Mother's safety." Was it her imagination or was the priest really trying not to laugh?

The cook arrived and placed a bowl of the smoked fish stew and a thick piece of freshly baked bread in front of Addy. Her mouth watered at the enticing fragrance. "Thank you, ma'am."

The cook smiled. "Does anyone want more?"

"Yes, thank you. That was delicious." Jacob handed her his plate. She blushed before bustling off to get him another helping. He turned to Addy, who was spooning stew into her mouth. "I still have to have a look at your leg, and then you can come with me to get you measured for some clothes."

Addy choked and sputtered, some of the soup shooting back into her plate and onto the back of her hand.

Jacob patted her on her back. "Are you okay?"

She tried to twist away from his touch. "Yes, thank you." She coughed and glared at him, but her tone was calm and light. "My leg is fine, and I told you I'm not leaving with you. I've decided to go home, so I can hardly let you buy me clothes."

His Holiness looked at her as if she had blasphemed. "You have to go with him. You are The Rose of Nerine, and he is sworn to protect you and deliver you to—"

"That's okay, Your Holiness. I haven't had time to explain everything yet."

"Oh, sorry. Yes, well, you can do that after lunch." The priest seemed to notice his stew, as if it were the first food he'd seen for weeks.

As uncomfortable as it was to be this close to Jacob — she could feel the heat from his thigh so close to hers — Addy had to deal with the situation. She looked into Jacob's eyes and ignored the warmth spreading through her stomach. He had lied to her by omission. He had a plan for her, and he had explained none of it. "Deliver me where and to whom?"

Jacob sighed loudly then pursed his lips, as if he had been caught just before he had gotten away with something — all his hard work had been about to pay off, but now it was being ruined. "I can't talk about it here."

"Where can you talk about *it*?"

The cook returned and placed a full bowl of stew in front of Jacob. He ignored it, his gaze never leaving Addy's. She heard the cook depart, could see, out of the corner of her eye, the priest not looking at them, his slurping becoming louder, more frantic.

Jacob stood, his chair scraping loudly on the flagstone floor. "Come on." He held his hand out for her, but she didn't take it.

Addy rose and followed Jacob out of the dining room and all the way to the women's dormitory. They stood in the hallway, next to the door. "Can you check there's no one in there?" Jacob asked.

She poked her head in the door. "All clear." Grabbing her knife before she went in, Addy stood in the middle of the room, giving herself space to move if the need arose. Jacob entered and shut the door.

He looked at the knife she held. "What do you plan on doing with that?"

"Just a precaution."

"What in all the hells has happened to you? I'm not going to hurt you. I would never."

He looked so sincere, wounded even, that she almost trusted him. *Almost.* She thought of slipping the knife back into her boot, but her hand trembled. She couldn't do it. "I'm sorry."

And she was.

She was sorry for the hurt in his eyes. She was sorry for the childhood she'd endured. She was sorry for all the woman and children she couldn't save. She was sorry she was being a problem. She was sorry for all of it. Before he could see her tears, she dropped her head towards the ground and blinked.

He stepped closer, but kept an arm's length between them. She looked up. "I can never hurt you, Addy. I'm your protector. Please listen to what I have to say. Venturan is on the brink of war. Our world is going to be destroyed, and I need you ... *we* need you to help stop it from happening."

She shook her head. "What are you talking about? I can't stop a war. Are you crazy? And who is 'we'?"

"I'll tell you if you let me take a better look at your leg. Please. You have your knife. And I promise I won't do anything."

Addy stared at the far wall. *Just pretend he's a woman. Nothing is going to happen. He could have raped you by now if he was going to.* Swallowing, she looked at Jacob. "Okay." Addy lifted her dress all the way up on one side, to expose her thigh. Skittish, she watched him, ready to run at the first suspicious movement.

Composed, his features relaxed and his movements smooth, Jacob stepped in closer. Before he bent to look at her leg, he met her gaze. "It's okay, Addy. Really. As I work, I'll tell you who sent me."

She blinked, nodded. "Okay."

He knelt at her feet and carefully placed her foot on his thigh, her leg bent. Keeping one hand on her boot, he raised the other hand. Palm flat, he hovered it over her scar without touching her. She shivered nonetheless, goose pimples forming on her leg — from fear of more pain or from his nearness, she wasn't sure. When he looked up to ensure she was all right, she saw concern in his eyes and something else she couldn't name. For the briefest of moments, she trusted him. Whatever he was going to do, it was going to be fine. Her heart beat faster.

He shut his eyes and a blue glow shone on Addy's thigh, warming it. The tingle in her belly, that she had last felt when he produced that weird light, had returned. As he worked, he spoke. "Queen Valtice of Nerine sent me to find you, although we didn't know who you were going to be. She sent me to find The Rose of Nerine. We must go back to Nerine, to your homeland." He opened his eyes and put his hand down. The glow had faded, but a warm vibration remained. He let her skirt fall to the ground, covering her once more. He stood. "I'm sorry, but there's a scar. If I'd been able to do it properly, there wouldn't be one."

"What do you mean, take me to my homeland? I was born here. Queen Valtice doesn't know me. There is no way she would want me for anything. How am I supposed to stop a war? And how do you do that … that thing with the glow, the heat? The night you burned my leg and closed the wound. How did you do it? And I don't care about a stupid scar. It will just add to my collection." She shrugged.

They were face to face. He was so close, and her earlier daydream of kissing him flashed unbidden in her mind. "I'll tell you everything if you come with me. All the secrets of using Ephrestine's gift will be yours. You already have the ability to use it. You are shelon."

All thoughts of kissing him fled, and the hair on her nape stood erect. Her words came out whispered. "B… but I can't be. My parents are Treloahn. This is insane. How would you know, anyway? Can you prove it?" She hadn't had much stability in her life, but her faith and love for Telouse was something that never failed her. Now he expected her to think her whole life was based on falsehoods? If she didn't have her identity and her god, what did she have left other than revenge?

"Well, no, b—"

She breathed out, relieved he was not going to substantiate her fears. "Exactly. Besides, even if I believed you, which I don't, there's still Radnok. I can't be at peace until I know he's dead. I'll strike a deal with you. If you help me kill him, I'll go with you to Nerine. But I will not set foot off Treloah until he's dead."

"Addy, every day we are here is another day Nerine needs us. Disaster is coming. We don't know how much time we have before it's too late."

"What disaster, and how do you know?"

Convinced and relieved he was wrong, his nearness was again distracting her. His shoulders were so broad, and the prominent muscles of his chest filled out his fawn shirt in such a tempting way. If she reached out, she would be able to touch his face. Feelings she had never known warred against her long-held beliefs and fears. She was the last woman who wanted to pine after a man and the last who would willingly give someone such power over her. Addy stepped back a pace.

"Ephrestine's Prophecy. It has guided Nerine for centuries. Most things foretold have come to pass. You must trust me on this. There is evil coming — the greatest evil our world has ever suffered. Millions will die; maybe all Venturan will become a wasteland where nothing can survive. We don't know how, or when exactly, but it is soon. 'When Pilone, Venturan cannot see, because he is hiding behind Aminty, waste and death will creep across Nerine, destruction of life ne'er anyone has seen....' I think that is self-explanatory, really. Not four weeks past, Pilone, the red planet that has graced our night skies for far longer than we have been alive, moved in alignment behind Aminty. He is no longer visible."

"But nothing has happened."

He stepped forward, imploring. "We don't know that. The disaster will begin in Nerine. Word takes three weeks to travel across the ocean, and if anyone is looking for me, I am no longer where I was."

"I'm sorry, Jacob. I have to kill him before I go chasing some fantasy of the Nerinian people. I don't believe in Ephrestine or your prophecy, but because you saved me, and if you help me kill him, I will go with you once it is done. I will have nothing holding me here."

His decision seemed to take an eternity. He stared past her, at the far wall.

"Well?"

He shot her an irritated look. "I'm asking for guidance."

"And?" Addy folded her arms. Guidance shmidance. He had two simple choices. How hard could it be?

No sign appeared to be forthcoming, but he answered anyway. "I'll say yes for now. I guess I can see how things go."

"Thank you." Addy suppressed a smile and chastised herself for reacting to his answer in such a fashion. She hardly cared about him. *You keep telling yourself that, stupid woman.* It would be good to have someone on her side for a while, even if he was doing it for Queen Valtice and the imagined destruction of the world rather than her. Relief exorcised the tension within her, and she was back to trying to trust him again. Addy wondered how many more times her faith in Jacob would be put to the test. Would she survive the emotional upheaval? "When do we leave?"

"The day after tomorrow. Let's get you measured for a bow and clothes." He went towards the door.

"Sounds good." She followed him out, finally letting her smile have its way.

Chapter Thirteen

By mid-afternoon, they had arrived at Anderson's Grove, a thick copse of trees halfway down a hill. After they waited a considerable time, the cloudy sky emerged from its drab cocoon to reveal a luminescent underbelly that was gently caressed pink by the setting sun. In the fading coral light, aimlessly drifting snowflakes, like hundreds of rose petals, meandered to the ground. Addy stuck her tongue out to catch some.

Jacob laughed. "I'm still not used to seeing you in disguise. Or being so … carefree."

"And I'm not used to snowflakes getting caught in my beard." Addy laughed too, not sure if she could remember the last time she had wanted to. She ran a hand over the facial hair that reached her chest. Apparently, it was beard hair from a real person. She scrunched her eyes tight and tried not to think about it. Her skin itched under the tree resin they had used to attach the beard.

They stood at a high point, just inside the tree line, watching for Kerwyn, and anyone else who may have followed him. Addy's horse nudged her back. "Hey, Charger. Careful." She turned and rubbed his cream-coloured nose then also rubbed her own bottom.

"That's what you get for lying, Addy. Why didn't you tell me you'd never ridden before?"

"I didn't think it would be hard. Besides, I've picked it up fairly quickly."

"You have, but you could have saved yourself three spills if you'd been honest. I would have given you some advice *before* it was too late. I also would have chosen a more appropriate horse." He eyed the strong-willed gelding at her side.

The animal stood sixteen hands high, his enthusiastic personality something Addy would learn to deal with. After the third time she had been bucked off in two miles, she had left her fear on the ground with her pride and climbed back on, this time talking to her horse and telling him what she wanted rather than just copying what she thought Jacob was doing. The horse, Charger, had apparently understood, as the rest of the day had gone without incident.

"Do you think Kerwyn will show?"

"I think he will, as long as nothing's happened to him."

"What if he was too late?"

"We'll leave here in a 600 count, with or without him."

Addy was glad Jacob ignored her question. "Can't we wait longer? What if he's a little late?"

"It's too cold to sleep outside. We'll only just reach the next town in time for the inn's closing. We're not the only ones who need to eat." Jacob rubbed his horse's nose. The black thoroughbred whinnied quietly, and the grey mare they'd brought for Kerwyn stamped a hoof.

As the pink bled out of the sky, replaced by murky twilight, a dark shape grew visible against the white snow. "Is that him?"

"Get behind that tree, Addy. Your aura!"

She had promised she would hide in the event they thought seekers were around, even though she didn't believe in the aura nonsense. It would make travelling easier if she acquiesced to Jacob's orders every now and then. Addy didn't have the energy to argue about *everything*. She crouched behind a wide trunk, her horse dipping its head to hers. "It's okay, Charger," she whispered.

Addy settled in to wait and heard Jacob unsheathing his sword. Taking a knife out of one boot, she listened intently.

The urge to stand and look down the hill was almost overwhelming. *Stupid aura nonsense.*

She waited.

She listened.

Jacob breathed out loudly. *Was that relief?* Then a whispered, "Wait here. If you hear me call out, take Charger and run."

"I will do no such thing," she whispered back.

His footfalls crunched away.

As a distraction, she silently counted to herself. One pig, two pigs, three pigs, four pigs.... At seventy pigs, she heard muffled talking that got louder, then laughing. "Addy?" It was Kerwyn! As she stood, Jacob lit his hand light thing. Addy let go of the reins and ran to him but then stopped before she threw her arms around him. "Kerwyn?" She tilted her head this way then that, studying his face.

The man she remembered was gone, and in his place was a clean-shaven individual wearing a brown woollen cap, but no hair showed underneath. His clothes looked well-tailored, and he didn't smell. The sword peeking out from under his coat and the confident way he held himself bespoke of great change.

Addy gave him a quick hug. "It's good to see you. I never would have picked you out of a crowd. What happened?"

He laughed. "And I you. Your change is more profound than mine. Never a prettier man have I seen. Any man would be proud to grow a beard that quickly." He winked.

Addy remembered her facial hair and laughed. "Oh, right. I forgot. Okay, you win."

Jacob retrieved his and Kerwyn's horses. "Let's mount."

Kerwyn nodded. "Thank you, young master."

"I'm no one's master, Kerwyn." Jacob's voice was quiet.

"You might as well play the part now we're on the road, and what are you going to do about Addy's aura?"

"I'm not sure. What did you find out about your family?"

Addy was glad Jacob had been the one to ask. She had avoided the question, although his demeanour would suggest they weren't dead.

"Well, this is where things get … difficult. I'm not sure where you're headed, but I need to get to the capital. It appears the king's men took them away."

"What? Why would the king do that?" Addy hadn't seen King Orlon since she was a child, but she believed him to be a good, fair king. Maybe he had taken them in consultation with Radnok — he was the king's man, after all — but the king would never murder them, would he?

"They have a better chance in the king's possession," Jacob said.

"Aye, that they do, but Radnok answers to Orlon. At least the king would never kill them without valid reason. That is why I need to see him — before Radnok can convince him to hand them into his care. I also found out there's a price on your heads, although the order is to take you alive, especially Addy. That disguise was a good idea."

"Yes, but we can't disguise her aura. She'll be visible to quite a few of the seekers. I've discovered they can't all see auras, but there are still scores who can. Seems like men with the sight are fewer than Radnok would have the world believe. The disguise will be good enough for the common folk, and I'm sure we can both tell a seeker from a mile away — they have a certain look. We'll just have to be ready to hide Addy from view when it happens."

Addy suddenly felt vulnerable out in the open at night. She couldn't see beyond Jacob's light, but, apparently, her aura was a beacon to seekers, if she really had an aura.

Addy furrowed her brow. "Does the king really condone the torture and murder of shelons? He doesn't seem the type."

"I don't know that he does," said Kerwyn.

"Can anyone develop the sight?" asked Addy.

Jacob interrupted. "No, and those born with the skill have shelon heritage. That fact has conveniently been ignored by generations of Treloahns so that today it is thought of as acceptable for a seeker to have these powers but shelons are still viewed as a threat. Any shelon can develop it, if they so choose. Are you starting to believe in this whole 'Ephrestine and The Rose pig shit' thing then?" She heard the smile in his voice.

"I wouldn't say that. I'm merely exploring the idea."

"So, will you help me get my family back?"

Addy answered, "Yes, but can I ask for a favour in return? Can you help me kill Radnok?"

Kerwyn nodded. "I can definitely help you with that, Addy."

Jacob sighed. "I would have said we don't have time, Kerwyn, but since I've promised to help Addy, and Radnok's next stop on his tour of Treloah is to debrief the king, I think it will all work out. I'll just have to ignore that Queen Valtice will be displeased when she finds out. If I'm caught spying or killing one of the country's top officials, it could easily start a war, which is what we're trying to avoid."

"If that's the war you're worried about, how much damage can Treloah do to Nerine from here? And why would the king want to do something to jeopardise his own people?" Addy asked.

"Sorry, let me correct myself. If I'm caught, Nerine will have two wars to fight simultaneously."

"Oh." Addy was quiet after that. If she believed all his babble about the world being destroyed, her wanting to kill Radnok and making them take this detour could have serious consequences. *But that was if Jacob was right, and there's no way he could be. Is there?*

A soft rustle then creak disturbed the silence among the trees. The wind picked up. Strong gusts whistled a haunting tune through branches, the discordant refrain vibrating through flesh, all the way to Addy's bones.

She pulled her coat tighter about herself and shivered, shrugging off the warning. Nothing was going to stop her killing Radnok.

Nothing.

Chapter Fourteen

The sun shone, suspended directly above. Row upon row of shirtless, tanned men fought in pairs — some training with swords, others in hand-to-hand combat. The sun raked eager claws over well-defined shoulders, backs and arms, drawing moisture away and leaving skin red raw.

From atop his black destrier, Smarnus admired the sweat that glistened and slid over the men's hard bodies as they expended effort just for him.

"Enjoying the display, Sire?"

Conran, his chief advisor, grinned up at him, shading his green eyes with one hand. The man wore a white shirt, buttons open to his chest, his long blond hair pulled back and tied with a leather thong. His other hand held out a small piece of parchment. "This just came."

The king took the note, enjoying the thrill that tingled up his arm as his fingers brushed Conran's. The thrill intensified as he read.

"Excellent. My brother should be ready within six weeks. He should be with King Orlon within the next day or so. Our troops are progressing well. How are the ships coming?"

"They'll be ready to sail within the month."

"King Felson's sympathisers?" A fly buzzed around Smarnus's face. He caught it, crushing it in his palm and wiping it on his horse's neck.

"Chained and ready to row when the time comes."

"Today is turning into a good day. Is everything ready for tonight?"

The sun was finally affecting Conran. The man usually looked unflappable, but he was hot enough to wipe sweat from his brow with the back of his hand. "Yes. Are you sure this is a good idea?"

Smarnus looked at Conran out of the corner of narrowed eyes.

Conran bowed his head. "I apologise, Your Highness."

"Don't leave until they are finished. I'll see you at dinner where you are to give me a full report on their progress." The king gave a single nod, turned his horse and let it walk to the castle. Conran would have plenty of time to contemplate his mistake.

King Smarnus returned to his study, a pile of parchment on his dark timber desk. He sat and read the submissions. The first was a petition from a farmer to be excused from taxes this year as his crop was half what it normally would have been. Smarnus put it to the left. The next was a man offering his second-born daughter, the only unmarried of three daughters, to the king's breeding program. In the future, they would need children descended from shelon — Var's priest had told him of this. They wanted only half-shelon, as they would be easier to control. This he placed on the right.

He read a few more then stood. Patience escaped him today. He blamed the heat rather than anticipation of the evening's meeting. His laugh sounded small and insecure in the high-ceilinged room. *Meeting* indeed. He was being initiated into Var's clan — a deal with the devil himself. He had but to exchange his soul in return for leadership of Venturan.

Again, he laughed. He had no soul. Var was getting the worse end of the bargain, in Smarnus's opinion. There was nothing he wouldn't do to have ultimate power, dominion over the world, and a prolonged life. He was actually curious to see what the god would require in exchange for Smarnus's chance to live six additional human lifespans in luxury, having his every desire met.

No, there was definitely no price he wouldn't pay.

The other thing that made this sweeter? He had beaten Radnok, again; his father would have been proud had he still lived. His brother would become one of Smarnus's underlings, forever under his control. It wasn't that he didn't love his brother; if he didn't love him, he would not have spared him. Smarnus was just competitive, that was all, and he knew he was destined for great things, unlike Radnok. Smarnus hadn't been his father's favourite for nothing.

Smarnus rubbed his hands together and approached his dressing room to ensure his robe for this night had been pressed. He wanted to enter into the next phase of his life as he meant to continue: as a formidable yet strikingly attractive man. He fantasised about receiving gifts and praise at the post-ceremony feast and promised himself he would hold onto this image for the remainder of the day. His version of events was much easier to comprehend than what Archid had explained would occur.

Archid, a short, pale man with black tattoos covering his face and entire body, was Var's chief representative on Venturan. During the initiation, Smarnus would receive a tattoo of the oath he made to Var, but that wasn't the unnerving part. At the apex of the ceremony, Var would possess his body, laying claim to his soul. Archid admitted Smarnus would probably wish he had not made the bargain at that point. Smarnus had believed Archid, his tormented eyes conveying the horrors he had endured. Even if Smarnus wished to die afterwards, it would not be possible. Once Var owned his soul, he would serve him for eternity, whether alive or dead.

As Smarnus ran his fingers down the soft red fabric of his robe, he tried to force his thoughts back to the pleasures that would be his when this was over. Unfortunately, the vision that stayed with him was Archid's ice-blue, afflicted eyes. It was too late to back out now; it had been too late as soon as

Smarnus had made his promise to Var. Besides, it was what his father would have wanted.

"Father, I will make you proud. Your first-born son is going to rule the world." He smiled, but for the first time, barbs of fear prickled down his spine. Smarnus needed a distraction.

Leaving his room, he grabbed the first person he encountered in the hallway — a curvaceous female servant, her bosoms filling out her black uniform enticingly. He smiled at her, and she smiled back. When he placed his hand on the small of her back and kissed her neck, she giggled. Placing his mouth on hers, he licked her lips before forcing his tongue between them, into her tantalising wetness and warmth. His cock hardened, pressing against his trousers, but even as he continued the seduction, he couldn't banish the dark thoughts from his mind.

What have I done?

Chapter Fifteen

Standing at a large arched window, Queen Valtice stared out, fanning her face with her hand. Even though she wore a loose-fitting, sleeveless robe, sweat dampened her face. A tendril of hair had escaped her bun, and she tucked it behind her ear.

Her whitewashed stone palace perched at the top of a hill, the highest point for three miles in any direction. Valtice looked past the formal gardens of hedges and topiaries that formed balls, cubes and even a horse, and the late-spring bulbs displaying fuchsia, yellow, purple and orange flowers, pruned fruit trees and rose bushes. Her gaze reached the ocean, two miles to the south.

She didn't really see any of it.

She imagined brown and dying fields, lifeless bodies with hollow eye sockets, parched skin flaking and blown by the wind across a sea carrying limp, bloated birds and fish in its cold, salty embrace.

Death crawled across Nerine, inch by inch, and she was as helpless as a newborn to stop it.

Fortifications in the form of high stone walls separated the gardens from the surrounding land. With the sea at her front and mountains in the distance at her back, the castle was easily defensible. Not that that had mattered during the past few hundred years — the shelons' reputation as a fierce, magic-using race had been enough to keep attackers away, but that time was over. Their enemy didn't need to scale their walls, not when they could suck the life right out from under them — literally.

She heard soft footsteps.

"Queen Valtice, I have the latest reports."

Valtice turned. Enyak handed her two parchments, the feel of them on her fingertips making her think again of dead things.

One report was from the west, the other from the east. Neither was good. The stress she had felt since viewing the blight for herself compounded with this new information. The decay had encroached another two feet in both sectors during the past two weeks, pushing the populations further and further towards the centre of Nerine. It wasn't critical at present, but in months it would be. And even if they stopped the attack soon, would the land forever be infertile, deadly?

Enyak fiddled with a button on the front of his sky-blue shirt. "Also, your sister has requested an urgent audience. She is waiting outside." His look was apologetic.

Valtice resisted the urge to sneak out the window and took a deep breath. "Send her in." Rather than standing awkwardly to watch her sister's no doubt dramatic entrance, Valtice spun back around to the vista, this time seeing the healthy plants, appreciating them. *We will win this war. We have to.*

Heels clicked on the white marble floor. They stopped. "*Daydreaming* again?"

Why did she say that like it was a bad thing? Valtice turned.

Sara stood in the centre of the room, under the apex of the domed ceiling, artwork of cherubs playing harps floating above her. She was also draped in white, but her dress accentuated her generous bosom, hugging every curve as it fell to the floor. Sheer drapery hung along the sleeves so that when she raised her arms, the effect was not unlike a colourless butterfly.

Valtice replied in her most deadpan voice. "Hello, Sara. Enyak told me you have an urgent matter to discuss." Where she could, Valtice tried to ignore her sister's baiting. Their arguments were never resolved, each sister having an entirely different way of viewing the world.

"Yes, I do. One of my scribes has decoded a valuable piece of the prophecy."

That was one thing she couldn't fault her sister for — as second sister to the queen, Sara was in charge of the Shelon Academy, which taught youngsters the ways of their magic, as well as researched better methods of drawing and using Venturan's power. They also excelled at deciphering the prophecy, having now made sense of more than half the enormous book. It had taken Nerine 300 years to get to this point. Older generations hadn't paid much heed to the prophecy, until one of Valtice's ancestors realised that elements of the prophecy had come true within the time frame suggested. Forthwith, serious study of the tome had begun, new discoveries researched and examined before the information was passed to the public. Well, sometimes it was passed to the public. It was at that time Treloah had distanced itself from their "crazy and fanatical" cousins across the sea, denouncing magic as evil and the domain of misguided heathens. The Treloahns feared Ephrestine and the prophecy.

In Sara's excitement, she appeared to have forgotten to act superior for the moment and approached Valtice. "The Rose is still the most important part, and of course there is The Arcane, although we are not sure exactly what part he plays, except in betrayal of The Rose. He may aid Nerine or be an advantage for our adversaries, whoever they may be." Sara took a deep breath and handed Valtice her parchment. "I present to you more information on … The Deserter."

The queen couldn't stop the thrill that bubbled inside her at this new, crucial information. She forced herself to read slowly, lest she miss anything in her rush to find out what this could mean. When she finally looked up, her sister was watching, her eyes shining in anticipation.

"Well? What do you think?"

"So, he's supposed to be the protector of The Rose, and he's in Treloah, in Courbel for the Snow Day Feast? That's wonderful news."

Sara's smile appeared guarded. There was something Sara wasn't telling her. "I know, Valtice! We need to send a message to Treloah, make sure our men look out for him. The Snow Day Feast is in two weeks. I'm so proud of my scholars."

Valtice nodded but her spirits sank; two weeks was too soon. "Have your scribes write this in three separate messages." Valtice looked over her sister's shoulder at Enyak, who stood unobtrusively near the arched doorway. "Get three tomyaks ready to fly." Her advisor bowed and left. She turned again to Sara. "Thank you. It seems your information has come at almost the right time. As it is, we barely have time to alert anyone, but there is still a chance. It's now in the hands of Druce." The fickle god of luck did not always favour the brave, as some liked to think. Valtice guessed luck depended on the god's mood. She prayed he was in a good one this day.

"What about the other information on The Arcane. Have you deciphered it? Do we know who he is?"

"No. We're working on it. When are you going to call my son home?" Sara folded her butterfly-sleeved arms.

Valtice should have known there was another reason for her sister's visit. *I wonder if she withheld that information until she had a reason to tell me.* The queen hated being manipulated. "Soon. We need more time. He's probably safer there than here with our own power being used against us, but we need as many good shelons as possible looking out for The Rose. You know that."

"But he's in danger. Radnok is not stupid. Jacob just has to make one mistake, one slipup. He's in the dragon's den, for Ephrestine's sake! We will never see him again." Sara stepped forward and grabbed Valtice's arm.

She didn't like it any more than Sara did, but she couldn't play favourites. Jacob had volunteered for the post, and to be honest, he was one of their best. They needed him to be there. If anyone could find The Rose, it was Jacob. Valtice didn't have any children, and her nephew was like a son to her. She removed her sister's hand from her arm and held it between both her hands. "He will be all right, I promise. I'm worried too. Just two more weeks and we'll call him back. I give you my word."

Sara pulled her hand out, her mouth a thin line. "If anything happens to him, it's your fault. Queen or not, sister or not, I will never forgive you." Sara turned, her long blonde hair flying with the force of it. Her heels click clacked loudly, echoing off the whitewashed walls, the noise reaching Valtice long after she was out of sight.

Valtice sighed and rubbed at her temples, the pressure of the past few weeks giving her a headache. Her peaceful day had turned to drama quicker than the sun turned to rain on an autumn afternoon. Things couldn't possibly get worse.

Enyak appeared at the door, wrinkles marring his usually smooth forehead. He glanced behind himself before looking to her again. "Your Majesty, you have a visitor."

A tall, balding man entered and stopped in front of Enyak. He bowed, but not too far, his portly belly interrupting his descent. "Lord Enderfield, Your Majesty. I have come to win your favour." He straightened and smiled. "High Mistress Sara wrote to me and said you expressed a desire to meet with me."

Valtice considered his words. It was an effort to keep the confusion from her expression. "Lovely to meet you, Lord Enderfield. Did High Mistress Sara say why I so desired to meet with you?" The queen risked a small smile that she felt might look more like she was suffering from stomach pains.

"Why yes, Your Majesty. I'm here to ask for your hand in marriage. I'm more than up to the task of helping you run Nerine, and between you and me," —he leaned over to whisper in her ear, the odour of his breath revealing his personal care was lacking—"I'm not too bad in many other areas." He winked. He actually winked at her ... at the queen! *This must be Sara's idea of a joke.*

She raised her brows. They were a relaxed royal court in comparison to Treloah, but this was going too far. "Enyak, please send for High Mistress Sara."

Yes, her earlier assessment had been incorrect. Worse was definitely the direction in which her day was heading. If worse was a thoroughbred racing for a cliff, she was on its back and they were leaping into mid-air.

Chapter Sixteen

They had been on the road for nine days and were only two days from Treloah's capital, Courbel. Seekers were more common on the roads, so it was safer to travel during the day. Addy glanced across at Jacob from time to time as they rode. His thick dark hair touched his shoulders, and he sat straight in the saddle, relaxed but strong. She blushed when she remembered the dream she'd had the previous night. In it, he'd not only kissed her, but they were lying naked together. She had woken herself before things had gotten to the sex stage, fear finding her even in an otherwise pleasant dream.

They had fallen into a comfortable friendship, she supposed she could call it. She respected him, and her trust in him had not been misplaced thus far. He had even revealed some of his precious information and had been teaching her how to mask her aura, but it wasn't working. Supposedly it was because she didn't believe in Ephrestine and her gift, so wasn't opening herself up to her power. Addy knew it didn't work because she couldn't see what it was she was supposed to do, the magic being invisible. The more she tried, the more she was assured she wasn't shelon.

In a shelon safe house, behind a shuttered door, Jacob persisted, while Kerwyn was out scouting their route to the city before hunting their dinner. Jacob faced her across a small, round table. "Maybe we're going about this the wrong way. Addy, could you just put aside your prejudices for one moment?"

"I'm trying! What if I asked you to believe that Ephrestine didn't exist? How easy would that be, huh?" She gave him a pointed look.

It was his turn to roll his eyes. He huffed. "You've seen the light that comes from my hand. You've seen me heal your wound. What is it about those events you don't believe?"

"Ephrestine isn't the only possible answer for those things."

"Hmm." He thought then slapped the table. "Why didn't I think of this before? I'm so stupid sometimes."

Addy was on the verge of agreeing with him when he grabbed her hand. She froze at the jolt that shot up her arm. Her chest tightened.

He smiled. "So, you felt that?"

She reluctantly answered, "Yes."

"I'll do it again." Another jolt stunned her, this one more powerful. It stung her skin, and she pulled back her hand. "No need to be cruel. How did you do it?"

"There's no point in me explaining, Addy, as you have to ask Ephrestine to let you use her gift, and she knows you don't believe in her."

Addy let her head sink onto the table. She banged it lightly twice before allowing it to rest there. She growled, and her muffled voice was full of frustration. "This isn't fair. What am I even doing here?" She sat up. "I could just walk out the door and go and kill him. He's at the palace; everyone knows he is. There's nothing stopping me. Besides, if Ephrestine wants me to help, if I really am The Rose of Nerine, wouldn't she just give me powers?" She stood.

Jacob shrugged — not the reaction she expected. "Fine. Go. You may or may not get close enough to kill him, but you won't succeed, and when he captures you, what's he going to do to you? Not only that, but you will have condemned our world to death. Every. Single. Person."

The bite of his words hurt more than when he had healed her leg. She didn't want it to, but his opinion of her mattered. *Is he right? What will happen if I'm caught?* And there was no shutting up the little part of her that trusted Jacob, believed he was telling her the truth.

"I have a plan, Addy. What do you have? You think you're so special because you can throw a knife and shoot an arrow?" He stood and came around the table. He was only a head taller than her, but it seemed as if he loomed over her from a great height. "You selfish bitch. You're going to get yourself killed for some all-consuming vendetta. What, did Radnok forbid you to go to a harvest festival, or maybe he wouldn't buy you the pretty dress you wanted? A spoiled runaway is what you are, playing at being a woman. Grow up and stand for something other than yourself, Addy."

Her mouth was wide open — she couldn't stop it. She blinked, trying to process his words, come up with a suitable response. Heat built inside her, and she wanted to scream. *How fucking dare he?*

The world slowed. She lashed out, but her hand seemed to move through quicksand, and she pushed him in the chest with it, sending him sprawling. "You shit-eating know-it-all, arrogant, pretty-boy shelon. You think you know me? You think you know my story?" She stood over him, all too aware of the knife waiting in her boot.

Frustrated by his damning opinion of her, heartbroken that he belittled her pain, she fought for control of her rapid breaths. She'd show him how ugly she was, how horrific her life had been. She'd prove him wrong. She removed her vest, letting it fall at her feet. "You want to see what it's like not to go to the harvest festival?" She tore her shirt off next and undershirt, throwing them to the ground. "What about not getting the pretty dress? Want to see what that looks like?" She undid her belt, aggressively pulled it off and flung it at him before grabbing the top of her trousers and forcing them down to her ankles.

Tears streamed down her face, and her breath came quickly, the only sound as Jacob sat stunned, his mouth shut and his eyes wide open, staring at her. He finally rose.

Almost naked she stood, shaking. Anger, shame, fear, pain muddled her brain until she couldn't think, found it hard to feel. It was as if she was outside her body looking down. She watched him with detachment as he stared at her breasts, her stomach. He walked around her as if in a daze. When he was behind her, he gasped.

She felt his gentle hand on her back, tracing the crisscross patterns she knew marred her skin. His fingers stopped in the three indentations where Radnok had burnt her with a scalding poker. He placed his hands on her shoulders and rested his forehead against the back of her head.

His voice muffled by her hair, he said, "I'm so sorry, Addy. I … I didn't know. I'm so sorry." He stayed that way for a time, his breath warming her head, his thumb caressing her shoulder. What thoughts were going through his mind? Would he pity her and treat her like she was broken? She didn't want or need that from him, from anyone. When he stepped back and took his hands away, her heart cried out at their absence. His touch was the first she hadn't shied from; it gave her comfort.

He bent and gathered her garments, dressed her as if she were a child. He pulled up her trousers and refastened her belt, his movements slow and sure. When he was done, he met her gaze with eyes that shone with tears.

There was more she could tell him, about how Radnok had forced himself inside her, watched while other men stripped her of her childhood, but revealing so much, reliving so much might finally break her. *You are worthless, Addy, nothing more than the daughter of a whore.*

Radnok's degradation of her was complete. Looking back, she wondered how she had ever had the courage to leave. She breathed deeply. Courage and the promise she had made to her younger self were all she had left. Her life had no meaning unless she could kill Radnok. While he lived, there was always the chance he would control her. No life should be lived under those conditions.

All the fight had leeched from her voice; there was only resignation. "Do you see why I have to kill him? I will never find peace, and as selfish as it is, I don't care if the world dies if I am dead and he still lives. But if the world survives, and we are both in it, I may as well be dead."

He nodded. "I don't agree that your life isn't worth living if he is alive, but I understand. I promise we'll kill him before we leave. We will find Kerwyn's family, and we will kill Radnok, then we will save the world."

Addy gave a small smile, her sorrow raw. "Thank you, Jacob. I promise you, if I survive killing him, I will dedicate the rest of my life to saving Venturan. I will do as you ask, as Telouse and Ephrestine are my witnesses." She hoped he could see she was trying. It took all her effort to not ask Telouse to forgive her for speaking of Ephrestine as if she were his equal.

Jacob cupped her cheek in his rough hand, looking at her with burning intensity. "We'll get this right, Addy, because if you can't mask your aura, you won't get within 100 feet of Radnok. Just give it a chance. Just for a few days — that's all I'm asking."

"Okay."

"Now, let's sit down and start again." They sat across from each other. "Addy, do you remember when we were escaping from Radnok's compound? When we first left the room and were running, but your leg hurt, I offered to carry you."

"Yes, I do. I said no because I'm quite capable of running by myself. Are you still upset about it?"

He gave her a look one gave to someone who has just missed the point entirely. "That's not what I'm getting at. When you insisted on running, your aura flared. The colour intensified. That's because you were drawing from Ephrestine's gift."

"I wasn't. I was concentrating on ignoring the pain."

"And how did you do that? Did you turn your thoughts inward, centring on your belly? And did you draw warmth from that?"

She looked at him as if he had just exposed one of her biggest secrets. How could he know what it was like to be her? Only her mother had understood, and even then she had passed it off as unremarkable and not something to tell people about. Addy had ignored her mother's advice, as children were wont to do, and she had tried explaining it to her friends, to see if they felt what she did, but they had looked at her as if she were crazy. So how was it that he understood?

He nodded. "You need to start from there. First, you must harness the power. Reach for the heat, as you would normally do."

Addy concentrated, shutting her eyes to block out the sight of Jacob. She didn't like the way he made her stomach feel like dragonflies swarmed inside, or that she had to resist reaching out to touch him when he was near. When she lay down to sleep at night, her thoughts alternated between ways to kill Radnok and what it would be like to kiss Jacob. She wasn't sure which man scared her more; it was unsettling to think both had power over her.

"Addy?"

She shook her head to clear it. "Sorry. Going now." Inhaling, she followed the breath with her awareness as it travelled through her nose, into the back of her throat, into her chest and lungs. From there, she imagined the little jump to her stomach and the warmth therein. Each breath fanned the flames of her internal fire, until she felt heat from inside.

His voice sounded slower, deeper to her. "Good. Don't make it too hot or you'll burn out."

Her eyelids snapped open, her connection disappeared, and the world resumed its usual pace. "What?"

"The heat you feel is the power being drawn into your system from the air around you. If you're standing near a ley line, the power will come through the earth. A person can only handle so much before it burns you alive. Your body can't process it fast enough, unless the energy has a controlled way to leave. I've seen fire burst from a shelon's belly, killing them instantly. It's not pretty."

"I imagine not, and what is a controlled way to get rid of the power? Do you mean like a fireball or something?"

"Yes, or it can come out in something physical — like a punch, a jump, a kick. You can harness the power to make you stronger. Fireballs are a little bit more involved, and not every shelon has the skill to form them. Also, the energy you harness takes strength from your body to process, so you can't do it indefinitely. There is always a period of tiredness after using Ephrestine's gift. With practice, you will become stronger, the tired episodes won't be as severe, but they will always occur."

Addy nodded then reached across the table to place her hand on top of his. "Thank you for helping me."

The intensity in his gaze cooled, and he looked at her as a teacher would a student. "It's my job, Addy. If you fail, we all fail."

She blushed, the earlier heat from her belly nothing in comparison. Embarrassment made her smile feel awkward. She drew her hand back. *Of course — you're his project, his way to make his queen proud. He would have been repulsed by your scars, and who can blame him?* "I know. I just wanted to let you know I do appreciate it. I know you're not really doing this for me. Let's get back to it."

She squeezed her eyes shut, blocking out his expression of sympathy. *Var's balls!* Why had she exposed herself and her secrets to him? Now he looked at her as some pathetic charity case he had to help just so he could save the world. He didn't think she was strong enough to do it herself. *Well, fuck, fuck, fuck, fuck, fuck him.*

Anger was the arrow to which she attached her focus. She speared it into her belly, plunging into the warmth. Her eyes still closed, she asked, "Now what?"

"Imagine you're grabbing the energy, like holding onto a blanket. Pull on it. Drag it around the boundaries of your stomach, up to your heart, around and back down again, completing the circle. Don't let go. And here comes the most difficult part—"

"Hang on. I'm not finished." The energy was viscous, hard to hold. If she moved too fast, it snaked out of her grasp. She had to retrieve it twice.

"Lucky no one has a sword to your throat."

Addy ignored Jacob and dragged the energy through her body, effectively creating a barrier between her organs and her flesh. As the power moved through her, it warmed everywhere it touched. At last, she had come full circle. "I'm there."

"Make both ends of energy touch, and focus on where they join. Focus until it's hot and you can see them fuse together."

She did as instructed. The power melded together, visible in her mind. It was like the heat and brightness within the bowels of a forge. The power was real. How could she not have realised it before? Did this mean she was dabbling in evil?

"When you have finished, release your hold on the energy."

When Addy released, she opened her eyes and was aware of the tickle as sweat slid down each side of her face. She felt contained somehow. Pressure squeezed her insides, not painful, more uncomfortable — the feeling one had at the onset of a stomach ache.

Brow furrowed in anticipation of her failure and more sympathy, she met Jacob's gaze. He grinned. "You did it, Addy. You did it! I can't see your aura."

"I did? Well, aren't I amazing." She smiled, more because of Jacob's reaction than her own happiness. Although she felt proud, guilt at what she had done against the wishes her god dampened her enthusiasm. *Telouse, forgive me.*

"You are, Addy. Really amazing."

And what was that look? Tenderness, as if he really cared about her. She ignored it. He was just relieved she had gotten it right. Any success meant maybe they would survive and make it to Nerine.

"Now what happens?"

"The energy is masking your aura, and will continue to do so until the two ends break apart, which will happen. It is up to you to check regularly to make sure it's still together, and if not, do it again. You will find it takes a small amount of energy when the power is tied off like that, so you may be a bit more tired than usual, but nothing too bad. It's how I've stayed hidden as a seeker."

"You have an aura too?"

"Yes. Mine is blue, which indicates strength in manipulating fire and water. I've also trained in using the power for physical combat."

"You said seekers, the ones who see auras, had shelon heritage. Wouldn't that mean they have some kind of aura themselves?"

"Yes. They have a smoky aura that indicates weak power. Mainly it's the power to see metaphysical things. They can sense ley lines of power as well, but not many know this skill exists. Radnok does, though. He keeps many secrets from his men and from the king."

"So what does a pink aura mean, other than signifying The Rose?"

"We're not sure, exactly, except that you have the ability to harness more power than any shelon in history. What you can do with that power is unknown, and we won't discover your limits until we get you back to Nerine to The Academy."

"Academy? You mean I have to study?" Addy wasn't sure if she should be excited or worried. Using the power went against everything she had ever been taught, but if it saved the world, wasn't that a good thing? Surely Telouse would forgive her. Maybe this power would make it easier to kill Radnok? But what if the shelon wanted to teach her how to handle power just to destroy Treloah? *Argh, brain, shut up! Don't waste time worrying about it now. Deal with it if it happens.*

"Yes, but that's information for another day. Let's survive killing Radnok first, and getting Kerwyn's family to safety."

The door opened, and they both turned. Kerwyn strode in, carrying two skinned rabbits and a pheasant. Snow drifted in behind him, and he hurriedly shut the door.

"Nice work, Kerywn! I'm starving." Addy jumped up and grabbed the bird. "I'll deal with this."

Kerwyn breathed in, about to say something. Addy assumed he was going to say it was too dangerous for her to go out, but then he stopped. "For the love of Ephrestine! Where's your aura?"

She grinned, pride outstripping her misgivings for the first time since she had failed to kill her bastard father. Addy was doing her best to believe in Ephrestine, and she figured Telouse knew she was not forsaking him. "Jacob finally did something useful and explained how I could hide it."

"And Addy finally did something useful and believed me for a change." Jacob poked his tongue out at her.

"Now, now, you two, no fighting or I'll have to put you in separate rooms for the afternoon." Kerwyn laughed. "It was good to expend some energy hunting. It's nice to forget about the world for a time. And the woods around here are full of wildlife. I could have caught a deer, but we won't be here long enough to eat it."

"I know what you mean about forgetting about the world. I hate doing nothing and waiting — too much time to think." Addy held the bird towards Kerwyn. "Can you hold this for a moment, please?" Kerwyn held the bird while Addy donned her coat. "Thanks." She grabbed the pheasant and opened the door.

Jacob called after her. "Don't be too long, and don't forget to check the seam."

"Yeah, yeah," she said as she closed the door. She breathed the cold air and giggled as flakes landed in her beard. Oh, the joy she would experience when she could rip this annoying thing off her face. Food dropped in it sometimes, and it was always itching.

Their log cabin was one mile out of town — a safe house kept clean and weatherproof by Jacob's shelon network. Addy wiped snow off a tree stump and sat, holding the bird so it dangled between her legs. Plucking the feathers with one hand, she methodically removed them section by section. There was something soothing about doing everyday tasks that reminded her of time with her adoptive family. Washing clothes, killing and preparing dinner, even sweeping the floor. She could get lost in those chores and pretend she was normal, pretend that life was mundane and simple.

The last few feathers dropped to the ground, and she stood. "Thanks, bird," she said, a habit she had picked up after she had run away. Before then, her meals had all miraculously appeared on the table, any questions as to their origins promptly fended off by her father as stupid and a waste of time. Addy had always believed animals had souls, could think and feel. She also knew it was the cycle of life that led one life to die for another, but it was right to acknowledge their sacrifice for her.

As she walked back to the cabin, a dizzy spell overcame her. She fell to her knees, gripping her head with one hand. An image flashed into her mind — a man in a grey coat, sword in hand. Fear emanated from the picture. *What in all the hells?*

From behind the house, towards the stables, the faint sound of a horse whinnying disturbed her. Addy raised her head. The noise didn't repeat itself. *Was that real or just my imagination?* Not wanting to take any chances, Addy left the bird on the ground and grabbed both throwing knives — one from her boot, one from her hip. She slowly made her way behind the house, running low from tree to tree until the stables, eighty feet away, were visible. Standing still and breathing as quietly as possible, Addy observed.

Finally movement. A man in a brown coat came warily out of the stables, his gaze darting this way and that. That wasn't the man from her vision. Was there another man hiding in the stables or was her weird episode a fluke?

There was only one way to find out. She would have to come out of hiding to kill this one; then it would most likely draw out the other. *Are they seekers or horse thieves?* Her instincts told her to kill first and ask questions later.

She was out of range for a killing shot, but to move would be to draw attention to herself.

Another vision knocked her off balance, and she gripped the tree trunk to stop from falling.

Green eyes full of anger. The black-coated man aimed the sword for Jacob's mare. No! Addy was seeing things from a horse's point of view. Was Charger communicating with her? Ignoring the absurdity of it, and figuring if powerful magic did exist, maybe this was part of it, she tried to throw an image back. Addy whispered, "Charger," and focused in the direction of the stables. She visualised a horse rearing and striking the man in the black coat.

Horse and man screamed simultaneously. The man in the grey coat turned to look at the stables. Addy ran out from behind the tree, her footsteps crunching on dry snow and twigs. She reached for the warmth — it always improved her accuracy — but she grasped at nothing. It was closed to her. The shock of it tripped her, and she only just managed not to fall.

She was forty feet from him. Thirty. Twenty. He turned. She threw, aiming for his neck. The blade sank into his flesh, cutting off his shout. His sword fell from his hand as he reached up to grab at the hilt of her knife. His fingers touched the silver weapon as he collapsed.

Addy picked up the sword, a weapon with which she was barely proficient. She moved carefully towards the stables as the other man appeared … crawling. It seemed as if Charger had received her instructions. A smile graced her face as she closed the last few steps and stood over the man.

The stranger saw her and looked up. He scrambled to sit, blood dripping from his temple. He put his hands in the air, in a supplicating gesture. "Please, don't hurt me. I was just seeking shelter from the cold."

Even though she had a beard, she couldn't disguise her voice, but it no longer mattered. He would be dead soon enough. "Who sent you?"

His eyes gave him away. He *had* been tracking them. Addy tried again. "I said, who sent you? Was it Radnok?"

His nonverbal cues were telling, plus the fact he wasn't denying it. "At least the rest of you idiots don't know I'm in disguise." Addy brought the sword up.

He reached over his head, his arms stretched high, hands trying to block the sword. Her decoy taken, she threw with her left hand. The knife slid into his neck easily, soundlessly. When she had used her power, which she hadn't known she had, things had slowed down. It was nice to know she could still hit her mark without the benefit of that power.

The man fell face first into the snow. Addy kicked him over and retrieved her knife, still warm and slick with his blood. Red seeped into the snow surrounding his body, and it kept coming and coming — a rivulet bubbling down his neck, steam rising from it into the freezing air, more and more of the frigid, white precipitation turning pink.

Addy stood and stared at the man for long enough that her fingers started to numb. Did he have a woman who loved him, children? She had just taken two lives. As that realization hit, dread settled about her, its oppressive weight lowering her shoulders, constricting her breath. An image of the prostitute surfaced — her surprised face, the way she had slid to the ground. Dying. Dead.

She retrieved her other knife and tried to clean both by rubbing snow over them, but really, she needed boiling water to scald the red stains from her knives and hands. Before she retrieved the bird, she checked the horses.

Two were in their stalls, calm now. Charger had broken through the half-height door of his. He stood outside Dusty's stall, nuzzling her, the two horses nose to nose. As Jacob had taught her, she ran a hand over Charger's shoulder, across his back and down each leg, making sure he had no injuries. When she was done, Charger placed his nose in front of her hand, asking for a pat.

"It's okay, boy. Thank you for warning me. It was you, wasn't it?"

He didn't answer, and Addy wondered if she was going crazy thinking she had communicated mind to mind with a horse. She put him in another stall and locked it, then returned to the house, a bird and sword in one hand, two knives in the other.

As soon as she shut the door, Kerwyn looked at her, his eyebrows shooting up. "What in all the hells happened to you? And where did you get that sword?"

Addy opened her mouth to explain, and tears came out of nowhere. Sobbing so hard she couldn't speak, she placed the weapons and pheasant on the dining table and grabbed a poker, prodding the fire under the kettle to make more heat. The last thing she wanted was for anyone to see her cry.

Jacob rushed to her and placed both hands on her shoulders, looking at her, checking for injuries she supposed, as she had done with the horses. Kerwyn grabbed his sword and ran outside.

"Addy, what happened? Are you all right? There's blood."

"It's not mine," she managed between sobs. Why did she have to cry? It was probably the shock, but what sort of a killer was she if she cried afterwards? It was another reason for the men to nod and agree women were weak. She breathed deeply, blocked her sorrow, and wiped the remaining tears with the back of her hand. "Two men, seekers, I think. I killed them both." She wasn't ready to open up about the visions, not until she knew she wasn't crazy.

"Here, let me do that." Jacob took the poker from her and added another piece of wood to the fire.

Addy sat at the table, staring at its timber surface. At the risk of getting blood on it, she ran her fingers along the wood, feeling each dip and groove. She wondered who had made it. Who had needed the safety of this cottage during the past? Who would need it in the future?

Jacob set down the poker and fetched a bowl from the cupboard. While he worked, he cast glances at Addy. Was he waiting for her to break down again?

"I'm okay. Just the shock, I think." She gave a wan smile, proof she would survive.

"Addy, before the other night, had you ever killed anyone?"

"No, of course not. What kind of a person do you think I am?" *A horrible one. You killed that poor prostitute. Have you even apologised to her family? You're more like Radnok than you thought.*

He nodded, gazing at her more intently. "If you need to talk, I'm here."

"And so am I." Kerwyn strode in and shut the door. "I've hidden them in one of the stalls. The ground is too cold to dig. When it gets dark, later, I'll get you to help me move them far from here, Jacob."

"Okay."

"Kerwyn?" Addy put all the sincerity into her expression as she could.

"Yes?"

Addy hated herself, and she knew it wouldn't bring the woman back, but it was the right thing to do. "I'm so sorry about that woman at the whorehouse. I really didn't mean to kill her. I'm sorry I killed your friend." Tears welled in her eyes again. She blinked and stared at the ceiling, willing the tears to disappear.

The older man approached her and knelt on one knee in front of her chair. He took both of her bloodied hands in his and looked into her eyes. His gaze held sympathy, understanding, pain. "I know, Addy. Lyssa was a beautiful girl with a beautiful heart. She worked there to help support her younger sister and sick mother."

"Oh, for Telouse's sake! What are they going to do now?" Addy frowned, and the dread of earlier, the dread one feels when they know they have done something horrible they can't undo, returned.

"I snuck back and retrieved her savings from the whorehouse before I met you. I gave it to them, but they will run out in a couple of months. We'll think of something, if you want."

"I want that very much. Thank you. It's the least I can do, and next time you see them, please tell them I'm sorry. I will never forgive myself for the pain I've caused."

Kerwyn nodded and wrapped his arms around Addy. She hugged him back, drawing comfort from his strength and forgiveness. What an incredible man that *he* was giving *her* comfort. It was a blessing he didn't hate her, for she surely deserved it.

"Your water is ready." Jacob's voice was gentle. She heard the liquid splash into the bowl as he poured it out of the kettle. "While you wash up, I'll get some more snow for tea."

"Thank you, Jacob." Addy stood.

Kerwyn patted Addy on the back. "That sounds wonderful. I'm sure we could all do with a nice cup of tea. Anyone got any mathis?" The strong, clear alcohol could just about dissolve skin, Addy had heard.

Jacob laughed. "No, but I promise you, when we get to Nerine, you can drown in all the mathis you like. Deal?"

"Aye, deal."

Jacob left, and Addy washed her hands, wrists, and coat sleeves. Blood seeped into the water, and Addy suddenly didn't feel like drinking tea. Tea couldn't fix what she'd done.

As she scrubbed and scratched her hands raw, she tried not to think of the nightmares that would come this night. Nightmares that would see her wake with tears on her face. Nightmares that would have her whimpering with self-loathing. Nightmares that would linger long into the day, spectres shadowing her every move. And the worst thing? She deserved every, single, one.

Chapter Seventeen

Shirtless, Radnok stood next to the fireplace and buttoned up his trousers. The ochre-coloured marble mantle reached his shoulders, such was its magnificent size. He held his hand out to the young seeker, who placed a small piece of parchment in his palm. After reading the short message, Radnok scrunched the parchment and threw it into the fire.

The news was bad, but even from unhappy news could come good. Two of his seekers had disappeared, which likely meant they were dead. They had probably died because they had found Adrastine and that weasel shit, Jacob. Why had he betrayed him? If all went to plan, Radnok would soon find out.

Radnok looked down at the messenger. "You may go."

The boy left, and the high seeker turned to the bed. "And you."

The girl looked at him, surprised. She was slow to exit the plush confines, trying to keep herself covered as she did. He stared at her even more, enjoying the way her cheeks reddened with embarrassment. Young and tight, just the way he liked them, breasts newly formed and perky, not like the saggy tits his wife dragged around. He had paid the mother well for her daughter's virginity. He hardened again and looked at her with regret. No time now. He was to meet with King Orlon soon.

As the girl left, he instructed a servant to change the sheets. He liked the sweet, dirty smell of sex, but not the fluids stiffening the sheets afterwards. One drawback was the blood the females always left. Messy business that. Women were, all at once, a pleasure and disgusting. So necessary, yet so irritating.

As he left, his guard of two seekers followed him, another servant trailing behind. He spoke to the white-liveried man. "Please bring my clean clothes to the baths. I will wear ceremonial garb tonight." He would look his best for King Orlon, and the throngs who would see them dine. Pulling the strings of his regent puppet would be easy. If that didn't work, he could always cut the strings and burn the marionette, which might be the only alternative if Orlon didn't name Radnok his successor the following night. And, if he did, which Radnok expected, his seeker network was there to protect him from his most powerful two rivals — Lord Bronstein and High Priest Tudos.

"Oh, and also, make sure my wife is presentable." He had taken away most of her drugs this past week, and she looked none the better for it. He would need her powers of persuasion this night, though, and, strangely enough, the king enjoyed her company. So presentable and coherent she must be. If anything went wrong now, he would pay a hefty price.

Before they had even reached the heated baths, sweat tickled his scalp and moistened his brow. *Druce, you fickle bastard, don't fail me now.*

***

Seated two places to the left of the king, Radnok sat tall and looked to his left ... at the empty seat his wife was supposed to occupy. The king caught him looking. "High Seeker, will your wife be joining us this evening?"

He clenched his fists under the table and smiled. "Of course, Your Highness. I imagine she's making herself as beautiful as possible for such an important event. You know how vain women are."

The king raised his eyebrows. "Some women yes, but the lovely High Lady Lilliana, I just can't believe it."

"And how is the queen?"

"She is not well, I'm afraid. When you get to our age, every day is a blessing. I thank holy Telouse I'm still here." He touched his fingers to his forehead then chest. "It is at times like this, it would have been nice to have had children. Offspring dote on parents far more than servants are wont to do." His grey hair was parted on the side, neatly brushed, his beard in a braid down his chest. Since Radnok's last visit, some four months ago, the king appeared to have lost weight. His blue-and-white robes hung so loosely, Radnok feared the man might disappear altogether in the folds, never to be seen again.

"Not all children, my king." Radnok let just the right amount of sorrow leak into his expression before looking at his hands. The king reached awkwardly across the vacant seat between them and patted Radnok on the shoulder.

"I heard about your daughter running away. Did you ever find out what happened?"

"No, and it has ruined my wife and me. If it wasn't for the joy I have in serving you, I may not have survived the last few years. Thank you for trusting me with one of the most important roles in your service."

Yes, the king gave him that paternal smile. "You have been like a son to me. I chose well when I chose you."

Radnok smiled, and it was genuine for a change. Pleasure welled up in him at the prospect of his plans falling into place so easily. He gazed around the vast hall, the ceilings high and patterned with silly flowers and cherubs pouring liquid out of giant vases. He may have that removed when it was his turn — a war scene would be far more interesting, and some naked girls. Yes, that would definitely please him.

Chin cocked like a wolf sniffing the air, he eyed his competition and happily noted that he and his wife, if she would ever fucking get here, had prime position next to the king. He would surely announce Radnok as the next king. The most important network, other than the soldiers, was the seeker network. Radnok had foiled assassination attempts on the king thrice, and, as far as anyone else was concerned, he was the king's biggest supporter.

He turned to compliment the king on his choice of entertainment for the evening — a six-piece string group whose music hummed pleasantly under the mindless babble of nobility and pathetic hangers-on, but the king was staring across the room. Following the king's gaze, he saw his wife.

Finally.

Admittedly, she looked beautiful in her flowing green dress, and she had managed to get those saggy tits to look like they had when she was twenty-five — their ripe fullness proudly elevated out of the top of her dress, her dark nipples almost exposed. Normally he would have said it was going too far in present company, but the way the king stared, he might start drooling at any moment.

Radnok stood to receive Lilliana and brushed non-existent dirt off his red collar. The roughness of gold threads caught his fingertips, reminding him how resplendent he looked. He took a few steps to meet his wife. He held out his hand, and she placed hers in his, then he leaned in to give her a kiss on the cheek — the things one did to satisfy public convention. He whispered in her ear. "You look beautiful, my love. The king is eager to see you. Do not embarrass me. Just smile and flirt, but say as little as possible." Standing straight, he led her to her seat.

The king half stood to greet her, and she bent to meet him, placing a kiss on his pale cheek. When they both sat, the king beamed at Lilliana, holding her hand while he talked. Satisfied that his wife was doing her job, Radnok was free to chat to the woman and man next to him, a married couple about his age, and cousins to the king.

"Hello. You may already know of me, but allow me to formally introduce myself. I'm High Seeker Radnok." Radnok inclined his head and kept his teeth hidden when he smiled, lest he look like a wolf about to devour a lamb.

The man, whom Radnok knew to be Lord Panover, probably thought he would be named as successor, but lines of succession only extended to siblings and children — neither of which the king had. And the lord, a wealthy merchant with holdings in Dubreat — the port city that dealt with exchange of goods between Treloah and Nerine — had not much else to recommend him other than his wealth and ability to make more money. However, that didn't mean he wasn't a threat. Lord Panover, in a lazy fashion, pushed his spectacles up his nose and tilted his head back to look down on Radnok.

The lord had not introduced himself, so Radnok pretended he was unaware of the man's heritage. If the man would not trade common courtesy with common courtesy, he had little more couth than the village moron, or a wild hog, and would be treated as such.

"So, High Seeker Radnok, are you enjoying your stint as leader of the seekers?" Lord Panover lifted his fork to his mouth, a dainty, feminine pinkie sticking up, just asking to be broken.

Radnok refrained from breaking the offending digit. "Yes, indeed. I've certainly enjoyed my time getting to know King Orlon. It's almost like having a father again, and I wouldn't want to speak too highly of our relationship, but he has said I'm like a son to him. Not like some of his relatives who never take the time to visit him. Very put out he was when no one came for his name day this year."

"Not all his family, I'm sure." The lord chased his confident laughter with a swig of red wine.

"Almost all, especially his family from Dubreat." Radnok leaned over, close to the man's ear. He looked around, finding a suitable quarry for his mischief. "In fact, I heard that Lord Carlton, over there, is very much in favour. I'm pretty sure the king's words were 'Carlton, out of any of my family, deserves my title.' And when I asked him who he least favoured, his response was, 'that greedy, pompous ass, Lord Panover. He mocks me; his declarations for tax have left out large amounts of produce. I let him get away with it because I pity him. He's married to an asinine woman who gave him five girls, and all fat. One has to have some softness of heart, lest one be deemed barbaric.' Yes, I'm sure that's what he said, and you know, I agree with him, Sir…?"

Lord Panover's face went from shock to red in an instant. He coughed into his hand, probably to wrestle control of his expression and to think of something to say that wouldn't be construed as treasonous. Radnok cocked his head, eagerly awaiting his response.

"Well, that is … interesting. I'm sure he's making the right choice. He is the king, after all. Now, if you'll excuse me, my stomach is somewhat upset. Roast pig doesn't always agree with me. I'm going for a spot of fresh air."

Radnok offered his best wishes and smiled as the man hurried away. He wondered if the lord would try to murder his cousin, or give up and go home. Either way, that was one out of the way. Panover may even get himself killed, whining to the wrong person. Radnok laughed.

Ah, yes, he loved court life.

Radnok stood. And now to butter up Lord Tensony. Another cousin of the king, he was a favourite of Orlon's, but his parents were first cousins, and he was dim witted. Lord Tensony was easily manipulated, so the king had provided him with a first-class advisor, and the head of his army was loyal to Orlon. Radnok had secured Lord Tensony's favour previously, but he meant to cement it this night. When Radnok was announced as king, he would have Tensony's support, and anyone else who valued the king's judgment. More soldiers for him to use to solidify his position against his opposition.

Seeing Lilliana deep in conversation with the king, and apparently enjoying it, he allowed himself to feel the prick of jealousy. The old man, given a chance, would fuck his wife in a heartbeat, Radnok was sure of it. Maybe Lilliana had already betrayed him with Orlon. There had been a time she had only smiled like that for him, but after he had taken her daughter to his bed, things had never been the same.

He recalled his last time with Adrastine, and his bitter smile turned lascivious. He needed to get her back, and not just for his amusement. Addy was the key to winning the coming war, and without her, he would become his brother's puppet. Not many believed in Ephrestine's Prophecy, but he did, and he knew whomever had The Rose of Nerine had the upper hand. He and his wife had been the only two to know of Adrastine's true identity — the girl herself wasn't even aware.

But first, it was time to secure his supporters. After he had the crown, he would capture The Rose. Ah, to feel the velvet of her petals again. He laughed.

Chapter Eighteen

Two days after murdering the seekers, Addy rode along a busy highway, Kerwyn on one side, Jacob behind. A foot of fresh snow banked up along the edges of the road, but the centre of the thoroughfare had been trampled down by heavy wagon, foot and equine traffic, and as a result, wasn't too hard going. The land was flat for a few miles in every direction. The patchwork of farms Addy remembered from the last time she was here was now cloaked by an unending expanse of white.

In the distance, the rounded towers and imposing crenellations of King Orlon's castle seemed to float above the ground. Surrounded by a wide moat, the mammoth structure was built upon a small rise, the land dropping away from the edge of the water-filled trench. The yellow stone seemed to glow against the inky backdrop of gravid clouds, their fullness a menacing presence threatening the structure.

The feeble light of midmorning did its best to break through the dismal overcast. No wind blew. The stillness unnerved Addy, and she chewed her lip. They would reach the outer village before lunchtime, where they were going to eat what they hoped wasn't a last meal before they continued to the castle.

Kerwyn and Jacob had donned disguises before they had set out that morning. There was no doubt that Radnok would have seekers out searching for them, not to mention the public who would love to get their hands on the ten gold pieces offered for their capture — enough for a family to live off for six months. The poster Addy had seen at the inn the night before had given fairly good likenesses of them, and more than one man had given Jacob and Kerwyn a second glance.

Yet Addy had seen their disappointment when they saw the young man Kerwyn and Jacob were with — not a woman as the poster had stated.

To appear older and more bard-like, Kerwyn had shaved his head and bleached his beard. Jacob had managed to grow two days' worth of stubble, the dark hair an attractive addition that roughened up his normally impeccable appearance. In order to hide in plain sight, he wore pants with one blue leg and one red. A court jester's red-and-green, three-pointed hat was tucked in his bag. Addy had been extremely impressed when, the night before, Jacob had demonstrated his ability to juggle five balls and walk on his hands — not at the same time, but skilful nonetheless. He was also adept at telling jokes — something unexpected if his constant serious expression was anything to go by.

Addy played the guard, bow tied to her saddle, quiver on her back. Even though she couldn't use it well, she had a dead seeker's sword at her hip. Kerwyn had given her some instruction to improve her basic proficiency, but she would never win against an experienced swordsman. Playing her role was fun. As her horse plodded along, she stared down any imposing-looking man who glared their way. Hiding behind a beard gave her added confidence. Who would've thought facial hair could do so much?

Being a man was interesting. Other men afforded her respect she never received as a woman, and women bent over backwards, almost literally, to get her a drink or a meal, and she had blushed both times women had offered her their intimate companionship. Men, it seemed, had things easier. The only negative had been when she received one of the offers of companionship; it appeared the woman's male "friend" hadn't approved. He had threatened to beat Addy to within an inch of her life. Addy had both knives in hand in the time it took to blink, and had held one to his throat and the other out in defence in case any of his friends got any ideas.

Kerwyn had stepped in and calmed the man, but Addy, heart racing, had retired to her room after that. There was no use looking for trouble. Jacob and Kerwyn were two of the only men to have ever treated her as an equal, something she deeply appreciated.

"Whatcha thinking about?" Jacob pulled up alongside her.

"Just how much power I have as a man. It's nice having people look at me as an equal for a change."

"You know, where I come from," —Jacob winked— "women and men are respected and treated equally."

"Is that why people here say all your men are useless dandies?"

"Who said that? Can you kill them for me?" Two luscious dimples. one on either side of his mouth, punctuated Jacob's grin, and his eyes shone with happiness. The way he looked at her melted her insides. He stripped her of caution, tempered her fear, and filled her with desire. She wanted to snuggle into his chest and find out if sex could be enjoyable.

"Ha ha, you jest. I suppose that's your job now."

"That it is, my good sir." He bent to acknowledge Addy, just as four of the king's soldiers rode past.

After they were gone, Addy winced. Her voice would draw attention. As much as she tried, she sounded like a woman trying to sound like a man. So far, she had avoided scrutiny by pretending she had a sore throat and had lost her voice, rasping her way through conversations and saying as little as possible.

"I smell snow," Kerwyn said. "It will arrive as we reach the city. Just in time for the Snow Day Feast." He rubbed his glove-covered hands together. His expression, as he stared into the distance towards the castle, alternated between hope and anger.

"We'll find them." Addy's voice cracked with the pretend illness. "I promise we won't leave there until they're found."

He turned his head towards Addy. "Don't make promises you can't keep. What if they're not there? What if my source was wrong? Will you search the whole of Treloah with me until we find them?"

Anger flicked across his eyes so fast she almost missed it. His pain was so raw, it begged for her to help end it. She resisted the urge to reach over and grip his arm — men did not comfort other men in public. *Stupid men.* Kerywn was hurting. People he loved most in the world were missing, and just as Addy would do anything to see Radnok dead, Kerwyn would do anything to see his family alive.

She was going to the castle to reap death and he to find life. How had they ended up on this journey together? And what was Jacob here for? A deal … a deal for which she had made a promise.

"Kerwyn, I promised Jacob that once Radnok was dead, I would return to Nerine with him. If he says we can help you, we will."

"For fuck's sake, A— Amon, you know we can't. This side trip is costing us valuable time as it is." Jacob scratched his stubble. "I'm sorry, Kerwyn. The prophecy…." Jacob had the decency to appear disappointed and sorry for the other man.

Kerwyn didn't hang his head or shout as Addy would have. He nodded, an air of composure and dignity fortifying his posture. "I know, and I would never ask you to jeopardise your mission. You do what you must, with my blessing."

Jacob nodded, the worry lines creasing his forehead making him seem older. As much as he appeared concerned, this wasn't personal for him, not like it was for Addy and Kerwyn. Had Jacob ever suffered at the hands of another?

Addy regarded him, the way he sat straight, met gazes with anyone and never showed fear or nervousness. He never worried that someone wouldn't like him or do what he wanted; he just assumed they would go along with his wishes, but not in an arrogant way. It was apparent he had grown up without fear, among people who valued and loved him. Even though Treloahn was not his native tongue, when he spoke it, it was with the lilt of the wealthy and educated.

"Are your family well to do?" Addy asked Jacob.

Incredulity replaced worry on his face. "What has that to do with anything?"

Addy shrugged. "I was just wondering. It's a fair question. I'd like to know what to expect when we reach your homeland." *It's also distracting me from thinking about Radnok.* Would she manage to kill him this time? And, if she did, would his men murder her immediately? She didn't want to die, but if it was her life for his, it was still worth it. The world would be better off without his kind of evil in it. Maybe that was what her saving Venturan was actually about.

"Yes, my family is wealthy, but I've always worked and studied. Learning how to wield the gift comes with great responsibility. I have an obligation to my family, my country, my mother, my goddess. Everything I do is for them." His mask of seriousness had returned.

Addy's voice was gentle as she asked, "Do you ever do anything just because you want to?"

He raised his brows, dipped his chin and looked up at her, his expression reprimanding. *Stupid man.* Addy blew out a breath and watched the road in front. *End of conversation, apparently.*

The city of Courbel curved around the castle in a wide semicircle, protected by its own walls, and leaving about half a mile between it and the seat of the royal family. Not much was visible above the fortification — a few orange-tiled roofs and four church spires that Addy could count. Most of the buildings hid safely below the top of the ten-foot, yellow-stone walls. In places along the masonry, steadfast grey stems of ivy held on, defying winter.

The entrance was a hundred feet away. Addy's heart beat faster, and she tried not to look as if she was staring at everyone, trying to discover recognition in their eyes that would see the three of them arrested. Seekers would be everywhere, since Radnok was here. Not to mention the king's soldiers. What had Radnok told the king? How many people were searching for them? When she thought about it, though, Kerwyn and Jacob were known by sight to more seekers than she was. Any one of them could be called out at any time. Goosebumps prickled the back of her neck, a wave of them rolling down her arms.

When they reached the entrance, Kerwyn cleared his throat, readying himself to speak and startling Addy, who remained hyper alert. But the guards didn't stop them. The couple behind — farmers riding their wagon, taking produce to market — were halted instead. Whatever the guards had to say to the unfortunate couple was lost in the din as the city enveloped Addy and her two companions.

Addy unclenched her teeth, her relief throwing off tension. The soldiers hadn't looked at them for longer than a breath.

Riding down the cobbled street, Addy surveyed the buildings on either side of the wide thoroughfare. A row of single-level stone terrace houses gave way to three single-level cottages and then to two-storey terraces. The stone was all the yellow stone that must be native to the area, and some of the homes were hewn out of timber planks. All had smoke drifting out of chimneys, and Addy envied them their warm hearths.

The odour of impending snow lay in the still air, clean and sharp. Addy was glad they were here in winter rather than summer when there was no missing the smell of rotting garbage, refuse and sweating bodies, and the wishtets would sting and buzz around one's face. She scrunched her nose.

"What is it?" Jacob asked.

"Nothing. Sorry. Just happy it's not hot. Summer in a city is full of flies and the odour of refuse."

"Not where I come from," Jacob said.

Addy nodded. "Yes, because I'm sure everything's perfect there."

"It is, actually."

She wanted to punch the smug smile off his face.

Kerwyn must have noticed, because he joined the conversation after holding his silence most of the day. "I know of a good inn. We'll grab lunch, get warm and go over things."

He said "things" as if they would be discussing the weather or the price of beef and not how they were going to carry out a plan to murder someone and potentially break others out of a dungeon. Calm should have been his name: Kerwyn the Calm. Addy smiled. She was glad, for the fiftieth time, he was with them. "Kerwyn, you must be the most easy-going person I've ever met. I'm glad you're with us."

"Why thank you, young man." Kerwyn grinned. "I may appear relaxed, but I'm just good at hiding the upheaval inside." His lips straightened, dropping the smile. "You learn to mask your feelings when you work for Radnok. He will use your emotions against you, and I learned early on to bury my true thoughts. It was a matter of survival."

Addy blinked. Kerwyn was right. Radnok had always known how to best hurt her, both physically and emotionally; it was some sickening skill he possessed. "I know only too well. I'm sorry he ruined your life too, but I'm glad you survived. The world is a better place for it."

Kerwyn looked at her, and his gaze held understanding. "Thank you. And I'm glad he didn't get the better of you, either. You have a lot to offer the world, but you need to believe it. And you have to know that not all men are like him."

"I know that now, because of you and Jacob, but sometimes it's easy to forget. Thanks for the reminder."

"Any time."

Two men rode towards them, and they ended their conversation. Goose bumps formed on Addy's arms. The feeling of someone staring at her made Addy check deep inside, to confirm her aura was contained. It had become a habit, something she did several times a day. She'd had to redo the seal last night. Feeling along the line where both sides of energy joined, she could tell everything was fine. She surveyed the approaching men, bustling crowd, and nearby windows, but nothing threatening appeared. Addy wished she could use her energy while shooting with her bow, throwing her knives, and fighting, but Jacob explained it would take a lot more training for her to be able to block the power to her aura only to try and draw it for something else simultaneously. He assured her it would require months of training in Nerine. Of course it would. Now that she had accepted magic was possible and not necessarily evil, he dangled that carrot whenever he had the chance. Although she wasn't ready to replace her god with Ephrestine, and she didn't know if she ever would be.

Near the centre of the city was a large intersection, where two wide thoroughfares bisected each other. A monument of a woman watering a garden, carved out of pink stone, and polished until it shone, stood in the middle. Snow had settled on the gardener's head and at her feet. She held a watering can, which may normally have had water pouring from it, but was lifeless in the freezing atmosphere.

"Who is she?" Had the woman depicted ever been real or was it just a fancy of the sculptor's imagination?

Kerwyn turned to Addy and smiled. "Some say it's Telouse's daughter, but I don't. The pink stone is too much of a coincidence. Do you know how far they would have had to cart it? I believe she's The Rose of Nerine, bringing life to the barren earth."

Addy swallowed, and her mouth went dry as his words triggered a memory from her childhood.

It dragged her under.

She felt as if she was drowning.

Her horse stopped, and she stared at the statue, but it existed in another season, at another time.

They had been here in the summer, Addy and her parents. Had she been six or seven? The wishtets had swarmed thickly around them, one even flying into Addy's mouth. She had coughed and spat it out before pointing and asking, "Who is she, Daddy?"

Radnok's smile had been luminous, his dark hair shining in the sun. Even then, her mother stood behind him, pale and biting her fingernails, not looking up unless she had to. "That is you, my princess."

Addy remembered thinking he meant to make her feel special, that she would grow to be a beautiful maiden who spent her days coaxing pretty flowers to grow. But had he meant it was The Rose of Nerine? That she was The Rose?

Her mind scrolled back through so many incidents, abuses, comments. There were too many to consider them all. Had this been behind everything? Had he thought she was shelon? Is that why he had punished her? But why, through everything, had he always been careful not to kill her? He had once strangled her as he raped her.

Sinking further into her shame, she didn't realise she bit her lip too hard until blood trickled into her mouth.

She could feel him on top of her — his substantial weight making it hard for her to draw breath. His hot palms pressed against the front of her throat, his fingers wrapped around and dug into her neck, and she didn't know what was worse, the pain where he pounded into her or the pain on her throat.

His twisted expression was branded into her mind, his concentration as he tried to achieve an orgasm that wouldn't come, until she whimpered before starting to black out. His groan of pleasure soured the air around her, before his slap stung her cheek. He had been making sure she was still alive. Calling her name. "Adrastine, Addy…."

The voice pulled at her, and her head broke the surface of her smothering memories. She started and snapped her head up, opened her mouth, and gulped in air, her breathing ragged and desperate.

Kerwyn and Jacob stared at her, worry evident in their eyes and the tone of Jacob's voice. "Are you okay? Where did you go?"

"I … I'm okay. Just a memory, that's all." Addy turned her horse away from the statue, to face Kerwyn. She took a moment before asking, "So, how far to this inn, Master Bard?"

Kerwyn looked as if he wanted to say something else to make sure she was okay, but instead, he said, "This way."

Letting her horse follow Kerwyn's, Addy tried to concentrate on the throngs dashing around. One woman wore a long red coat, the colour vibrant against the mainly darker coats of people around her. Fur lined the edges of the hood, and shiny golden buttons cascaded down the front. Why would a woman of means be running around in this weather? Addy imagined different scenarios: the woman was late for high tea with her great aunt; the woman needed more bread and they had run out of flour, her servant sick with a winter illness. And, walking in the opposite direction, almost knocking into her, came another woman wearing a serviceable grey dress and plain coat. She carried two parcels so large she could barely see over them. Where was she going, and what was in those parcels?

In this way, Addy passed her time and staved off the memories until they reached Wayward Inn. A timber veranda fronted the three-story, red-brick building, and a path leading to the back hugged the side of the structure. Kerwyn dismounted, gave his reins to Jacob and wandered inside. Shortly thereafter, he returned. "They have rooms and stables available. Jacob, can you get a table for us? Amon, you help me with the horses."

Addy dismounted. She didn't mind the new name. When they had created her disguise, they had asked her what name she preferred. She had often thought that if she had been born a boy, she would have liked that name. So Amon it was.

As she led Charger through the cold slush to the stables, the horse pulled on the reins. She stopped and turned. He had jerked his head up to look at the sky. She patted his neck. "It's okay, boy. It's just another snowstorm coming. We'll be all right." The horse whinnied but let her lead him on.

The clouds had darkened, and an eerie stillness thickened the air. Addy didn't blame the horse for reacting to the changing weather; he was an animal, after all, and was more sensitive than she. Once he was settled in his stall, the familiar odour of hay and horse dung around him, he calmed enough to dip his head into a feedbag and eat.

Addy patted him once again and whispered, "That's a boy. I'll be back to check on you later." Charger lifted his head to nuzzle her shoulder before dipping into his feed again.

Kerwyn was still settling Jacob's horse, so Addy headed for the inn by herself.

Whispering to avoid being noticed was tiring. The sooner Radnok was dead, the better. She had been hiding in fear too long; it wasn't any way to live. This night would be the end of it. Either she could live her life free, or she'd be dead.

She stomped the ice and slush off her boots before entering the large common room where warmth hit her numb cheeks and nose. Through the smoky torchlight, she found Jacob sitting at a table in the far corner. His chair back was against the wall, and he noticed her as soon as she walked in; at least he was vigilant.

Addy sat on the same side of the table as Jacob — having her back to the crowd made her feel on edge, and today she definitely didn't need anything adding to the tension.

Jacob looked towards the door again. "It's getting darker out there."

Addy adopted her gruff tone, the one that sounded as if she had lost her voice. "Big storm coming. Charger was skittish."

"You know we'll be out in it tonight, if things go well."

"I know, but only for a while. The bard has somewhere safe for us to stay until dawn."

"Before dawn." Jacob shook his head. "If we make it."

Addy breathed out. "Yes, well, thanks for the reminder, Lord Positive." She leaned over, fist on the table. Her voice was low, the emotion behind her words heating her face more than the burning logs in the hearth. "We will make it, and if *I* don't, I will take him with me. Nothing … nothing will stop me. If you have any doubts, keep them to yourself. My whole life I have waited for this. Get in my way at your own peril."

He grabbed her thigh under the table, squeezing hard, and Addy froze, her heart slamming against her ribs. "Don't threaten me, *Amon*. If you die, we all die. The whole fucking world will die, and I will get in your way if I have to. And just in case you haven't noticed, I care about you, Amon. I won't stand by and watch you die, not while I have breath in my body." Jacob released his grip.

Addy placed her palm on her sore thigh. Jacob and Addy stared at each other, and her heart raced, both from their heated exchange and his revelation. Did he mean as a friend or a lover? It didn't matter which; she was lucky he cared at all, but why couldn't he understand what she needed to do? "I'm sorry, Jacob. I'm not doing this to be spiteful. I have to do this to find peace. Please understand. And don't ever grab me like that again." Anger flared through her before dying. She shook her head, sadness a leaden burden constricting her heart. How could he ever comprehend what she'd been through? In a way, she was glad he couldn't understand; she wouldn't wish her experiences on anyone. She would have to keep her own counsel and pray that everything worked out for the best.

Kerwyn reached them.

The older man looked down at them, narrowing his eyes. "What's going on?"

Addy took a shaky breath but didn't say a word. What was there to say?

Jacob was just as quiet. Kerwyn shook his head and removed his gloves, setting them on the table. "Whatever it is, you leave it at the castle entrance tonight. We're a team, and if either of you ruin my chance of finding my family alive...." His gaze burned into theirs before he turned and stalked to the bar.

Neither Addy nor Jacob spoke while Kerwyn was gone. He returned with three mugs of warm ale. "I've ordered us lunch."

Addy and Jacob mumbled, "Thanks," simultaneously.

When the barbecued venison swimming in fragrant gravy arrived, Addy had lost her appetite. The men devoured their lunch, but Addy picked at hers. They had gone over their plan scores of times and had allowed for different things to go wrong, chance things, but there were some things that could never be planned for. What if Kerwyn's family was already dead? What if they weren't even there? What if the two friends he had in the castle no longer worked there? And what if one of them had already been recognised, a spy already running to tell Radnok and the king that the criminals were at the Wayward Inn?

Addy stood. "I'm going to check the horses." She put on her gloves and pulled up her hood. As she walked past the few occupied tables — not many braved this cold if they didn't have to — she envied the men their simple, honest lives. Not like her angst-ridden existence, which was filled with pain, loneliness, danger and shame. Come to think of it, how could Telouse allow an innocent child to be subjected to the tortures she had been forced to endure? Now *she* was the one who was on the run, treated like a criminal, not the man who really deserved it. Had her faith been misplaced? She had given Telouse her love and obedience her whole life, and she had received nothing in return. Was the god narcissistic or just uncaring and oblivious? Did he even exist? Addy was travelling in dangerous territory, and she half feared being struck down. Would she bring bad luck on herself for thinking these blasphemous thoughts? She was normally a logical person, but had pushed aside logic for too long where Telouse was concerned. Maybe it was time to give Ephrestine a chance, a real chance. After all, Jacob and Kerwyn believed, and they were still here, both of them having better lives than she up until this point. Addy had a lot of thinking to do.

The path to the stables was no longer harmless slush but slippery ice; the temperature had dropped noticeably. Addy cautiously made her way to Charger, her hand out ready to grab the wall if she slid. The horse nickered when he saw her. She smiled. Ah, animals — she could just be herself with them. When this was all over, she was moving to a farm as far away from people as possible.

They would be here for a while, so she removed his saddle and brushed him down, placing his blanket back over him when she was done. The exertion warmed her somewhat, and she watched the plume of her breath dissipate into the frigid air.

She put her arms around Charger's neck, rested her head against his rough mane, and closed her eyes. What would happen to him if she died? She supposed someone would find him and decide he was theirs.

"Okay, boy, I'm going to practice throwing. I'll see you in a little bit." She couldn't wait around doing nothing until tonight or nervousness would eat away at her resolve. She wouldn't admit it to anyone, but she was afraid to die — not that she wouldn't sacrifice herself to kill Radnok, but she didn't have to like it. Supposedly there was a heaven waiting for those who believed, but if the past few weeks had taught her anything, it was that the world she once believed in had become unstable. What if nothing waited? What if they were pawns of the gods while they were here, but they ceased to exist once the gods had tired of them? She knew, logically, that it was a silly fear, as she wouldn't know any different when the time came, but to not be here, aware of life was a depressing thing indeed.

A gate behind the stables led to a lightly forested area. She picked a tree trunk, drew her knives from her boots and threw. Time after time, she hit her mark, so she made it harder for herself. She ran towards her target, across the target, stopped and started, throwing at various times. She only missed once, but once was too many times. That once might be the only chance she had.

She ran and threw, ran and threw.

"Hey, Amon."

Addy stopped, breathing hard from her exertion. After retrieving her knives from the tree's chopped-up bark, she turned. Jacob approached, calmness having replaced his earlier aggression. He looked around to make sure they were alone, she guessed. Then he faced her. His voice just above a whisper, he said, "I'm sorry about before. I know you don't care about anything but killing Radnok, but I do. I care about *you*, Addy. I care about our world, my family, my friends, my home. Without you, it will all disappear."

She hated how his nearness caused her heart to race and her stomach to feel as if a hummingbird had taken up residence, tickling her insides with frenzied wing beats. "You only care about me insomuch as you're worried what you think will happen if I die. You don't really care about me as a person. If you did, you wouldn't have grabbed me like that. You men are all the same: aggressive and forceful when you don't get your way."

"That's not true. I'm nothing like Radnok; I would never do what he did. I'm sorry for grabbing you, hurting you. I didn't think. I like you, Addy. I like you a lot. Please forgive me." He took one step forward, the step that had been the only thing between them. He wrapped his arms around her and kissed her forehead. "I don't want anything to happen to you, to Addy the person. Even if you weren't The Rose, I would still feel this way."

It was as if her forehead burned where his lips had been. Her cheeks heated, and she closed her eyes, enjoying the thrum of sensation vibrating throughout her body and between her legs. She hugged him back and tilted her head to look into his eyes. She wanted to believe him, this beautiful, intelligent, patient, strong person who made her laugh and cry, all in the same day. But it was damn near impossible to ignore a lifetime's worth of conditioning. Even if he did care for her, love was not for her. Love, from what she could see, mostly entailed pain, and was rare. What her father and mother had for each other wasn't love. What Kerwyn had was love, but look at how that had worked out. And Jacob. Who had he loved before, and why was he here by himself, an attractive man who could have any woman he wanted. Was there someone from Nerine he pined for? Was there someone he would return to? Was she just a way to pass the time?

Shut up, Addy. Stop overthinking everything. Pushing her negative thoughts away, she tried to enjoy the moment. His lips were so full, so close, and she just wanted to lean forward and touch them with her own, but then she remembered her beard, and that would just be weird. She laughed.

"What's so funny?"

"Have you ever kissed a man?"

"No, can't say I have."

"I was just thinking...." She risked looking at him with passion she had never shown anyone. He returned her stare, his pupils large, and he licked his bottom lip but made no move to kiss her. She shook her head, blushing at her own foolishness. Keeping her tone light, Addy said, "It's okay. Do you promise not to get in my way unless there's no hope for killing him?"

"No. I can't. It's not what I want, Addy, to see you hurting because of that depraved piece of shit, but I've made promises to others. Promises I must keep, even to the death. Please understand."

The sincerity in his eyes touched her heart. He was telling the truth, and he was torn. Who was she to demand he set aside his whole life, his training, and his belief system for her? *Although, isn't he asking me to do the same thing? Ha, but I don't have a life worth living right now. He knows what it is to be happy.* She nodded. "It's okay, Jacob. I just … I have to do this. I can't let him hurt anyone else. I won't take any more risks than what I absolutely must. And, by the way, I still think you're mad. Do you really expect me to be able to save Venturan when I can't even kill Radnok? Seriously, have you thought about it?"

"With my help and Nerine's shelon army, you will." He pulled her close again, and they stood that way for long enough that Addy's toes started to numb. The freezing air consumed the warmth from her earlier running. "Let's check the horses then go inside."

"Okay, Addy. And don't forget we're in this together. You and me." Before he dropped his arms from around her, he kissed the tip of her nose, his warm lips and sweet breath bringing heat flooding to her cheeks. His smile touched his eyes.

Uneasiness niggled at Addy. "Jacob?"

"Yes."

"What promises have you made to your people back home?"

His smile fell. A ridge formed in the space between his eyes, and his gaze turned wary. "I have many duties to fulfil when I return. Nothing you'd find interesting. Come on, didn't you say we should check the horses?"

He led the way to the stables, the yawning divide that had just opened between them as cold as the weather. He was hiding something from her, something he knew would upset her, but she wasn't going to push right now; they could die this night. If they survived, she would have her chance. In the meantime, she tried to close off her feelings for him — her affection toward him would do more harm than good — and focus. Tonight was her last chance for revenge.

At the barn, she surveyed her blades before placing them back in her boots. "I've got some sharpening to do."

After Addy honed her blades and Jacob checked the horses, they trudged back to the inn. The sky darkened further, the clouds low and black. The unnatural stillness cocooned them, but Addy felt the false sense of comfort. When heavy flakes started falling, quickly covering their tracks, Addy couldn't help but shiver. A storm was approaching, and none of them would escape without scars, if they escaped at all.

Chapter Nineteen

Smarnus fought to wake from the nightmare. Suffocating darkness surrounded him, and a malevolent being approached. He couldn't see it, but he sensed it was there; it hovered close, waiting to strike. Smarnus tried to run, but his legs wouldn't move. *I need to wake up. Wake up, damn you.* Terror overrode his ability to think, and he cried, knowing he was about to die. The air in front of his face stirred. *No. Please no! Ephrestine, save me. I'm sorry, my goddess, please forgive me.*

His eyes sprang open, breaking the hold of the night terror.

Sweat coated his body, and his heart raced. He reached fingers to his cheek to pat the tears lingering there.

Bright daylight made him blink. His breaths came in a shallow, rushed tempo until he saw his pristine white sheets and Conran sitting in a chair next to his bed. The relief on Conran's face worried him. Then Smarnus recalled the night before. How close had that prick of a demon summoner, Brak, brought him to death?

The last thing Smarnus remembered was the ritual, standing under a full moon and repeating some unintelligible words Brak had instructed him to say. Then he sucked blood from the sliced belly of a young woman, her shrill screams almost ruining his hearing. He shuddered as he remembered the metallic taste and the sickly slide of the blood down his throat.

The night had then turned blacker than it had any right to. The moon had still been there, but oily shadows had reached up from beneath his feet, a sinister mist rising and smothering their small group. When the inky force had closed over his head, the moon had been lost to him.

That was when the powerful entity reached black claws into his heart and mind. His chest had felt as if it was going to explode. Pressure had gripped his head, squeezing his skull, like a giant hand crushing his brain until he thought he would lose consciousness. Then it was he who had screamed, louder than the woman. He had wanted to collapse, but the repulsive energy had held him aloft, his feet leaving the ground, until he floated.

Var had claimed him.

"Sire?" Conran reached for Smarnus's arm, but stopped before touching him and drew back.

"Why do you fear touching me?" Smarnus's voice croaked and cracked; he must have screamed for a lot longer than he remembered.

Conran stared at Smarnus, wariness and uncertainty in his gaze. "I just wanted to make sure it was you. You've been asleep for two days, and you scream sometimes, talk in a brutal language I can't decipher. And now ... your eyes." Conran handed his king a small mirror.

Smarnus sat up, his muscles sore and spent. What the fuck had they done to him? He grabbed the mirror, and before losing his nerve, held it in front of his face. He gasped before clenching his jaw to hold back a scream. What in Var's name had they done to him? What had he agreed to? His unlined, pale face reflected back at him. His younger appearance was not the problem. His red eyes were.

The strong, dense crimson of blood. The glowing red of the hottest coals.

And behind his red irises and black pupils, something dangerous flickered. Something he didn't know. It was him, but it wasn't.

Who or what had he become?

"Conran, run me a bath then help me dress." He held his hand out to the man who was closer to him than any other. Smarnus didn't love anyone, but he cared for Conran, lusted after him. It was almost love, but Smarnus would always put himself first, and Conran must serve him.

Naked while he waited for his servants to do as Conran asked, Smarnus sat in a timber chair in front of his full-length mirror. His hair had not escaped the ravages of Var and had turned so white that Smarnus imagined it might glow in the dark. His body hadn't changed, though. He admired his muscular physique and broad chest, avoiding scrutinising his face. If he found gazing into his own eyes unnerving, what must it be like for everyone else? Conran was braver than he thought, not running as soon as his master had awoken with Var's mark upon him.

Sweat, an effect of the warm weather and the recent dream, gave his now pale skin a sickly sheen. He had rather liked his tan and would miss it. What hellish process could strip the colour from a man? Was he becoming a creature of the underworld?

And then, a scarlet glow pulsed, cascading over his body in waves. When he looked up, he met his reflection in the mirror. The stream of light came from his eyes. He shut them, hoping to stop the unsettling incandescence, but a vision settled before his sight nonetheless. A bearded young man with a rosy glow about him glanced around nervously. He sat with some kind of court fool, and a bald man, all drinking mead in a common room while snow fell outside.

Smarnus jumped when commands accompanied the vision.

The voice slithered through his mind, and he physically recoiled at its touch, but he couldn't escape. It was an ancient, unmerciful voice that held worse than death in its tone. Its rasping tore into his brain, cut it open and revelled in his suffering. "You must find them and bring them to me. The Rose of Nerine, The Deserter, and The Arcane. You fail, you die."

"Why. Who are they to us?"

Smarnus cried out at the feel of pincers squeezing his head.

"The girl is The Rose of Nerine. While she is in the hands of the shelon, we cannot win, but the young man, he is pliable. If we have him, we can get to her. But he cannot be forced. You must cajole him. And the Deserter must die. He will stand in our way while he lives."

Smarnus didn't dare question Var again. The god hadn't given his name, but Smarnus knew inherently, the way one knew how to breathe without being taught. "Yes, Master."

"Good. I will be watching."

The presence was gone, and Smarnus found himself on the floor, curled into a ball. He gripped the chair to pull himself up, not wanting anyone to find him in a weakened state. He needed to rule while being ruled, so no one must know how easily Var controlled him. Maybe there was a way he could defy the god and keep some thoughts to himself, but that wasn't smart thinking for the present. He was new to this, and if he wanted an eternal life filled with luxury and every excess he could imagine, he would have to begin today.

Conran returned. "Your bath is ready, Your Highness."

Smarnus followed him to the adjoining room where black mosaic tiles covered the walls, and a painting of a blue sky with clouds and wheeling seabirds decorated the ceiling. An octagonal bath was set into the floor in the middle of the room, large enough to fit ten adults. Smarnus stepped down the four steps and sank into the warm liquid.

He leaned back and shut his eyes. "Conran."

"Yes?"

"I have a journey to undertake. We will be gone indefinitely, and I want to take fifty of my best men. Boats and horses will be needed. We need to leave on the morrow."

"Will there be anything else?"

Smarnus opened his eyes, desire building within him. "Yes." He reached under the water, gripped his own erect penis and stroked his hand up and down. He licked his lips. "Get in."

Tonight Conran would be his, and tomorrow he would make his claim on the world.

Chapter Twenty

The windows and shutters were closed to keep out the worst of the cold. Torches burned in wall sconces, a bright accompaniment to the fire crackling cheerily in the hearth. King Orlon finished warming his hands and went to the bed, where he stepped on a footstool then climbed on. His wife lay on the far side, and he sat next to her.

He took her hand in one of his and stroked her soft white hair away from her forehead with the other. She smiled up at him.

"How are you feeling, my love," Orlon asked.

"Tired." She coughed, her whole body shaking.

"Not long, my love. Not long. Tonight is the night we have been waiting for. I just don't know how it will go."

"Then you'll be free to join me?" She coughed again, and the king winced. The spasms were worsening, and she had taken to spitting blood with them. He wiped the scarlet moisture from her lips.

"Shh, no need to talk, but yes, I will join you one way or the other. Tonight, we come into the prophecy, for ill or for good. But there are two possible outcomes. One good for Treloah, one bad. In both, we die. It is nothing to fear. We will be together, and you will be free of your ailments." He smiled and brought her hand to his lips. He closed his eyes as he tenderly kissed the back of her hand.

Her skin felt gossamer thin to his lips, her bird-like bones easy to detect underneath.

"I know your secret, my darling Orlon, and it's all right." This time she swallowed down her cough.

He would have denied it had she been better, but there would be no secrets in the afterlife, and he didn't want her to force it out of him, lest the coughing kill her. He didn't want her to go yet. Every extra moment was precious. He gently squeezed her hand. "I'm sorry for keeping it from you. I didn't want to bring you shame. You didn't deserve that, but there was a time when I loved another. The love died long ago, but the future of my legacy did not."

"Ephrestine has a plan for us all. I love you, Orlon." This time the coughing lasted so long her pallor turned an alarming shade of blue. Orlon leaned over her, helpless, a tear following each wrinkled indentation as it slid down his cheek. As soon as she breathed again, he held her in his arms and rocked her. *She has become so light; she may be taken to the afterlife with her body.*

"Just hang on until tonight, my love, then we can go together."

Eyes closed, she nodded. The king stared into the soothing fire and felt relief. His job in this life was almost done; he just prayed it wasn't all for nothing.

Chapter Twenty-one

Feeling refreshed after having bathed, Addy donned four layers of clothes before checking her beard was on properly and her aura contained. She finished by lacing up her boots and examining the shiny gleam of her knives in the candlelight. Her room was shuttered — the innkeeper had predicted high winds, and one of the worst storms of the season was approaching, so she had no idea how high the snowdrifts were. She hoped it wouldn't hinder their short ride to the castle.

It wasn't easy to move in so many clothes. She closed the ties on her bag, gathered her bow, and carried them downstairs to meet Jacob and Kerwyn.

Kerwyn had gone out after lunch to run some last-moment errands before their foray to the castle. Addy remained ignorant of the details, but she did know he was calling in favours to make sure they were granted access to the castle and for their escape afterwards. He had procured extra horses for his family, although, how his children would fare in the freezing cold, Addy wasn't sure.

She found the men sitting near the fire eating pea soup and bread, Jacob's face painted white, two round rouge circles on his cheeks. Addy sat next to Kerwyn. "Looking suitably creepy, Jacob. You can hardly tell it's you."

Jacob smiled. "Yep, Kerwyn helped. It's a bit itchy, though."

Addy turned to Kerwyn. "How'd you fare this afternoon?"

"Good. Everything's ready."

"Can I ask a question?" Addy wanted to know more about this kind man who had helped her despite the danger. He was a man who had lost all hope before she had come along, it seemed.

Kerwyn shut one eye and looked at her with the other. "You can ask. Doesn't mean I'll answer." And that was something she knew too well. She smiled as she recalled their brief time in Radnok's cell.

"What's your family like? What do they look like, you know, in case one of us stumbles across them?"

Kerwyn pulled two small, black-and-white ink pictures out of his pocket. One was of a beautiful woman with long, dark hair and large eyes. She had high cheekbones and thin lips that were curved into a vibrant smile. The artist had even managed to capture a cheeky glint in her eyes. The other was a boy of about nine, his straight hair forming a fringe across his forehead. His eyes were large and round, like his mother's, but he had Kerwyn's fuller lips and nose.

Kerwyn cleared his throat before he spoke, his eyes soft and brimming with tears. "This is Jorgan." He pointed to his son. "My eldest. He'll be turning thirteen in midwinter. And this … this is the woman who stole my heart when I was but a lad, soon after I started with the seekers. She knew I was different, seeing the auras and all, but she loved me just the same. Her name is Mayna."

Jacob studied the pictures. "When was the last time you saw them? Have they changed much?"

"I saw them only a few weeks ago. I left them, but I still went to see them from time to time. They never knew I was there, but Mayna would have known, as I often left something for them, whether it was an armful of apples or a coin or two. The pictures are three years old. Mayna looks the same, maybe sadder, and Jorgan's hair is longer, his face a touch fatter." He glanced at the pictures one last time, kissed them once each and stowed them safely in his inside shirt pocket. When that was done, he resumed eating.

"Why did you leave if you still love them? Did Mayna make you go?"

"I had to spare them the shame. I failed as a seeker. I couldn't provide for my family. Three weeks before I left, Mayna had to take a position as a seamstress, and the women there looked down on her. People knew I'd left my job because I wasn't tough enough.

"She shouldn't have to work — she was from a wealthy family. But when she fell in love with me, it was against her family's wishes, and she chose me over them. But her father was right. I wasn't worth it. I could never be good enough for his daughter. Worst of all, if I stayed, my family might have become targets of the seekers. There are always seekers trying to gain favour with Radnok, and punishing me by killing or harming my family would have eventually occurred to one of them."

Addy was surprised Kerwyn had thought so little of himself. From what she had seen, he was steadfast, caring, capable. He was superior to most people she had met. "Even so, you should have stayed. Isn't marriage supposed to be forever? Things got tough, but it would have been easier to get through it together. She would have had to work with or without you there, but you just made it so she had to work *and* be lonely. You could have moved, gotten away from those who knew you?"

Jacob pursed his lips and breathed deep through his nose, his tone acidic. "Addy, shut up. We can't all make the perfect decision every time. Right now you're an excellent example of that. Way to make him feel better."

Addy's face heated, and she shied from Jacob's scrutiny. She wanted to tell him to piss off, but deep down, beyond her pride, she understood he was right. "I'm sorry, Kerwyn. I sometimes speak before the sensible part of my brain gives me the go ahead, and it didn't come out how I intended. Jacob's ... right." It hurt to say that, and Jacob's smug expression didn't help. "We all make the wrong choice sometimes. You know you're worth her love. She still knows it, I'd wager. Don't give up on yourself. You're one of the bravest, most decent people I've met, and living on the streets, you meet a lot. I lived rough for a couple of years before an elderly couple took me in. If you can survive out there, you can survive anywhere."

He patted the hand Addy had rested on his. "It's okay. You're right, but I'm not going to wallow anymore. When I thought I'd lose them … really lose them to death, I knew I'd wasted too much time. If I'd stayed with her, I would have found work eventually. I hated myself enough for both of us, but I'm not going to live like that. Radnok will not determine how I live anymore."

Addy smiled. "It'll be hard for him to control anything when he's dead." Her smiled widened to a grin, and Jacob and Kerwyn laughed.

Laughing helped release the tension that made Addy's jaw and head ache.

Kerwyn stood, sliding his arms into his thick coat. He buttoned it, slipped his gloves on and pulled his hood over his head. "I picked the wrong time of year to shave." When he smiled, dimples formed at the corners of his lips, and Addy imagined he would be more fun to spend time with in different circumstances. Sadness overcame her when she thought of how much he missed his wife, and how much his family probably missed him. She had promised Jacob she'd return to Nerine as soon as they had killed Radnok, but she couldn't let Kerwyn save his family by himself. Hopefully, they would all soon be on the boat bound for Nerine.

Outside, the fattest snowflakes Addy had ever seen poured out of the sky. Small gusts of wind stirred the flakes one way and then the other. Snow covered the ground and the two steps up to the inn, drifts collecting against the front wall under the awning.

The menacing charcoal sky absorbed what little afternoon light there was, and the street torches had been lit. The walk to the stables was safer now the snow had covered the ice. Addy sank shin deep with every step and was glad she had Charger to carry her to the castle.

Before long, they had saddled the horses and were riding into the main street of Courbel, but this time there were no people rushing to finish errands. Sensibly, everyone was inside where it was warm and safe. The houses that sheltered them were mere shadows in the gloom, a small number given away by hazy light shining from rare, un-shuttered windows. Addy felt like a wraith, floating through a deathly, abandoned landscape. She patted Charger for comfort.

"Hey, baldie, I hope you know which way you're going," Jacob commented.

"Course I do. I was stationed here for five years before Radnok was given his own seeker academy and compound at Querse. A little dusting of snow won't bamboozle me."

Jacob laughed and shook his head.

Addy remembered Querse, a port city to the south filled with whitewashed houses, turquoise water and sand dunes. "I think I was born in Querse, but we moved to Targen when I was seven." She opened her mouth to catch snowflakes, diverting her thoughts from memories that wanted to squash her down and snatch her confidence. She wouldn't be able to kill Radnok from the bottom of a pit of fear. She refused to succumb to memories of Radnok and her mother.

The gates at the far end of the city came into view when they were just about upon them. Such was the lack of visibility. The gates were shut, and Jacob dismounted then knocked on the door of the three-storey round tower. Cheery, yellow light shone from its small, rectangular windows. Charger stomped a hoof and snorted, and Addy sensed he was eager to move, to keep warm.

The door to the tower creaked open. Jacob exchanged muffled words with a soldier, who turned back inside and motioned to someone else. Another man appeared at the door. Addy thought maybe they had recognised Jacob and wanted to check who accompanied him. Ready to kick her mount into action, she swallowed and watched the tower door intently.

The two men didn't approach her, though. They hastily reached the gates and unlocked them, grumbling their reluctance to be out in the cold. "Hurry up. We haven't got all afternoon," the first soldier whined.

"Thank you, good sir," said Jacob as he mounted and their little group passed through.

Out in the open, Addy felt more vulnerable, but to the elements rather than the seekers. To her left, the tree line started not far from the road, but she couldn't see it through the downpour of white. But she could hear the creaking branches and the rush of wind weaving amongst the trees.

The wind blew harder than when they were in the city, and the rustle of leaves reached her in the softness of thickening snow. Addy hunched in on herself, trying to escape the biting cold. She dipped her head and trusted that Charger would follow Kerwyn's horse. Jacob stayed behind her, and true to his word, took the role of protector.

"We'll be there shortly." Kerwyn's deep voice floated back to her, and Addy wondered if his neutral tone was meant to calm her. If she could only believe they really were the visiting entertainment, with feasting and laughter the reception they could expect. "Let me do the talking, and Addy, look mean and dumb. In fact, pretend you can't speak. I don't want anyone accidentally giving us away. Jacob, get your balls out and show them some tricks as we walk in."

"Are you sure that's appropriate?" Jacob laughed, and Addy snorted. That would be a sight.

"The balls that are a handful, so that would not be the two in your pants. If I'd meant those, I would have said marbles."

Jacob breathed in sharply and, feigning offence, in a sarcastic tone said, "Ha ha. Very funny."

Kerwyn continued, "They'll show us to the performers' hall, which is usually a room adjoining the great hall, with a door covered by a curtain, so Jacob can make a dramatic entrance at *performance* time.

"By the time Jacob is ready to go out, I'll be searching the castle for Mayna and the children. My sources in there tell me some people were brought in and put in the dungeons over a week ago, and that they saw children with them. I don't know for sure if it's them, but I'm going to start there. Addy, you'll want to position yourself in the great hall before the performance so you can get a feel for where everyone is. After the performance, when the acts are allowed to join the feast, you should've figured out how to kill Radnok and get out of there. Don't wait for me."

"But what if you get caught?" Addy couldn't believe Kerwyn was going to wander the castle by himself. Anything could happen.

"I won't. I have friends inside. The seeker oath requires us to always do good for Treloah and her people, so I did, and it earned me many friends at the castle, not that all seekers abide by the oath." He shook his head. "I'm grateful they remember my good deeds rather than my failures, and to be honest, not many like Radnok. They know ... what he is."

"A childhood-stealing pervert who treats women and girls like shit. I want him dead. Fucking. Dead." Addy wanted to cry. She wanted to skewer Radnok like a pig on a spit. People knew what he was. Why didn't anyone do anything about it? Why? Were they all like that, men, so they protected each other? They couldn't be. Kerwyn didn't seem to be.

"What did you say, Addy?" Jacob's voice had taken a menacing edge.

"I want Radnok dead. You know that." *Shit, I've said too much. Stupid damn mouth.*

"I saw things I didn't like when I worked for him. Twice I saw children leaving his room at a late hour." Jacob kicked his horse into a trot and came around in front of Addy, stopping his horse and forcing her to do the same. "Did he do that to you? Please tell me he didn't."

Addy shrugged. "It's not something I make a point of talking about." She felt nauseous, ashamed. What would Jacob think of her? Would he think it was her fault? Had it been her fault?

Jacob's eyes darkened, and his lip curled into a sneer, showing a hint of white teeth. "That fucking Var-loving bastard! How dare he! How could he? His own daughter. A child. I can't … it's beyond horrific. I'll kill him myself. Addy, what you went through is … I can't even find the words. I'm sorry. I'm so sorry." He nudged his horse to stand next to hers, and he held out his hand. She took it, tears moistening her eyes, making them sting in the frigid air.

"Thank you, Jacob. I'll be okay." She was sure they all heard the lie in her words, but by saying it, she wanted them to know she was trying, and she would fight until she finally got there. "Now you know why I want to kill him, not that the physical scars he inflicted on me aren't a good enough excuse."

Kerwyn had stopped too. His eyes held sympathy and anger. "You'll get your chance, Addy. Just don't be overeager. Take your time, and wait for the right moment."

Addy stared at her gelding's neck, too ashamed to hold Kerwyn's gaze. "I'll do my best."

Jacob squeezed her hand before letting go. Addy pushed her pain away, ready to change the subject. She didn't want Jacob and Kerwyn staring at her as if she were damaged beyond repair. She was still a strong woman, and she would make things right in her life. Addy would heal and be happy, the best revenge aside from killing Radnok she could think of.

"Kerwyn, are you sure you don't want us to help you find your family first? Maybe get them out before we kill Radnok?"

"I'm planning on finding them before you kill that filth, and in the commotion of that, I should be able to sneak them out. No one will be looking for a family."

"Oh, wow, thanks." Addy and Jacob were decoys?

Jacob's tone was gentle but firm. "Addy, you said you wanted to do what you could to help Kerwyn. He's gotten us in, and we'll do what we have to and run. Simple. Everyone gets what they want." Jacob made it sound as if what Kerwyn proposed was the most logical thing in the world, and she supposed it might be.

"If I get them out, I'll try and make it to the north, to Marcern in time. If not, I'll send a message later to Queen Valtice to pass onto you."

Jacob replied, "Sounds like a plan."

The roadway was lost under snow that continued to descend. Maybe two inches had fallen since they had left the inn.

"What if we get snowed in?" Addy asked.

Kerwyn surveyed their surroundings. "Head to the lower levels below ground. There are tunnels and secret places under the castle that my friends know about. If the snow is too thick, they will hide us until we can get out. They'll also take care of our horses and hide them with the king's."

"You're pretty good at all this planning. I'm glad you came along," Jacob said.

Kerwyn shrugged. "Maybe Ephrestine knew you would need a hand."

"If Ephrestine knew we needed help, why couldn't she just strike Radnok down with a lightning bolt or something? Honestly, what use is a god if they let someone like him walk the land? Radnok's like a jellyfish or wasp. I don't see what benefit he brings to the world, only pain. He doesn't need to be here."

"Don't speak like that," Jacob admonished. "She can hear you, you know."

"Oh, great. Hey, Ephrestine!" Addy yelled into the whiteout, snow blowing into her mouth and eyes. "Can you stop the snow and make it warmer. I'm bloody freezing. Thanks. Oh, and can you get the carrot out of Jacob's arse?"

"Addy! You can't talk to a god like that."

"Oh, Jacob, lighten up. Seriously?" *Why does Jacob never understand my sense of humour?*

"Jacob's, right, Addy. The gods can't control everything, or she wouldn't need you, but there's nothing smart about being rude. One day, when you need her the most, Ephrestine may be able to help you, but whether she'll want to or not...."

"If Ephrestine is like anyone else I've ever met, she'll only help me if it benefits her. I loved Telouse, worshipped him as I was supposed to, but he didn't stop any of the shitty things that happened to me. Seems to me gods are more like people than everyone thinks. I mean, who cares if the whole world dies? We won't know any better, but there'll be no one left to worship any gods. It's in her best interests to help us."

"Whoa, Addy, you're really pushing our friendship. Please don't deride the god I love. You're insulting the motivation for what I'm doing, and you're spitting in Ephrestine's face. Who do you think gave us the gift?" Jacob's accent slipped through as his anger rose, and as he said "the gift" it sounded as if it had been pushed through clenched teeth. He stared at her with a dark gaze. If Jacob's anger manifested into energy, it would have melted the snow.

Addy decided to keep her opinions to herself from that point onward. "Sorry. I didn't mean to insult you. I'm just nervous about tonight and frustrated. We're the ones in the right, so why is it so hard to stop him? Anyway, don't answer that." Addy pulled up her horse and gazed past Jacob. "I think if that massive shadow is anything to go by, we're here."

High stone walls loomed in front of them, only just visible in the negligible light. The castle was a dark form that could have been anything — a dragon (not that anyone had seen one for five hundred years) a group of trees, a giant from a fairy tale.

Kerwyn kicked his horse into a walk, and they travelled to where the drawbridge lay across the iced-over moat. Four guards in heavy coats greeted them, but Addy felt as if someone else was watching her. When she looked up, she noted two archers outlined in dim light, one in each of the two towers that flanked the front entrance to the castle. But that didn't assuage her discomfort. In all likelihood, if she could see two, there were more she couldn't. She shivered.

One of the guards spoke to Kerwyn, his tone gruff, warning no nonsense would be tolerated. "Names?"

"We're the entertainment. I'm Bard Vaganty, this is my juggler, and that is my guard. I believe Mistress Hanover is expecting us." Kerwyn bowed in his saddle.

Addy surveyed their surroundings to stop herself from staring nervously at the guards and appearing suspicious, not that there was anything to see but white in a thirty-foot radius.

"Dismount and wait down here." The guard pointed just to the right of where they were. Then he turned and nodded at one of his companions, who left to presumably find Mistress Hanover to vouch for them.

Addy was about to complain that there should be somewhere warm to wait, but then remembered her un-manly voice. *Var's balls, that was close.* Her saddle creaked as she swung her leg over and jumped to the ground. When she landed, she sank up to her knees. Addy had never fought in deep snow, and she hoped she wouldn't have to this night. Fighting in snowdrifts favoured the tall.

The gusts grew stronger while they waited, the wind's mournful song a fitting accompaniment to the dark sky as it raced around and through the battlements. Flags flapped noisily from above, and jingling tack sounded from behind. Addy shivered and tried to breathe warmth onto her gloved hands. Maybe running on the spot would stave off the numbness that had stolen feeling from her extremities. Not wanting to look ridiculous — she was supposed to be a guard after all — she stepped from foot to foot and drew her coat tighter about her. *Hurry up, for Telouse's and Ephrestine's sakes.*

Turning, Addy saw dark shapes approaching. She discretely pulled her dagger from her hip scabbard. Outlines didn't materialise into riders and horses until they were well within striking distance. It would be so easy to sneak up on someone in the snow if one had good hearing. Addy felt even more vulnerable. Her scalp prickled as if ants were crawling all over it, and she glanced around quickly, seeing nothing but white. She took deep breaths to calm herself.

The party reached the large gates, crowding Addy, Kerwyn and Jacob. The first two men dismounted — taller than Kerwyn with wider shoulders. Addy didn't imagine their group would be a match for those men, and she wished she had been able to learn more about how to use her powers — whether they were a gift from Ephrestine or not, she could admit they existed and that Telouse wouldn't strike her down for using them.

The men addressed the king's guards before being asked. "Lord and Lady Tenesh, by invitation from King Orlon. We were scheduled to arrive this morning, but one of the horses pulled up lame."

The guard produced a piece of parchment from his coat and moved into the torchlight to read. "Please come through. Let's get you out of the cold." He nodded to another of his guards, who escorted the party of eight through. Two were the lord and lady, one looked to be their daughter, and the others were guards.

'Get you out of the cold?' What about us?

The large party reached the other side of the drawbridge. Once they had attained the inner courtyard, a woman in a cape and long skirts came across the bridge towards Addy's group.

The guard who was doing all the talking folded his arms. "'Bout time you got here, Mistress Hanover. I don't have time to babysit your charges."

In a stern, teacher-like voice, she answered. "Farlon, it is your job. Don't be an ass."

Addy's shoulders shook from suppressing laughter. Mistress Hanover's insult had caught him off guard, and he had no response.

"Please come this way. I'm sure the king doesn't want your performances affected by having to wait in the cold for so long." She gave the guard a pointed look then ushered them over the bridge. On the other side, a large stone arch opened to a snow-covered courtyard. Jacob grabbed a small pack from his saddle before young men took their horses, and Addy stood for a moment watching them leave. Mistress Hanover must have sensed Addy's concern because she said, "They'll take them to the stables where they'll be given food and water. It's warmer in there as we have quite a crowd tonight." She made a point of turning her head to look at Kerwyn before again facing Addy. "Don't worry over your animals."

Jacob spoke to cover for Addy. "Thank you so much, Mistress Hanover. We really appreciate it." None of them knew who Kerwyn's contacts were — he had insisted, in case any of them were caught and tortured. Also, seekers might be watching, or someone who wanted that reward. They would remain in character until the end.

The hairs on Addy's neck stood, making her shudder. She scanned the courtyard to see who was watching. No one. She tilted her head to check the windows facing the courtyard. The shutters were closed. For the tenth time that day, she checked her aura remained hidden. Yes. Whoever was watching them may just be observing any new arrivals, and if her aura didn't glow, they would never suspect her. *You're safe. Stop worrying.*

Mistress Hanover led them through the double front doors into a utilitarian foyer that was austere rather than grand. A large, peacock-blue rug covered the flagstone floor, and weapons hung on the walls. Two crossed swords hung to Addy's right and next to that a battleaxe as tall as herself, which she imagined would take a giant to wield.

They followed Mistress Hanover past a staircase and down a hall. Taking the second door on the right, they traipsed through a medium-size reception hall where portraits of kings lined the walls. Lounges and single chairs sat against walls, while a fireplace blazed in a hearth that was big enough that Addy could have walked into it.

The door opposite led to another corridor. Two more turns, one to the right and one to the left, and they arrived at their destination. Before stepping across the threshold, Addy checked behind them, but no one followed. She entered the large, crowded room and stood just inside the door — there was no way she was going to rush in without assessing the situation.

Two iron light fittings hung from the ceiling, scores of candles in each. A vast timber dining table had been pushed against the far wall, leaving the red-and-gold rug in the middle of the room bare. Addy counted thirty other performers who practiced their craft. A harp player in one corner tuned her instrument; on the rug, five acrobats dressed in white, tight-fitting clothes, climbed over each other, forming different human towers; a magician and his assistant discussed something near the stone fireplace; and a choir warmed up, voices as smooth as the best Nerinian honey flowing through the room.

There didn't look to be any seekers. Addy unclenched her jaw.

"There's space to practice over there." Jacob pointed to an unused corner.

"Before you warm up, I have need of your services, bard." Mistress Hanover smiled at Kerwyn.

He bowed. "Of course, Mistress Hanover. I would be honoured to help. Now what is it you need?" Kerwyn gave a nod to Addy and Jacob, an intense goodbye in his eyes.

Addy blinked, the sudden urge to cry surprising her. Not wanting to alert anyone to anything unusual, Addy gave him a close-mouthed smile, hoping he could see she wished him luck. If anything bad happened to her friend, it was her fault. If not for her, he wouldn't be in this mess.

Jacob touched her arm. "Time for me to practice. I'll need an audience." He raised his eyebrows.

"Of course, master juggler," she answered quietly then turned to watch Kerwyn leave.

But he was already gone.

Chapter Twenty-two

Wearing his ornate red jacket with gold fringing on the shoulders, Radnok stood with his back to the giant portrait of King Orlon's father, King Payton, and faced his men. He rested one hand on his hip, the other on the bejewelled hilt of his ceremonial sword. He was aware of the way his gold buttons shone in the candlelight.

Twelve of his seekers stood at attention, their faces intense in reverence. The rest of his men were stationed throughout the castle, ready to quell any disruptions after Radnok was announced as the new king. None of his men had reported seeing Adrastine, which was a shame. He would have loved for her to observe his greatest moment. Once he was crowned, he would have plenty of resources to defend himself against an army, and then it wouldn't matter who knew of her existence. He also wanted to punish the traitor who accompanied her. Although, could he blame the boy? The gods knew the lure of cunt had led better men than Seeker Jacob astray.

Radnok smiled. "Well, here we are, on the cusp of a momentous occasion." He paused to let his men smile and enjoy the moment with him. "Because of your exceptional service, you twelve seekers have been chosen as my honour guard. You will be the first to protect the new king." More than one of his men smiled wider, their shoulders pulling back further — he had never seen them so proud.

Radnok ran a hand over his hair to smooth it. "We want to make a good first impression with the people, so, as much as it pains me, I'm instructing you to capture and imprison rather than kill anyone who opposes us, where possible. There will be many of our brothers stationed throughout the crowd to make sure the transition is as smooth as possible." Radnok had snuck in 200 extra seekers to increase their numbers to 400 — still not enough but any more would be noticed. The king had approved a team of only 200 — Orlon wasn't as stupid as everyone thought. He was aware Radnok was popular. Another 600 seekers awaited his instruction at their nearby compound.

Radnok raised his voice. "Who are we?"

His seekers answered loudly in unison, "We are the seekers. The protector of innocents, the destroyers of evil."

"Who do you serve?"

"The High Seeker. High Seeker Radnok is our leader and saviour. Without him, we are nothing."

Radnok nodded, his chest swelling with pride. These were his men to the death.

A knock sounded from outside. The door opened, and one of his guards stepped in and bowed. "High Seeker Radnok, High Lady Lilliana is here to see you."

"Send her in."

The guard stepped aside and opened the door wider. Lilliana sauntered in. Radnok both loved and loathed his wife. At this moment, he loved her exquisite curves. Her dress was the exact red of his coat, cut low to show her cleavage, which she had thankfully lifted with an undergarment, and he had a sudden desire to bury his face there and lick her skin. She knew she had everyone's full attention; it was obvious in the way she smiled and the way her gaze stayed on him.

When Lilliana reached him, she kissed his cheek and linked her arm through his. All the seekers watched her every move, and two of them licked their lips.

"You look stunning, my dear." He needed her to behave. This was a crucial time, and she had always responded well to him when he was nice.

She smiled. "And you look like the magnificent leader you are."

Radnok was very aware, even after all these years, of her bosom as it pushed against his arm. She was playing games, seeing if she could distract him. Well, later, he would give her what she asked for.

Radnok addressed his men. "Let's go." Then he bent his head, putting his lips to his wife's ear. "Tonight, my love, we will have much to celebrate, thanks to me. The world will soon be mine, and if you're a good girl, I'll let you come along for the ride."

Her smile faltered. Where before, in her demeanour, there had been confidence, there was now self-doubt. He was skilled at keeping those around him off balance, and he enjoyed that he could choose to support her so she continued standing or he could push her so she fell. Mere words were all it took.

As they proceeded to the great hall, no one spoke. His men walked proudly, ceremonial swords glinting at their hips, their footfalls on flagstone floors echoing off the walls. With his men in formation around him, their black cloaks flowing behind as they moved towards his destiny, Radnok already thought of himself as king. By the end of this night, so would everyone else.

Chapter Twenty-three

Kerwyn stood in a dim corridor three floors below ground, breathing in the musty aroma of his nightmares.

Mistress Hanover had led him to the lower ground level on the pretence of gathering a sack of flour. It had taken all his nerve to walk past each of the six guards they had encountered on the way. She had left him one level above where he had taken a secret passageway that came here and also led up, to a first floor bedroom.

Kerwyn had his sword drawn as he crept along the little-used hallway. No colourful carpets adorned the floor. No paintings hung on the walls. If he raised his sword, he knew he would bring it down with cobwebs. He tried to breathe quietly as he walked so he could hear anything, from an enemy to a crying child. Imagining his children locked in a dungeon brought vomit to his mouth. If Addy didn't kill Radnok, *he* fucking would once his family was safe.

Mistress Hanover had been a godsend. She had subtly let him know that extra horses would be saddled and waiting for him and his family once they escaped. Unfortunately, his friend had not been able to tell him exactly where his family was being held. She hadn't seen them brought in, and, having kept her ear open for gossip, had heard no one else mention it. What if they weren't here? His heart beat faster, and he tightened his grip on his sword hilt. *Stay positive. They're here, and you're going to get them out.*

It was hard to hear over the blood pounding near his ears. He willed his heart to slow. Stopping for a moment, he held his breath and listened.

Nothing.

Walking on, he reached a T intersection. He had gotten to know these corridors well when he was stationed here. There were not usually many prisoners, but whenever Radnok had been in residence, there was always one. The high seeker had sworn his men to secrecy; the king was weak of stomach, he had claimed, and he didn't want him upset by what they had to do to keep Treloah and their monarch safe. The atrocities they had carried out down here more often than not led to death, and Kerwyn had never told anyone, not even his wife.

He thought he heard a faint scream — a sound muffled by thick walls. Or was it a memory, a haunting from one of the men he had helped torture and murder?

Leaving the seekers, even if it had meant losing his family and his sense of self, was the best thing he had ever done. Maybe now he had finally found his real self again — the man who believed in redemption, in helping others, and serving his god. Radnok had twisted Kerwyn's beliefs until it was as if depraved Radnok was the god. Not many acted against the high seeker as Kerwyn had done. He wondered why he was still alive; he had expected his life to be forfeit when he deserted his post.

He peered both ways down the hall and waited. There it was again. Muffled screaming from the right, but he couldn't tell if the voice belonged to a man or a woman. His heart raced from fear and anticipation. Was he about to see his family again? Were they all right? He took a deep breath and jogged towards the sound.

Another scream floated towards him, louder.

He moved faster, knowing he would reach the cells soon. Stopping, he listened. Shuffling came from behind, from the other hallway. "Shit," he mouthed. All was silent again. It could have been a rat, a cat, or a person. He swivelled his head this way and that. Should he go back and potentially face soldiers, or go forward and find his family. *Fuck it*. He ran towards the cells. He was so close now. If he died without seeing his family and telling them how much he loved them, it would be the greatest tragedy of his life.

Another scream, this one raising the hairs on his nape.

As he ran down the hallway, feet pounding loudly against the stone foregoing any attempt at stealth, he heard the definite sound of other booted feet behind him.

He reached the cells — two rows separated by the hallway with iron bars so occupants could look across and see each other. The first two were empty. The next two, empty. He checked one after the other. They were all empty. Only two cells remained, and they were closed rooms. The only way to see in was to open the door. He reached for the handle of the first room, hoping it was unlocked. His fingers curled around the cold metal.

The pounding of boots drew close.

Ephrestine's piss. Kerwyn let go of the handle then turned. Six soldiers, wearing the blue-and-black livery of Treloah, ran into the cell area. The one at the front spoke, his sword drawn. "What are you doing down here?"

Kerwyn shrugged, his mouth going dry. "Just checking things out. My lord wants to build a castle, and he's researching dungeon design." *Where the fuck had that come from?*

"What's your name?" The soldier approached, slowly, warily, one of his companions next to him. The hall was only just wide enough for two men to fit side-by-side.

"Oscar Wilton." Kerwyn took a step back for each forward step of theirs.

"Didn't your mother tell you it wasn't polite to lie … Kerwyn?"

How the fuck? Who had betrayed him? He needed to find his family. *It can't be over.* His heart thudded, the powerful beat of his blood pulsing against his neck in a quick rhythm.

"The king is looking for you, Kerwyn. His orders are to return you alive, so don't do anything to make us *accidentally* kill you."

Kerwyn turned to run. But four more soldiers blocked his way. How could he have failed so badly, so quickly? Ephrestine was definitely not smiling on him. Maybe this was punishment for being Radnok's evil servant, and if the king knew Kerwyn was here, what about Addy and Jacob? Were his friends still alive?

The men surrounding him were dressed in armour, and in this tight space, he would have trouble swinging his sword. He could try to run through them in a surprise bid for freedom, but he would have to get through two rows of men. And that was if he didn't get skewered first. *Fucking Var's balls.*

He dropped his sword and raised his arms, admitting defeat. If Orlon's soldiers were men of their word, he might see his family again. If not, well, he had tried.

Mayna, please forgive me. After all the years of hiding and living in fear, he was ready to meet his fate.

Chapter Twenty-four

In a corner, safely distanced from the other performers, Jacob faced Addy and practiced juggling; Addy watched, her back against the wall. It was soothing watching the shelon toss the five batons into the air. Throw, spin, catch. Throw, spin, catch. He had only dropped two sticks, which was impressive, considering he didn't juggle regularly.

"You're quite good," Addy whispered, eliciting a smile from Jacob, even though he still concentrated on his sticks.

"Thanks. I like juggling. It's fun." He caught the sticks one after the other until he held them all. He placed them on the floor then picked up six balls, handing three to Addy. "When I say 'when', throw me a ball, for my right hand."

Addy examined the bright orange ball she held. The stuffed leather was firm and slightly squishy on the outside. Jacob tossed the first ball into the air then the second, and then the third. Once he achieved a comfortable rhythm, the three balls spinning up, down, and around, he said, "When."

Addy complied. He caught it and sent it into the spinning loop with the other three.

"When."

She threw the ball gently. He deftly scooped it up, and it joined the other balls spinning faster and faster through his hands.

His tongue stuck out as he concentrated. "When."

Addy held her breath and tossed it to him. She expected him to drop them at any moment, but they kept spinning in a circle, until he changed things, and now they soared through the air in a figure eight before returning to his nimble hands to rise again. *He's really good.* "Could you teach me how to do that?"

Jacob caught the balls, one after the other, and looked at her. "We'll have plenty of time on our boat trip. It would give us something to do." His sly smile made her think he might be suggesting there would be time to do things other than juggling as well. He stepped over to her until only a few inches separated them.

Her body seemed to heat up without any encouragement from her brain, and she leaned against the wall, trying to put more space between them. He leaned in closer. Her bottom and the back of her head bumped the wall.

"What are you afraid of, Addy? I would never hurt you. Never. I am *not* your father."

"I know. I really know, but I'm still scared sometimes. Scared of doing what women do. What if he's all I can think about?" She hoped he understood what she meant without having to explain it in all its embarrassing detail. What if she was destined to relive Radnok's torture again and again for the rest of her life? A tear ran down her cheek. When she tried to wipe it away, she touched coarse beard, which made her smile. "I must look terrible with this thing on."

"You don't look terrible, exactly. I'll admit, you're much more attractive without it." He leaned over, resting his hands and the balls on the wall to either side of her face, and whispered in her ear. It sent tingles to the swollen softness between her legs. "I would even say you're beautiful." He kissed her neck, just under her ear lobe, and she almost moaned. Despite her fear, and the fact that others could see, she wanted to wrap her arms around him and pull him in as close as she could. But she didn't. She closed her eyes and enjoyed it for what it was — a brief moment of fun before they did something there would be no going back from. They would likely be killed.

Addy reached up and placed her palm on his cheek. Then she lifted her head and softly touched her lips to his, the feather-light contact setting her body aflame. They stood that way for a few moments, breathing each other's air, just being. "Thank you," Addy whispered. "Thank you for everything, Jacob."

A male voice from the other end of the room called out, "Choir, positions please. After the choir, we want the juggler ready to go."

Addy started and gently pushed Jacob away, looking over his shoulder. "Looks like it's time for your performance. Break a leg, preferably Radnok's." She giggled.

Jacob's smile promised everything would be all right, but his eyes were grave. "I'll do my best, Little Rose."

She helped him carry his props to the door, but he had to take them through by himself. From the doorway, she could see into the enormous room. Rows of tables held laughing and eating guests, all dressed in their finest clothes, a happy patchwork of reds, greens, blues and yellows. Laughter floated over an undertone of constant chatter and a chorus of fiddles.

Where was Radnok? She hastily gazed around and noticed a viewing gallery above the room. She hadn't finished yet, but the master of entertainment was shooing her into the practice room. Just as she leant back through the door, she spotted the king's table. That would be where Radnok was — he always knew how to weasel his way in with people. She imagined that was how he had caught her mother, or maybe it had been the drugs he had readily supplied her. Well, her mother wasn't the first person fooled by his duplicitous ways. The king was Radnok's friend, or had been when she was a child. She supposed nothing had changed. As much as she hated Radnok, he had charm and charisma. If he had been a plant, he would have been a Bug's Soup — the flowers emitted a sweet smell, only to lure bugs and spiders into a liquid acid trap deep within its cup of petals.

Back in the waiting area, she wiped her sweaty palms on her coat. As much as she wanted the easy movement being coat free would provide, it had been too cold to remove it outside, and if she took it off now, she might lose it in the fray that was sure to follow Radnok's murder.

It was time for her to find a better position, one from where she could kill Radnok. Assuming the entrance to the gallery was on the floor above, once out the door, Addy turned right, back towards the entry hall. Relief coursed through her when she reached the main foyer and staircase without encountering any guards. Harried servants rushed around carrying empty and full dishes, bottles of wine and spirits, but no guards stopped her.

Addy slipped her knives out of her boots and took the steps two at a time. She checked her aura was contained while she ran along the hallway, marvelling that her ability to focus inward while doing other things had improved greatly.

The hallways were eerily deserted. Maybe it was because what was happening downstairs was too important. Rumours circulating the city today spoke of King Orlon announcing his successor, but in true King Orlon style, he had not confirmed it. The amount of attending dignitaries, if the same rumour mills were to be trusted, suggested an important event was taking place other than the Snow Day Feast. She hoped she wasn't going to ruin everything for the king, but she had to take whatever opportunity presented itself.

She had slowed to a walk, not wanting to draw any attention to herself if she did meet anyone. The door to what she assumed was the gallery was visible down the hall on the left. The giveaway was the two guards outside. The king was more cautious than Addy would have thought. They were observing everyone coming in and out. *Great.*

Even if they let her in, there was no way they would let her out if they saw her killing Radnok. Addy knelt, pretending to do up her bootlace. Giggling came from behind her and the swishing of skirts. The air caressed her cheek as two women rushed past, talking excitedly. "... and then he lifted my skirts..." The women tittered, their voices fading once they reached the guards, who looked to ask them a few questions before allowing them entry. *Ephrestine's piss.* If they were suspicious of elegant women in dresses, what hope did she have?

Addy swallowed and made the toughest decision of her life.

An oil slick of hate for Radnok floated on the surface of her emotions, suffocating the happiness underneath. Two more innocent people may have to die. She hoped it wouldn't come to that, but she couldn't take any chances. If the choice were between her and them, she would choose herself every time. Ultimately, she would blame Radnok and everyone who let him get away with his excesses and depravities. *Ephrestine, give me strength.*

Knives concealed in her coat sleeves, Addy approached the soldiers and smiled.

"Name," one of them said.

"Radnok."

"Ha! Just like the high seeker." The man relaxed, and Addy felt sick for what she was about to do.

"Exactly," she replied, sounding as if she was losing her voice.

The men were taller than her, broader of shoulder and thicker of neck, both wearing chainmail. She had to get this right the first time.

"Oh, what's that in your beard?" Addy asked the one who stood in front of her left side.

He reached up to feel in his beard, and his companion leant over to look. Blocking out reason, logic and regret, lest she lose her nerve, Addy worked both knives into her hands. Radnok's face appeared in her mind, his cruel eyes taunting her. Anger surged through her being, tears glazing her eyes.

Addy thrust her left arm forward and her right arm up. Her knife met minor resistance then slipped into one soldier's groin. Simultaneously, her other knife popped through the delicate skin of the other soldier's neck. Leaning forward, she pushed it in all the way and wrenched her arm to the right, slicing him open. Blood flowed out, running down her knife and onto her hand. She pulled both knives free.

The first soldier doubled over, clutching his wound. The other soldier, his face a tortured façade of pain and shock, held his hands at his throat, but blood seeped through his fingers. His eyes met Addy's gaze, his expression asking why. Then he fell.

She didn't have long. The first soldier raised his head and reached for his sword, keeping one hand on his groin.

Addy sliced at the hand protecting his injury. Blood beaded quickly then flowed down his hand. He tried to step back, but the door was closed. Quarters were too tight for him to pull out his sword. He brought up his free hand, to punch Addy's face, but she swung up her forearm and knocked his arm to the side. She wanted to step in and stab him in the stomach, but his chainmail protected him. He let go of his wound, and his face contorted with pain. He grabbed her around the neck with both hands and squeezed.

In the haze of battle, the feel of the man's hot, slimy skin against her neck transported her mind to a large bed where Radnok lay on top of her. Her nose again smelled the head seeker's masculine scent; it was Radnok's stench overpowering her awareness, not the blood and fear of the soldier strangling her. Addy tried to scream, but only a choked sound escaped.

The soldier's blood-soaked hands had cut off her air supply. Desperately trying to breathe, she twisted, attempting to slip out of his deadly hold, which was too much like Radnok's. She twisted her torso, brought her arms up to one side and pushed her hands together, careful not to drop her knives. Then she twisted back and slammed her arms down across his. He grunted, and his grip faltered as he was forced down and to the right, bending at the hip. Addy wheeled her right arm across, sheathing her knife in the side of his neck. She jerked the blade back and forth to open a wide gash. Ruby liquid surged out, coating her blade and fingers with its unfettered flow.

When his hands slipped from her throat, she gasped in one sweet breath after another. Blood cascaded from the soldier's neck onto the floor. His body soon followed, landing in a dark puddle of his own blood.

Addy had never seen so much blood; there was even more than in the snow the day she had killed the two seekers. It trickled along the hall, following the slope of floor, inching along dips in the stone and the joins between. It reached her boot, and she stepped out of the way.

Breathing hard, she dragged the soldier away from the door and hurriedly wiped her hands and blades as clean as she could on his pants leg, the only thing not already soaked in the russet tinge of death.

She opened the door, relieved that only the two women from earlier and a group of four youths occupied the viewing area. The area formed a U shape around the main hall. About twelve-feet wide, it was dimly lit, the only illumination coming from the low-hanging chandeliers above the room below. Addy was aware that blood was smeared on her face, so she kept her head down. The scarlet would be invisible on her dark coat, at least.

Knives tightly secured in each fist, she moved to the edge and peered over the balustrade. Warm air and delicious smells of the feast rose from below, wafting past her face. Sweating, Addy wiped perspiration off her brow and cheek with the back of her hand and checked it. It was pink, as if her pores had been leaching blood. She turned back to the door, to make sure no one was sneaking up on her. It wouldn't be long before someone found those two soldiers and raised the alarm.

Gazing back down to the crowd below, she soon found Jacob. She breathed out in relief that he was still alive. The throng around him was enthralled, watching him spin his sticks, higher and higher, until Addy thought he would miscalculate and drop them.

Addy searched the room for the king's table, but it was under the overhang to her left. She moved right, until it came into view. King Orlon sat at the head of the table, nodding and smiling at what the woman next to him said.

What in all the hells? Addy recognised the woman. Grief and anger burst inside her, the invisible pain doubling Addy over. If someone had taken a hammer to her elbow, it wouldn't have hurt any less. She shook with aftershocks of raw emotion, blinding tears tracking a river down her face.

The woman in the red dress was supposed to have protected Addy and loved her more than life itself, but here she sat, at a ball, indifferent to whether her daughter lived. Lilliana laughed. She flicked her fair hair off her shoulder, to expose the creamy skin of her breasts. She ate food straight off the fork of a man sitting on her other side then giggled coquettishly when sauce dripped onto her cleavage.

The last piece of Addy's love for her mother shrivelled and died. Her adult heart shed the desiccated skin of a trusting child's dreams, emerging stronger, poison dripping from its fangs.

Addy had loved her mother, even when she had hated her, and it was only now that she allowed herself to admit she would never receive that love in return. Her mother had never searched for her after she had run away. Addy would not make any more excuses for her. Her mother had chosen Radnok over her own flesh and blood. *How the fuck could someone do that? What is wrong with me that my own mother hates me?*

Addy leaned a fist on the railing, trying to regain her breath.

Pull yourself together. Addy straightened then brought her attention back to the king's table. Radnok sat on the king's other side. Addy's ears buzzed with the increased tempo of her heart. *This is it. I'm not going to cock it up this time.*

The angle wasn't the best, but she had a clear shot. No one else was in the way.

Radnok smirked at the king and nodded.

Addy leant over the railing and took three steadying breaths. She drew her arm back.

She almost dropped the knife when a serving woman arrived next to Radnok, leaning across and in front of him, blocking her shot. "Shit," she said through clenched teeth. She remembered Kerwyn's friend and shook her head. She wasn't going to do that again.

The woman poured some beverage out of a decanter into the king's tankard then Radnok's. She stepped back, moving to Lilliana.

Addy's shot was clear again, but the king held up his hand, and a well-dressed man in a burgundy coat, high boots laced up on the outside of his pants, stepped between Addy and Radnok. She rolled her eyes. If this continued, she would be running downstairs to stab him from close quarters. Maybe she should have dressed as a serving girl.

She checked to see where Jacob was. He had finished his performance and stood against the wall behind and to the left of the king, drinking something and blending in. His presence calmed her, and she nodded to herself. *This was going to happen.*

But then the man in the burgundy coat rang a bell the size of his fist. *What in Var's anus is going on now?* Gradually the room quieted. Music stopped, and guests placed knives, forks and goblets down until everyone's attention was on the man with the bell.

In a clear, loud voice that easily reached Addy's lofty position, he enunciated each word in the polished speech of the upper class of Treloah. "Lords and ladies, good evening. On behalf of King Orlon and his wife, Queen Verella, we would like to welcome you and thank you for braving the inclement weather to attend this most auspicious and momentous occasion."

Addy's hope sank. There was no way she was going to kill him with everyone watching. How much longer would she have to wait? She turned to look at the door — the guards had most likely not been discovered yet. How much time did she have? Maybe she should go downstairs, take a chance getting close to Radnok. There were so many people, but what if the rumours were true and Orlon was announcing the next king? Addy opened her eyes wide. *Ephrestine's piss, Radnok had a place of honour next to the king. Surely not?*

Nausea danced mischief in her belly, and acid grazed her throat as her lunch threatened to return in the most spectacular of ways.

The man with the bell spoke again. "King Orlon is aware that rumours of tonight have circulated within and without the city. Why are we here, you might ask? We are celebrating the Snow Day Feast, however, it is also a day for Treloah and her allies to rejoice. King Orlon has presided successfully over his people for over fifty years. He has been a generous, noble, and well-loved king, and he would like to address you, his people." He bowed to the crowd then the king. "I will now ask High Seeker Radnok to accompany King Orlon to the stage."

The elevated platform in the centre of the room, where Jacob had just impressed the audience, was empty and flanked by two guards. Two servants entered, carrying a heavy throne-like chair, obviously straining to hold its weight. They placed the gilded, high-backed chair in the middle of the red-carpeted stage.

The room was silent. Even Addy held her breath.

Fear unfurled in her belly and slithered throughout her body. She had to kill Radnok before he was announced as Orlon's successor. If she didn't, he would have an army to hunt her down, and no one would tell him no — not that anyone ever had, but everything he had done so far had been contained. There would be no moderating his desire to capture her when he ruled the land. And what implications did that have for the kingdom's children? He could snatch and abuse any child he wanted. No one would be safe.

Movement in the hall below caught her attention. Radnok stood, pride in his features, his chest puffed out like a cock about to crow. Lilliana watched him, her face glazed over with adoration. Addy wanted to scream.

Radnok offered the king his arm then accompanied him to the stage, where he assisted him up the four steps. Radnok made sure Orlon was seated comfortably before he stood behind and to the right of the throne. More guards moved to surround them. Well, there went her chance of running down and stabbing him. She would have to finish what she started from her current position. There was only a small chance she would hit the king, ensuring her certain death. She smiled mockingly. *Just your luck, hey, Addy.*

She would be accurate, and the shot would be guaranteed if she embraced her powers and didn't dim her aura. It would attract the attention of every seeker in the room, including Radnok, but by the time they reacted, her knife would be in his chest. It was a chance she was willing to take, again. And, if she embraced her powers, she would have more speed and strength, allowing her a better chance to escape.

King Orlon's voice filled the silence — not as loud as the man with the bell, but loud enough. "Greetings, my subjects. No doubt, many of you have heard the rumours about why we're all here, this night." The elegantly dressed diners nodded. The king smiled. "The rumours are true. Tonight I will be announcing my successor." Some guests gasped, some nodded, and Radnok wore a self-satisfied smirk.

Addy clutched her knife and prepared to draw back and access her energy.

The king continued into the expectant silence. "But there is something no one knows, a secret so great, it has lain heavy on my heart for the last thirty-five years."

Addy paused, raising her eyebrows.

The gathered nobility sat forward in their seats, and Radnok's smirk slipped into a frown.

"This night, you will find out my secret." A commotion formed at the entrance to the hall. Addy couldn't see what it was at first — the entrance was hidden from her under the overhang of the upper level. The guests could see, however, and they reacted with confusion. Radnok's brows furrowed, and he narrowed his eyes.

What the hell was going on?

Finally, Addy could see what everyone else saw, what now had Radnok open-mouthed. Four guards surrounded one man, one on each side of him holding an arm. They placed him before the king, and his back was to Addy, but Addy knew who it was. She sucked in a quick breath, and it felt as if her stomach had dropped to the floor. *No, no, no!*

Kerwyn's head dipped, showing respect to the king or defeat, Addy couldn't tell. She had to save him. They must have caught him sneaking around. Unleashing her aura would definitely create chaos enough, and so would a dagger in Radnok's heart.

Addy breathed deeply and concentrated on the sealed cauldron deep inside her belly.

The king rose, but Addy closed her eyes. The activity in the hall was distracting, and she couldn't focus properly. Addy only half listened as the king spoke. "You have all waited long enough, and I am overjoyed to be relieved of this terrible burden I have carried for too many years. The person who will succeed me is … my son. You will have to excuse how he is dressed. He is as ignorant of his parentage as all of you, and the method I used to bring him here was rather unorthodox. I thought him safer in anonymity. Welcome home, Kerwyn, prince and future king of Treloah."

Addy's eyelids sprung open. *What the fuck?* Gasps sounded from the hall, and more than a few people sat slack-jawed in shock.

Orlon started down the stairs, towards Kerwyn.

Radnok's face twisted into unfettered anger. Crazed aggression emanated from him, from his clenched fists to his manic gaze. Addy knew she should act immediately, but she was momentarily rooted to the spot, a crush of thoughts scrambling through her mind.

Orlon reached Kerwyn, and the guards released his arms. A smile lit up the king's face, and he threw his arms around his son, enveloping him in a hug. Kerwyn didn't move for a moment, but then he raised his arms and returned the king's affection. Addy felt tears forming, and joy started to replace shock.

Radnok raised his arm in the air and shouted, "Seekers, claim my throne!"

A man clad in black, who had been hiding in the crowd, moved from behind Radnok, the silver gleam of a short sword flashing in front of him. Orlon's soldiers drew swords and closed ranks around the king and Kerwyn. If only she'd brought her bow in. *Damn!*

Enough is enough. Addy reached into herself and tore open the fetters holding in her aura, unleashing her power. She winced as searing heat shot through her belly, but it was gone in an instant. As she grabbed the sweet energy, her body felt more alive than it had in a long time. Her blood thrummed vibrantly through her veins, and her perception of time slowed, as it always did.

Her actions were enough to draw attention from the seeker attacking the king and Kerwyn. His head snapped up, as did Radnok's and some of the other seekers in the room. They stared at her. She stared back. *Well, apparently I really do have some huge glowing thing around me.* She grinned.

Something else opened deep within her, Addy's awareness unfurling a little more. She looked down at her body and saw pulsing rosy radiance, golden flecks glinting within in. The aura, a two-inch dazzle of pink light, framed her arms, her legs, her torso, and it moved when she moved. She blinked, unsettled by the glow. *Wow.*

Shouting drew her attention. Seekers were running from the hall, no doubt coming for her, all glowing with their own auras. Some had dull white, and some had grey, one even had yellow. She didn't know what it meant, and there was no time to find out. Swords clashed below, seekers and soldiers in red uniforms fighting with the blue uniformed soldiers loyal to the king.

Radnok stood on the stage, his face schooled to passivity, but his eyes told a different story. His intense gaze was for Addy alone, and it caught her, freezing her limbs. Elation at her newfound powers was replaced by fear so tangible it seized her limbs, and she believed she would never escape. He would always own her; it was only a matter of time until she would be under his control once more.

Someone shouted, "Addy! Addy! Run!" She shook her head, released from Radnok's spell. Jacob. He was near Kerwyn; hopefully, he would be able to get him out of there. The shelon, arm above his head, waved frantically at her to leave.

Addy twisted around to check the door then pivoted back to observe Jacob. A seeker was behind him, sword raised, the scene playing out at a fifth the normal speed to her power-enhanced senses. Addy yelled, "Jacob!" Her heart slammed with the terror of it. *Not Jacob!*

Jacob turned just in time to block the strike. Chaos flooded the great hall. People screamed and fled. Soldiers shouted battle cries, clashed swords, punched, and stabbed. A table was upended, knives, forks, plates and food crashing to the floor, a fleeing servant slipping on the mess and slamming into the ground. And Jacob and Kerwyn were in the middle of it.

With a final scathing look at Radnok, who stood tall with his hands on his hips and smirk back in place, Addy shouted at him. "Fuck you, you fetid smear of shit. I haven't finished with you yet!"

She spun and ran for the door.

Chapter Twenty-five

Addy yanked open the door, bent and grabbed one of the dead guard's swords. At one with her energy source, she knew her skills would be much improved. The sword felt lighter than it should, and she bounced on the balls of her feet, savouring the energy buzzing throughout her; if someone asked her to run fifty miles, she felt it would be an easy task.

Shouts and footfalls came from the hallway leading to the main stairs. There must be another staircase she could use to reach the great hall, but did she have time to find it with Jacob and Kerwyn in danger? She decided not. The men coming to attack her were seekers.

Addy ran down the hall, towards her enemy, and met them when she reached the top of the stairs. Three seekers stood shoulder to shoulder on the wide staircase, two steps below the landing where Addy had stopped. They tensed, each man sizing her up. Not wanting to give them any time to decide what to do, she threw the knife in her left hand into the seeker on her left. He wore no armour, and the knife sank hilt-deep into his stomach. Addy held up her sword to block the thrust of the middle seeker while she kicked the injured one in the midsection, sending him back into two of his comrades on the steps below.

The seeker standing directly behind the injured man fell backwards under his weight, and they both crashed down the stairs. Addy moved into the gap created by the two men while pulling her dagger from the scabbard at her hip. Her back to the balustrade, she blocked a tentative strike from the man in front of her. It was as if he wasn't trying to kill her, just disable her, or maybe he was testing her skill. *Stupid me! Radnok's told them not to kill me. Of course.* That should make things easier, although she wouldn't underestimate them.

The seeker on the top step opposite Addy moved onto the landing and came around to attack her from her right. His movement also gave the seeker in front of her space to step back and engage her properly. She almost rushed her moves, desperate to reach the main hall, but she tried to push that from her mind lest she lose focus and give these men an opening. *You can do this.*

The seeker in front of her thrust forward, trying to run her through the leg. She swept her sword down in an arc from left to right, meeting the other weapon with a loud clang. The impact, which normally would have jarred her fingers enough to possibly make her drop the sword, hardly registered. The energy from her tingling belly buzzed through her arms and legs, giving her unnatural strength.

With her altered perception, her enemies' every action was slow and predictable. She had time to prepare, time to see. When she had blocked the other strike, the man above had drawn his sword back. Addy let her sword arc continue until her blade was raised over her right shoulder, to block his attack. She smiled at his surprised expression. Simultaneously, before the seeker on her step could recover, she lunged forward, pushed her dagger into his stomach, and wrenched it across. When she pulled her weapon out, his innards followed.

Addy coughed, trying not to gag as she focused on her next move. A putrid stench permeated the air as the contents of his bowels spewed over his clothes. The sweat and now fear of those around her assaulted her heightened sense of smell.

The seeker fell sideways, and the two below him just managed to get out of the way. Seeing her opportunity, Addy ran down the stairs, past the scrambling men. Near the bottom, the two seekers who had fallen earlier lay in a mangled heap, blocking her way. She thrust her dagger into its scabbard and bent down. "I'll have that back, thank you," she said to the dead man and pulled her throwing knife out of his stomach. Straightening, she grabbed the railing with her left hand and pushed off. Addy vaulted the bodies, sailing over ten steps to land at the bottom of the staircase, ending in a crouch to protect her knees.

She didn't stop for anyone. Her friends could be killed at any moment. Radnok could escape. She rearmed herself with her dagger, grabbing it in her left hand, the sword still in her right. "For King Orlon!" she shouted as she entered the great hall, making sure the king's soldiers knew on whose side she was. She didn't need to be fighting two different groups.

Orlon's soldiers fought the soldiers dressed in red tabards; she didn't know where they had come from, but they seemed to be fighting with the seekers. So, Radnok had managed to find an ally. *Where is that traitorous bastard?* Addy glanced around and spotted the head seeker, his sword out, fighting back to back with a nobleman. That must be who owned the other soldiers. Addy was jostled as she entered the fray, with no time to see where Jacob was. She stepped over a body and engaged a red-clad soldier. He met her stroke for stroke at first, his face twisted in concentration and discomfort. Sweat rolled down his face and into his eyes as he blocked Addy's blow. He blinked. It was the opening Addy needed. She spun and crouched, sweeping a foot across his ankles. The soldier lost balance, knocking into another of his comrades as he fell.

Addy, kneeling next to him, plunged her knife into his neck, killing him.

She hastily assessed those fighting around her before she stood. Where was Jacob?

She jumped up and looked towards the place she had last seen him and Kerwyn with the king.

A group of soldiers, still in a circle, their backs to the inside of it, slashed, blocked and parried, fighting off the seekers and red-uniformed soldiers swarming them. Addy hoped her friends were safe inside the human barricade. The soldiers were hard pressed, one of the king's men taking a sword to his chest as Addy watched. The man tried, with the last of his strength, to slash his attacker, but, instead, he fell to the ground. Sadness nudged the edge of her focus. *Too much death.*

Addy eyed Radnok again, a swell of loathing threatening to overwhelm her, and she wanted to run to him, stab him repeatedly, but she remembered her friends. Her revenge would have to wait for later. Jacob and Kerwyn needed her now. Addy checked behind her before running to help the king's guards. With the intention of causing a brief distraction, she screamed a battle cry, the power running through her amplifying the scream until it sounded like a bird of prey.

The fighters near her stopped and turned, the seekers among them hesitant about staying where they were or moving to attack her. In her slowed-down world, she saw the twitch of one seeker's leg, the indecision on his face, and another seeker start towards her.

Addy attacked.

The seeker already coming for her had a knife in his throat before he knew what had happened. Addy pushed him into two other seekers and slashed her sword at another. The soldier parried and swung. Addy seeing his movement early, stepped aside. By the time the man realised what she had done, he was committed. Out of the blade's way but still within reach, Addy stabbed her sword into his side, not easy through his chainmail, but not impossible with her increased strength. She pulled the sword out, heard the rustle of someone behind her, turned and slashed, connecting with another seeker's sword.

Sweat poured off Addy as she defended and attacked. She had made a difference though; the king's men were attaining control of their section of the room. *Baby steps.*

Addy still couldn't see her friends, so she called out while blocking a seeker's strike. "Jacob! Jacob!"

A faint response came from the other side of the circle. Before Addy could answer, Jacob was behind the man she fought. She hadn't seen any weapons on his person when they arrived, but Jacob had two knives — one in each hand. *Ephrestine's piss! They're his juggling sticks. Nice.* What good forethought the shelon had. Addy grinned as he felled the seeker. He grinned in return, and they stood back to back, protecting each other as they cut through enemy soldiers and seekers.

Blood slicked the floor, and Addy almost fell twice.

One of Orlon's men shouted, "We need to get King Orlon out of here."

Addy glanced over to the guard. The circle of king's men, whom Addy assumed still protected Kerwyn and Orlon, shuffled towards the door as they fought. Enemy colours of black and red dominated the other side of the room. Addy raised her voice to be heard over the din. "Jacob, we need to clear a path to the door. There're too many of Radnok's men for us to win this battle."

Jacob hastily scanned their surroundings. "In a moment. Cover me?"

"Yeah, sure." Addy kept her focus on two soldiers in red who circled them, their faces wary, their breaths coming in laboured gasps. Addy turned as they moved, keeping them in her sights, her sword at the ready.

"Done," Jacob proclaimed, before holding one of his juggling balls in front of himself.

"What? Are you being stupid? Juggling is n—"

The ball flew threw the air, hit one of the enemy soldiers, and burst into flames as soon as it struck him. The fire raced down his arms and legs, across his torso, and slid quickly into his hair. He screamed, dropped to the floor, and tried to put the flames out by rolling around. The conflagration jumped from him, latching onto his friend. The other soldier tried to pat the small patch out with his gloved hand, but it spread rapidly until the man fell to the ground, his tortured shrieks drawing the attention of others.

With a space opened up in front of her, Addy glanced around. The mob had thinned, many dead or dying on the ground. *Where the fuck is Radnok?*

Addy then stared at Jacob. "What in all the hells?"

"One of my shelon skills is fire. The juggler's balls are flammable. I had to ignite them with my power. It takes effort, but I can will the flames to go where I want, provided there's little space between where it is and where I want it to be."

The stench of burning flesh coiled around Addy, and she dry heaved. She slammed her hand over her mouth, the feel of coarse whiskers reminder her of the beard. *Time to ditch the whiskers.* Addy ripped them from her face. "Ow! Bloody, ow. That hurt."

The smouldering bodies in front of Addy discouraged an attack from that quarter, but a seeker came in from the side, his sword sweeping towards Addy's arm. Jacob stepped across, knocking the seeker's strike wide. Before the man could recover, Jacob smashed him in the side of the face with his fist, while Addy's blade butchered his head as he fell.

"Addy, we have to break them up." Addy turned to where Jacob indicated.

A group of six seekers and enemy soldiers blocked the exit, waiting for King Orlon's men to reach them. Addy tilted her head towards them. "More flames?"

"Ask nicely."

Addy rolled her eyes. "Seriously? People are dying." Jacob raised an eyebrow at her, his mouth curled up on one side. "Oh, for Ephrestine's sake. Please make more flames, oh master of all that burns?"

Jacob smiled. "Hmm, I like my new title. And I liked you better *with* the beard." He winked.

Addy jerked her head around. Two seekers from the group at the door were advancing towards them. She slapped Jacob's arm. "Just burn them already, idiot."

"Your wish is my command." Jacob threw three balls, each one hitting a different target, erupting on impact. He concentrated, waved his hands from side to side, and the flames jumped from their host to the person next to them. Within moments, all the men were alight. Skin blistering, acrid smoke pouring off them, they died screaming. Burning was the least pleasant way to die, Addy decided, shielding her face with her arm as the bright, orange mass flared with almost unbearable heat.

The king's soldiers stared horrified at the blazing decimation of their enemy. Two of the soldiers double over and vomited. Addy ran to the group. "Is the king in there?"

One still-shocked man nodded, his red curls sweat-flattened and dark against his forehead. Peace had graced Treloah for such a long period that Addy doubted these men had ever fought in such harrowing circumstances.

Addy nodded at the soldier. "We can help. Jacob and I will go ahead and make sure the way is clear."

He briefly considered her offer, scanned the immediate area, and returned her nod. He turned to his comrades. "Men, to the door. For Treloah!"

This battle would leave more than physical scars on these men and on Addy. She pretended there would be no nightmares, that she hadn't failed to kill Radnok, in order to be able to keep going. Scanning the room one last time, she spotted Radnok fighting alongside the lord dressed in red. Shaking her head, she grabbed Jacob's arm. "Let's go."

He nodded and followed her out, a throwing-stick knife in one hand, a ball in the other. Addy held her breath and tried not to look too closely as they jumped over the charred bodies. *Nightmares, here I come.*

The hallway was clear of people. It seemed Radnok had all his resources concentrated in the great hall, but he would have more seekers in reserve, like the king had more soldiers. Both forces were scattered throughout Treloah. Were other skirmishes taking place at present? Addy hoped not. The king's forces, while much greater in number than Radnok's, would have been taken by surprise. What if Radnok had other allies than the one here this night?

Jacob stuck his head back into the hall and said to the soldiers, "The way is clear. Hurry!" Jacob stepped aside to let them pass. They strode two abreast. Their bloodstained uniforms were ripped, and one soldier limped.

In the middle of the bedraggled cluster was Kerwyn.

Addy's heart went out to him. He carried his father, the king, who had his arms wrapped around Kerwyn's neck. The aging monarch looked childlike in Kerwyn's strong arms. Orlon's wispy hair stuck up this way and that through his gold crown, which sat askew on his head. His cheeks were sunken, and deep sorrow darkened his eyes. He must have been exhausted or injured for he rested his head on Kerwyn's shoulder.

His face sombre, Kerwyn acknowledged Addy and Jacob by meeting their gazes as he made his way down the hall surrounded by his father's men. Addy tried to pick the similarities in their features. They had the same shaped brow and nose, but even with time slowed for Addy, they were gone before she could scrutinise them further.

Jacob followed them. "Come on, Addy."

Addy jogged to catch up. "Your aura is purple."

The shelon glanced at her briefly before looking ahead once more. "Congratulations, you've learnt something. How long?"

She knew he meant how long had she been seeing auras. "Tonight, when I was upstairs. It just kind of happened." She shrugged. "I think Kerwyn's news is more surprising. I'm still in shock."

"When he was brought in, I considered attacking the soldiers. I'm glad I didn't. Amazing how things can turn around in the course of an afternoon."

"You're telling me." Addy shook her head. What Kerwyn's new-found parentage would mean for them, Addy had no idea. If Radnok wasn't currently trying to overthrow the monarchy, things would be more clear-cut. As it was, should Kerwyn stay and fight, or run? Things happened so quickly, and news of his succession would not have reached anywhere outside the city, so he was unlikely to have anyone's loyalty — he was a stranger to the Treloahns, whereas Radnok was well-known, if not revered by many. Was there a way Kerwyn could turn it to his advantage?

As they walked, Jacob and Addy made sure they weren't being followed. The shouts and sword clangs had grown quieter. The fight had been almost even, but Radnok's men looked to have had the best of it. There was no clear winner ... yet.

The party climbed one flight of stairs then proceeded down a long, wide hallway where portraits of past kings and battle scenes lined the walls. At the end of the corridor was a wide door that the lead soldier opened. They went through, Kerwyn following two soldiers through the outer room to the king's inner chamber. Addy and Jacob went as far as the door to the king's bedroom.

A fire in the hearth and torches in wall sconces suffused the room with soft light, yet the chandelier hanging in the middle of the room remained unlit. A blue-and-gold-patterned rug covered the floor, and a large four-poster bed sat against the wall opposite the fire, its gold-and-blue canopy presiding over a small shape hidden under white covers.

Kerwyn laid the king on the bed, removed his crown and set it next to Orlon. Then he bent his head close to Orlon's, and they spoke quietly. Kerwyn sat carefully on the edge of the bed and held the older man's hand.

Addy felt as if she was intruding, watching such a private moment, but she had so many questions for Kerwyn. How could the king have hidden this secret for so long, and Kerwyn's mother — she must have known. And why had the king let Kerwyn sleep on the streets for so many years only to bring him in now?

King Orlon sat up, with Kerwyn's assistance. When he spoke, his voice was not as weak as Addy expected. "Captain Rondessy, please fetch Advisor Comlyn, and send someone to bring him travelling clothes."

The captain, a short man with the bulk of a well-honed fighter, bowed then gave instructions to the guard next to him before they both left. The captain, his sword already drawn, paused in the outer room to give his men more orders, before he exited to take his chances in the dangerous expanse of a compromised castle.

The king spoke again. "Adrastine, Jacob, please join us." Addy started, not expecting King Orlon to address her, let alone remember who she was.

Everything had been going at the slow pace, and she was so used to it, she forgot she held her power. As she approached the bed, she released her hold on the energy. Her legs collapsed, sending her crashing to the floor. It was as if the strength had been syphoned from her limbs in a rush. A whirlpool of dizziness spiralled inside her head, and she closed her eyes to stop the room from spinning.

She heard more than one pair of boots thudding on the rug. Someone placed a hand on her back, and Jacob said, "Addy, what happened? Are you all right? You don't have any injuries you didn't tell me about, do you?"

Addy kept her eyes closed. "No, no, I'm fine. I just released the power."

Kerwyn spoke, his voice coming from above Jacob. "Jacob, pick her up and put her in this chair." Addy heard a chair being dragged across the room.

Jacob placed an arm under Addy's back, and she sat. "I can walk. Maybe just help me up." Addy opened her eyes and swallowed down lumps of vomit. *At least the room's stopped spinning.*

Before she rose, Jacob pinned her with a worried gaze. "You aren't used to drawing power for so long. You need to build up to it. If you're not careful, you could kill yourself. Unless you're specifically drawing energy from external sources, you are also drawing on your life force, channelling it for a specific purpose. You will be weakened for some time, and we have a long way to go tonight … in the freezing cold."

"Maybe you should have warned me before. It's not like you haven't had time. Anyway, I needed the power to survive. I doubt I could best six seekers by myself otherwise."

Jacob raised his brows. "Did you kill all of them?"

"Three, I think. I left the other three with something to think about."

Jacob nodded. "Nice work, Little Rose."

Addy frowned, which made the shelon smile.

"If you two have had your conversation, do you think you could hurry up? We're on limited time," Kerwyn said from his perch on the king's bed.

Gingerly, Addy stood and, leaning heavily on Jacob, made her way to the chair Kerwyn had placed next to the king's bed. She shouldn't be thinking of it at a time such as this, but she relished the feel of Jacob's strength and warm body next to hers. It wasn't exactly skin on skin, but it felt good. When she was safely seated, he stood and moved to the foot of the king's bed. Addy was careful to hide her disappointment at his retreat.

Closer now, Addy could make out the lump in the bed. The queen. Pale, her short white hair was parted at the side and combed down neatly. The queen slept on her back, unmoving. At first Addy thought she might be dead, but then she emitted a faint snore. Relieved the queen was alive, Addy met the king's gaze.

The king's voice was smooth, calm with an underlying pleasantness, as if traitors hadn't just ambushed him. "Welcome to my quarters, Adrastine. Kerwyn tells me you're The Rose of Nerine." Addy didn't want to disappoint the old man, so she stayed silent about her misgivings. Yes, she did believe she had power, and she could see her pink aura, but until she had read this prophecy, she wasn't going to claim her title. Besides, she didn't want it. She was not cut out to save the world. She could barely live her own life without stuffing things up.

"You have an enormous task ahead, but I believe you can do it, and my son has promised to do all he can to help you." Orlon gazed lovingly at Kerwyn, who wore a half smile. Yet Kerwyn's posture was stiff, showing he was still unsure or uncomfortable with that fact. Addy didn't blame him. The man must have so many questions of the king. Was he angry that the king had all but abandoned him until he had desperate need of his services?

"Thank you, King Orlon, and I'm sorry for Radnok's actions. I've always hated him, but I never thought he'd betray you." Addy bowed her head, not sure whether she'd overstepped etiquette for mentioning such a thing to the king.

"Worry not about him, Adrastine. Things have a way of working out for the better, and those who commit crimes such as he has will pay their reckoning when they meet Ephrestine, or Var, as the case may be." The king reached for her hand and patted it. Addy looked at him. "You need to believe in yourself and trust in Ephrestine and her gift."

"You believe in Ephrestine, Your Highness?" How strange. He was the king of a nation who believed in Telouse.

"I do, young lady. I also believe in Telouse, but Ephrestine is the goddess who rules the lesser gods. Generations of faith is hard to change, and I didn't want a religious war fought on Treloahn soil when it wasn't important."

"But what about all the shelons Radnok and your seekers have murdered?" Jacob looked at Addy as if she had gone mad, but there was respect in his gaze.

"I'm afraid I wasn't aware of Radnok's true agenda until recently. He managed to turn more than one of my spies to his way of thinking. By the time I found out, it was easier to pretend I didn't notice. I'm truly sorry. In this, I have failed." The king looked at Jacob then. If Orlon was waiting for forgiveness, it looked like he would be disappointed. Jacob matched the man's gaze before finally looking down.

Awkward silence pressed on them until Addy heard the door to the outer room open. By the time it shut, the captain stood at the doorway to the king's bedroom, a taller, thin man by his side. Both bowed. "Comlyn, Your Highness."

"Thank you, Captain. Before you go, I have something I wish you to witness." The captain bowed and straightened. Everyone watched King Orlon and waited. The king reached a shaking hand to his bejewelled crown and picked it up. He ran his fingers over the diamonds, sapphires and rubies, admiring them before he raised his head. "My last duty as King of Treloah is to bestow the title on my beloved son. Kerwyn Patrick Courbel, you are hereby pronounced king of Treloah. You are entrusted with her safety, and the health and wellbeing of her people."

King Orlon reached up a shaking hand, the effort evident on his face, and placed the crown on Kerwyn's head. Kerwyn said nothing for a moment while he tried to wrestle his shocked expression into something neutral. Addy's heart swelled for him, to get such acknowledgement from his father, but the pressure on him to win back Courbel and Treloah was a heavy mantle to don.

Kerwyn touched the crown on his head and stood. "King Orl … Father, thank you for this honour. I hope I can be half as good a king as you were. Your people love you, and even though I didn't know of our relationship, I have always admired you as my king." He took his father's hand and bent, kissing the back of it.

Addy glanced around at her sombre companions. They were probably as surprised as she and Kerwyn that this would happen now, in the middle of an attack, but no one spoke out against the king's choice. Addy knelt in front of Kerwyn. "I will serve you in whatever way I can, King Kerwyn."

He gazed at her as if she'd just suggested they disrobe and run in the snow, but then the others followed, each man kneeling and promising their service to the new king.

What an incredible thing to be witnessing. Addy shook her head in amazement.

The king smiled, relief smoothing some of the wrinkles that had tarnished his forehead. He laid his head back on the pillow. "Captain, thank you for your years of service. You have done your country and I proud, and I am grateful that you will continue to support my son, King Kerwyn. Now I will ask you to please wait outside. We won't be long. When we're finished, please take your men and ensure my son and his friends make it safely away."

The captain nodded and bowed. He turned to leave, but a boy, who looked maybe eleven or twelve summers old, appeared at the door, out of breath, leaning his shoulder against the doorframe. Blood coated his right sleeve, and his arm hung limp. As soon as the king saw him, he bid him enter.

The boy scrunched his face in what appeared to be pain as he bowed. "Your Highness, an army is at the gates. The men are fighting as well as they can, but we'll be overrun soon."

"How many, and whose colours do they wear?"

"They wear red and black. Their banner is a falcon sitting on two crossed swords, a white halo around it, on a black background."

Jacob moved to the boy. "Let me take a look at that." He parted the sleeve where it was sliced and looked at the wound. Laying his hand on the laceration, Jacob closed his eyes.

The boy cried out, "Ouch! What are you doing?" He tried to move away, tried to pull Jacob's hands off with his free hand, tears welling in his eyes, but Jacob held him still for another ten count.

"It is done. Your arm is all better now."

The boy looked at his arm, rubbed it with his hand. The look he gave Jacob held reverence touched with fear. "Th-thank you."

"Don't thank me, thank Ephrestine. It is her gift I have used. I am shelon, and we are not to be feared as you have been taught." Jacob turned and eyed the king. "I fear you have done my race an injustice, King Orlon. I know it was not of your creation, but you have encouraged a long-held false belief with your silence."

"It was in part because of your mother, Jacob, and your aunt, Queen Valtice, although yes, it was easier on me to do so." The king chuckled. "Don't look so shocked. I am the king. It's my job to know what's going on around me. Ask them about it when you return home, and send them my regards. I will be sure to give yours to Ephrestine, may she guide and protect us."

Addy realised her mouth was hanging open. *Oh, what a secretive person he is. Royalty? Shit!* Addy glared at Jacob. *How many other secrets does he keep?* Would she reach Nerine and find he had a wife and six children?

Jacob gave a brief nod. "Thank you, King Orlon. I will let them know."

Kerwyn placed his palm on his father's shoulder. "Your Highness—"

"Please call me father, just one more time."

Kerwyn cleared his throat, his cheeks flushed. "Father … the banner represents Lord Tensony and Lord Hetford. If the boy's description is accurate, and we all can see the halo represents the seekers and Radnok." Kerwyn turned his head to spit on the ground. "May he rot in Var's halls."

"We don't have the numbers to defeat them. Both lords have sizeable support. Seems I didn't know as much as I should. Of course, there was always going to be resistance to my decision, but I didn't expect this." The king shook his head.

"You must leave now, my son." Orlon paused to smile. "Go with them, Comlyn. You are my son's advisor now. With most of my troops divided between north and south keeps, we are sorely undermanned. Our long-held peace is at an end. We may have lost Courbel, but we have not lost Treloah. Kerwyn, it's up to you now. You are the true king of this nation, but you must escape to Nerine. They will help you. Return and aid Captain Rondessy as soon as you can. May Ephrestine be with you." The king pulled Kerwyn down and kissed his forehead before whispering something and releasing him.

"Now, my wife and I have somewhere to go. The most exciting adventure for us yet, isn't it, my love?" The king turned to the slumbering woman, but she didn't answer.

When Kerwyn turned to leave, Addy saw tears in his eyes, his composure fractured. He stopped. "Please come with us, Father." He pivoted around to face the king. "I can't leave you here to be slaughtered. I won't."

Sorrow and regret softened the king's face. "You must. This country needs new blood. I am tired, son. I'm sorry we didn't get more time together, but I did what had to be done. I've always loved you, and I'm sorry I wasn't there for you. I will carry that love with me into the next life. It's up to you now, King Kerwyn."

Kerwyn stared at Orlon, Kerwyn's shoulders drooping.

Jacob gripped Kerwyn's shoulder. "Ephrestine's speed, King Orlon." Jacob bowed. "Come on, Your Highness." The shelon manoeuvred Kerwyn around, gently guiding him to the door.

"Thank you, King Orlon. It's been an honour." Addy bowed and joined her friends who filed out the door.

Comlyn had leaned over the king's bed as they left. They waited for him in the outer reception room. Finally, he appeared, his expression bewildered, tears shining on his cheeks in the firelight, his mouth closed, lips pressed firmly together. He grabbed and donned a peacock-blue coat that he must have thrown onto the couch before he had entered the king's bedroom. He took gloves from his pockets and slid them on.

Kerwyn confronted the captain, his voice terse. "So, you're just leaving him here?"

"Those were his orders. I don't like them any more than you do, but while he still lives, he's the man I obey." If the captain felt uncomfortable about the decision to leave Orlon to be slain by Radnok's forces, he didn't show it. He was displaying leadership. Addy didn't envy him, but she respected his commitment to his king's wishes.

"We must take him with us." Kerwyn's hands were on his hips as he loomed over Rondessy.

The captain shook his head, and Comlyn broke the silence with a quiet voice, full of regret but steadfast. "He wants to die with his wife. She is not well enough to travel and does not have long left. Without her, he would be lost. Those are his wishes. After everything he's done for our country, he deserves this much. Besides, how long do you think he'll survive out there, in the bitter cold? We have little chance of outrunning the enemy forces as it is. Speaking of which, we need to leave. Now."

Addy placed a hand on Kerwyn's arm. "We'll serve King Orlon best if we do as he asks. We're with you, Your Highness."

"Thank you, Addy, but can you not call me that? I prefer just plain Kerwyn, especially from you and Jacob." Kerwyn took a deep breath. "Okay, then, you all win. Let's go."

As much as Addy avoided physical contact with most people, she longed to give him a hug and tell him it would be all right. He needed his wife. He needed his children. Where were they? Did they know they were royalty? Addy suffered a jolt of panic that vibrated inside her chest. That meant they were in even more danger. Addy whispered to Kerwyn, "What about your wife and children — where are they?"

Kerwyn stared at Addy for a moment. "I can't tell you until we reach Nerine, but Orl ... my father has told me where they are and has assured me they will be safe. The fewer people who know, the better."

"Okay," Addy said as she made her way to the door.

Captain Rondessy took a torch from the wall and led the way into the hall. Addy's tired body tensed, on alert. After what Jacob had said, she would only draw power reluctantly. Once she was on her horse and had her bow in hand, she would feel safer.

The empty hallway echoed with distant sword clangs and muffled shouting. The enemy were still occupied downstairs, but if an army waited outside, they had little hope of even making it to the stables, let alone over the drawbridge and away. The men kept looking behind, the tension of expecting an attack causing Addy to clench her jaw.

The captain led them into a reception chamber and study, and the captain stopped in the latter. Bookshelves lined two walls, and a third wall was home to a small onyx fireplace, the black stone dull in the muted light of a single torch.

Comlyn navigated around a small table near one bookshelf and bent, feeling along the book spines.

Addy's brow creased. "You can't take books, ah, Comlyn. We don't have enough space in our saddlebags." *What in Var's anus is he doing?*

"Don't worry, Mistress, I'm not taking any books." He paused then found what he was looking for. "Ah." He pulled at a book. *Click.*

Oh! Standing where one wall of bookshelves met the wall with the fireplace, Captain Rondessy pushed on a shelf. A section of wall moved inward. *A secret door.*

"That's unexpected," Addy said quietly.

"And that's the whole point," said Jacob, his smile smug.

"Well, obviously." Addy rolled her eyes almost hard enough that she thought she'd injure herself. On the other side of the shelves was a dark tunnel. Captain Rondessy's torch illuminated enough for them to see they would only fit in single file, the floor sloping downward. The torch burned the cobwebs ahead as they started forward. Addy wished she'd grabbed a torch too, but it took all her strength to keep walking. "Does anyone want a sword?" It was heavy, and she didn't have a scabbard for it. Her fingers ached, and every now and again shooting pains danced across her hand.

Right behind her, Jacob said, "Keep it. You might need it before we're done here." He had leaned in close, and his warm breath on her ear made her shiver. *Oh, gods, why does he make me feel this way?* She longed for him to wrap his arms around her. *Argh, stop it! What in all the hells is wrong with you, idiot?* Her focus returned to her aching hand and arm.

She wanted to turn and complain, tell him how tired she was, but what was the point? Either she dropped the weapon or she kept it; neither called for commentary. Picturing what might happen if they managed to reach their horses, she decided keeping it was better. Her bow was good if she had space, but what if she was in close quarters with mounted foe? The disadvantage would be all hers.

Shadows bounced off the walls, distorted copies of Addy and the men. The stone walls rose to a low curved ceiling, and it was as if the stone closed in on them. Addy felt their enemy's presence as if she were prey. Her heart raced, and she reached out to touch the wall to ground herself in a reality that was hard to grasp in this nowhere place in between the castle walls.

Illumination came from behind Addy, and she smiled. It was the yellow-hued light she had often seen bobbing above Jacob's hand.

"You'll have to teach me that sometime."

"We'll have plenty of time on our way to Nerine, Little Rose."

She hated that name, but when he said it, luscious warmth spread through her stomach. She had never liked roses. They were pink — okay, some were red, but she had only ever seen pink ones. They were the flower Radnok had given her mother when he was trying to make things up to her, which had seemed like every other week when Addy was young. Not only that, but everyone said pink was a girl's colour, meaning it was a colour for the weak, for the sweet. Addy wanted to be strong. Pink was not her colour; she preferred blue or green. Even grey was better than pink. And as for being some long-awaited heroine who was supposed to save the world.... *Yeah, right.*

They had walked down the ramp-like passageway for so long, Addy thought they must be below ground level by now. What was happening above? Was the king still alive? How much had he told Kerwyn? What must Kerwyn be feeling at this moment; his whole world had shifted to the realms of fantasy. Where was Radnok? Now was not the time to ask anything. The shuffle of their feet against the stone floor, and the occasional cough were the only sounds accompanying their flight. Everyone kept close counsel with their own thoughts.

The gradient finally evened out. The cool, lifeless air held the secrets of the dead, of those long buried, the ones who only had scuttling beetles and worms for company.

Addy whispered, "Are we nearly there?" Even that sounded too loud. Was the enemy listening?

Captain Rondessy answered, "Yes. Just around the next corner, we'll turn to the right, and we're almost there."

"Does Radnok know about these secret passageways?" Addy asked.

Comlyn answered, his voice quiet yet confident. "No, at least I didn't tell him, and I know King Orlon never did. Not many know of these tunnels, or what would be the point of having them? They're here for such a time as this. For times of war."

Someone let out a sobering breath in a *whoosh*, and Addy shivered.

So this was it — the war Kerwyn and Jacob told her was coming, and she hadn't believed them. *Maybe it's not the war they thought. Maybe it's coincidence.*

Her faith was being called into question. She believed Ephrestine did exist, especially since she didn't have to disbelieve in Telouse in order to acknowledge the goddess. Could Addy really be important to Venturan's survival? That didn't seem possible. What could be happening that would require Addy, or the amazing Addy-Rose person, to do something no one else could? She wasn't amazing; she wasn't skilled at anything thousands of others weren't; she wasn't special. *Even if Ephrestine does exist, they're wrong about me. I can't even wipe that smear-of-shit Radnok from the world. And I'm damaged, so ridiculously used, no one could ever want me for anything.*

When they made the right turn, brightness beckoned from the end of the corridor, and the pungent odour of horse manure reached them. A warm sensation shot through Addy, her senses on alert. She hoped it was their horses waiting for them and not enemies with swords.

Rondessy stopped and passed his torch to the soldier behind him. He motioned for everyone to stay where they were and be silent. Jacob's yellow-tinted light extinguished. The captain snuck quietly towards the light at the end of the hallway.

Addy rested her sword tip on the ground and counted her breaths. The moments seemed stretched out. Torture was what it was. Had they made it this far only to be ambushed so close to freedom?

Addy jumped at a touch on her person; Jacob had curled the fingers of one hand around her waist. His thumb rubbed her lower back soothingly, his heat burning through the many layers of her clothes to the sensitive skin beneath.

What in all the hells is he doing that for? Was he playing games, or was it meant to just calm her? Whatever he was trying to do, he was stoking a fire in her she didn't want, a fire that would burn her to an ashen husk in the end. Nothing good could come of her lust for him; it would end in rejection or she would get what she wanted only to have him treat her like shit later. *As nice as he seems, he is a man. Never forget that, Addy.*

She focused on the ache in her sword arm and tried to ignore his hand.

Rondessy's silhouette, now at the end of the corridor some forty feet away, paused before disappearing around the corner. Addy counted her breaths again, *one pig, two pigs, three pigs* ... tightening her aching fingers around the sword hilt. A horse whinnied up ahead. Was that Charger?

The captain's voice filtered down the hall — calm, talking-to-animals sounds. Then he appeared at the doorway. "All's clear. Come and claim your mounts."

It felt as if everyone exhaled at once. Addy smiled. She was going to be reunited with her beautiful horse. Mistress

Hanover had done well. Addy wished she could thank her and hoped Radnok's traitors hadn't slaughtered her.

The passageway opened to a large room with a curved ceiling. Torches along two walls cast homely yellow light, and straw covered the ground. Two groomsmen attended to their horses. Addy's, Kerwyn's, and Jacob's were there, as were four others — horses probably meant for Kerwyn's family. Curiosity tickled her tongue, but she knew Kerwyn wasn't going to tell her where they were. At least it seemed they were alive.

Kerwyn took the reins for his mount. "These others are spare horses, Captain. Comlyn, you'll need one. Pick whichever you want," he said, his voice monotone, defeated. Kerwyn addressed Rondessy. "You're welcome to the others. We won't be needing them."

"Thank you, Prince Kerwyn." The captain gave a small bow. "I can't call you king until tomorrow, until I know King Orlon is dead."

"You'll get no argument from me, Captain. I didn't ask for this." Kerwyn frowned, ran a hand over his face and rubbed his eye. He took the crown from his head and made space in his saddlebags. "This won't be of any use where we're going."

Addy thought she knew a little of how Kerwyn felt — being burdened with news about yourself you couldn't quite believe. At least he had proof — the king's word, no less, and he had the crown. What proof was there that Addy was The Rose of Nerine, other than the ramblings of a stupid prophecy? Her aura might just be a benign light, not a sign that she was Venturan's saviour.

Addy sighed, grabbed Charger's reins, patted his nose, and made kissing noises. The horse bent his head so she could kiss his nose. "You gorgeous boy. I've missed you. Mistress Hanover took good care of you, didn't she?" Addy checked her saddle packs and retrieved her gloves. As she was about to put them on, she had a good look at her hands. A thin layer of dried blood tarnished her palms and the backs of her hands. Dark maroon crusts sullied the underside of where her fingernails grew over the tops of her fingers.

Brushing hair away from her face, she noticed the strands were stiff and smelled like smoke from burning bodies. She wanted a bath, wanted to scrub the death away, but instead, they would be riding in driving snow, hoping Radnok's men weren't right behind them, ready to strike. At least Addy and her two friends had survived thus far.

Addy checked Charger's saddle and looked over his back at Jacob. The shelon returned her gaze, his focus intense. *Is that an angry look for ignoring him or a questioning look?* As if fighting one war weren't enough. She didn't have the energy to argue with him, and her heart ached, knowing he was probably unhappy with her. She should look away, but she was drawn to him in a way she couldn't explain or ignore. His mouth finally relaxed, the fire leaching out of his blue eyes until they just looked sad. All she wanted was to go to him, but only pain would follow her down that path.

She eventually broke their connection under the guise of adjusting her stirrup, the loss of their connection reverberating through her heart. Sighing, she decided to figure it out later, because, right now Kerwyn, who had grabbed a torch from the wall, was leading his horse into the next passageway, following Captain Rondessy's lead.

They soon came to a fork in the tunnel. "This is where my men and I leave you, Comlyn, Your Highness. Follow that passage." With a jerk of his head, he indicated the right-hand tunnel. "And you'll reach a cave that faces north. Once we reach our destination, I'll send you a bird. We're headed south, to the keep at Querse. May Telouse protect you and guide your way." Forgoing an emotional goodbye, he walked to the left, his men trailing behind.

Kerwyn veered into the right-hand tunnel, Addy behind, with Comlyn and Jacob at the rear. Addy counted as they walked, since no one was in the mood to talk. Would it take 100 counts to reach the exit or 200? Was King Orlon being murdered right that moment? Addy bit her lip and dug her nails into the leather reins. *Argh, stop thinking stupid things.*

Addy's counting reached 300 before the floor began an incline. A wisp of cold air slid past her face indicating they were nearing the exit. Addy breathed in the sharp, clean smell of snow.

Nervous, she itched to draw on her power, but that would be foolish as exhaustion weighed down her limbs. Would their enemy be waiting?

The air grew colder, the gentle stir becoming a constant breeze. Charger snorted, and the horses' hooves clopped a steady, slow rhythm. Their torchlight didn't reach more than ten feet ahead, and Addy almost tripped when the floor changed from smooth stone to uneven ground.

She found herself in a small cave where dirt and dead leaves, borne by the wind, chased each other in small circles. Addy shivered. Once they had all exited the tunnel, they stopped to listen. Wind moaned outside, occasionally whistling when a stronger gust entered the cave — a haunting melody to accompany the newly deceased, of whom there were too many, on their journey.

Kerwyn held up his hand, and Addy nodded, knowing he wanted her to stay put. The newly crowned king gave his reins and the torch to her and approached the cave mouth, some fifteen feet away. One of the horses stomped a hoof. The muted sound made Addy jump, but was immediately snatched by the wind.

Addy swallowed hard as she watched Kerwyn. He had reached the far wall and pressed his back against it. *Shouldn't Jacob or I being doing that? Surely the king shouldn't be putting himself at risk.* This change in their roles was so new that Addy wasn't sure of the protocol they should follow. Hadn't the king said Jacob's aunt was the Queen of Nerine? *I'm surrounded by royalty.* After tonight, she had better start helping more, putting herself in harm's way to protect her friends.

Kerwyn's sword made no sound as he slowly drew it before he inched towards the opening. When he reached the edge of the cave mouth, he crouched and peered out. Then he carefully stepped into the darkness.

Her jaw ached from clenching it, and she held her breath. Waited. Listened.

One ... two ... three ... four.... Addy counted and quietly released a breath then took another. Her mouth filled with saliva, and she swallowed again.

Shit, why didn't I untie my bow? Too late now.

Kerwyn finally re-entered the cave, brushing snow from his head and shoulders. When he reached them, Addy relaxed at his relieved smile. The worry lines that had marred his face the past few days had smoothed away. "I don't want to curse our luck, but there's no sign of Radnok's forces, or anyone for that matter. There's a cottage two hours' ride of here. We're going there to quickly clean up, eat, and drink our last hot beverage. After that we'll have a ten-day ride over the mountains to the harbour. But as soon as daylight comes, Radnok will be on our trail, and eventually we'll be passing through enemy territory. Lord Hetford's keep is at the base of the mountains on the other side, and there is no way to avoid the area. There's only one safe way through. At least our tracks will be covered while the snow falls."

Jacob moved to stand next to Addy. "Sounds good to me. Ah, just a question. How would you like to be addressed? King Kerwyn, my king, Kerwyn?"

The forehead lines returned, and Kerwyn flinched. His voice held a sharp tone Addy wasn't about to ignore. "I said before, Kerwyn will be fine."

Comlyn cleared his throat and waited until he had Kerwyn's attention before he spoke. "You're going to have to claim the title at some point. Our soldiers will be fighting for you. If we want to rally our troops and reclaim Courbel, we need to follow someone."

Kerwyn's fist clenched. "No one is going to be rallying behind me any time soon. I'm committed to going to Nerine. Besides, I'll need Queen Valtice's help defeating Radnok. By the time we get there, he will have forced others to support him. Each day that passes will bring him more strength."

Comlyn replied, "We will need our king back eventually. Just don't leave it too late, *King* Kerwyn." The advisor raised one brow and folded his arms.

Addy had to admire Comlyn; he was certainly determined.

"Addy?" Jacob touched her arm, diverting her attention. "Can we talk for a moment?" There was no fight in his voice as she had expected, but something more like hope registered to her ear.

"Oh, okay."

Kerwyn eyed them. "Make it quick."

Addy and Jacob nodded.

The shelon moved far enough away from the others so their conversation would remain private. Addy followed reluctantly, afraid of what he might say.

When they found a spot to talk, Jacob stared into Addy's eyes. *Why does he have to be so damn handsome?* She wanted to reach up and run a thumb along his bottom lip and only just stopped herself in time. If he didn't say something soon, she was definitely going to do something she would regret.

Luckily, Jacob finally spoke. "Where do you stand with Ephrestine and who you are?"

"I don't know. I believe I have powers that others don't, and I can't explain where they come from, but whether it means I'm The Rose of Nerine, I can't say. Let's just say, I'm exploring my new relationship with Ephrestine."

Jacob bit his top lip. "Addy, I need you to believe in who you are. How are you going to commit to what's needed if you don't?"

"I'll find a way. I promise." She wanted to, she really did, but changing a lifetime of believing things were one way and having to do a total about face wasn't easy.

"Please, Addy. You've already come so far. Learning how to hide your aura is a skill rarely accomplished by a novice, yet you did it, which tells me you're strong in the gift. Please believe me. A lot of lives are depending on you. Your life is at risk too. The power you've wielded so far is nothing compared to what's needed, and the only way you'll achieve it is to totally commit to Ephrestine and accept who you are, what you are."

She shook her head and looked at him. She wanted to tell him that the world was about die in that case, but there was no point antagonizing him. "I said I'll find a way, okay?"

"Okay, but please, for me?" He tilted his head, waiting for her answer. She nodded, and his small smile was her reward. "There's one other thing. Are we still friends?"

"Of course. At least, I think we are. Why?"

"I thought I might have done something to upset you … in the tunnel. I just wanted to make sure we were okay."

Addy huffed. "No, it's just that, well, I wasn't expecting you to touch me. It took me by surprise. It seemed a bit intimate for a *friend*."

"Well, I didn't mean anything by it — I thought you might be scared. Sorry if I gave you the wrong impression. I care about you, Addy, but like a sister, you know?" This was an about-face she should have expected. *Men.* What about their kiss in the practice room? And the way he currently gazed into her eyes was not the way one would look at one's sister, at least she thought it wasn't. Unless … maybe it was in his country.

At the risk of offending him, or maybe wanting to offend him after his confusing signals, Addy asked, "Do people have sex with their siblings in Nerine?" His words said one thing, his actions another. There was something he wasn't telling her, but even knowing his secrets were holding him back was not enough to stop sharp pain scoring her heart.

Jacob's mouth fell open, and his brows drew down in disgust. "What? Of course not. That's sick. What's wrong with you?"

"*Sorry*. I don't know what you do over there. I thought…. Anyway, it doesn't matter what I thought. Friends, *Prince* Jacob?" Addy lifted her chin and folded her arms, hoping she'd make him feel guilty. "I wonder what other things you've lied about."

He blushed and folded his arms as well. "I didn't lie. I just didn't tell you everything. You didn't need to know."

"Lying by omission. It's nice to know I have a friend who doesn't trust me."

"I'm sorry, Addy. I'll tell you my story later if you like, but for now, know that I am your friend."

She narrowed her eyes. *See, Addy, you were right not to trust him.*

He reached up and ran the back of his fingers down her cheek in a very un-brotherly way. "I like you much better without the beard."

Addy couldn't be more perplexed if she tried. "Nice way to change the subject, *Prince* Jacob. I think we should go. Kerwyn looks like he's about to wet his pants."

Jacob turned and they watched Kerwyn lean from foot to foot, obviously eager to leave.

Addy walked to Charger, buttoned her coat, and pulled her hood over her head before she mounted her horse. The more she thought about who everyone around her was turning out to be and who she was supposed to be, the more it scared her. If she really was The Rose of Nerine, she didn't know herself at all. What sacrifices would she have to make, other than the one she already had? If it wasn't for her promise to Jacob, Addy would have stayed and found a way to finally kill Radnok, but she was leaving things undone. It didn't sit well with her.

And there was something else that had been on the edge of her mind since she had first been told she was The Rose. That ungraspable feeling of pre-cognizance she had carried around with her finally revealed itself, and she understood why she didn't want to believe in who or what they said she was.

It went back to when she was eleven, just before Radnok had started abusing her. She had had a nightmare in which she had been on her hands and knees, alone — so lonely — and surrounded by death and decay, the air clouded with pink-tinged smoke and dust. Her hands and forearms had been buried in the ground, and as she had pulled and strained to free herself, sweat poured down her face, the salty fluid stinging her eyes. She had screamed out in frustration and fear, her sobs finally choking her into silence.

She had known she needed to run. Run fast. *It* was coming. It had killed everyone else because she had failed, and now It wanted her. Pink light glowed around her, and when she examined it through her tears, it was not just around her — it was coming *from* her.

The terror — monster, demon? — drew closer. Dust blocked her nose and caked in her throat, making her cough. Her fingertips burst in searing pain. She couldn't see them, but she had known, as one did in dreams, that her blood was running through her fingers into the ground. Pain squeezed her as she was sucked dry, dizziness becoming all she was. Just before she shut her eyes, the pink glow around her had flickered, dulled.

In the moment before her dream-self had died, It arrived. It spoke to her, each sound it uttered was a brand burned into her soul. "Adrastine, Rose of Nerine, you have failed."

And then It laughed.

Addy jerked in her saddle, becoming aware. They had left the cave, and she hadn't noticed. Snow gusted in droves around her, thick flurries sweeping across her path, Charger's mane and eyelashes white with it.

She shrank further into her coat, until only her nose protruded, but she couldn't escape the biting cold, because the chill puckering the skin under her coat didn't come from the grim night.

The chill came from deep within her soul.

She was The Rose.

They were all going to die.

Chapter Twenty-six

Radnok took the steps two at a time, ignoring the dead bodies sprawled upon them. Four guards trailed him — two his seekers and two Lord Tensony's men. Radnok stopped at the top of the sweeping staircase and turned around, enjoying the view. This magnificent staircase with its carved timber banister was his. That chandelier hanging above the foyer was his. The men he could hear talking at the entry doors were his. The whole castle was his. He smiled. The city was his.

Except for one small detail.

Turning again, he strode along the hallway. His grin pushed the apples of his cheeks high enough that they encroached on his vision. He should have bathed and changed for his final act of victory, but he couldn't wait. This whole becoming-king thing had drawn out all his patience, and he would enjoy what he was about to do whether he was clean or dirty.

Radnok took a moment to appreciate the feel of the cool air on his face as he marched down the hall. He nodded to one of the portraits as he passed — King Horain the Second, dead for 270 years, and the only king during the past 500 who had ruled as Radnok would — with total, unsympathetic control.

At the end of the hallway, he stopped in front of a yellow-hued timber door. A white vase, blue vines and flowers decorating the swell of porcelain, stood on a marble plinth. Radnok picked it up and caressed the smooth, cold surface. He had always liked this piece.

And now it was his.

Radnok carefully placed it back on its stand and faced the slightly open door, which he pushed all the way open to reveal King Orlon's private sitting room. *My private sitting room.* Satisfaction warmed him from his fingertips to his toes. He motioned for his guards to wait then entered the royal bedroom alone.

Ugh, old-person smell. Radnok reached the bed and gazed down at King Orlon and Queen Verella. The high seeker tilted his head to the side, observing. *This is going to be too easy.*

Radnok tapped the king's forehead with two fingers. Orlon opened his eyes, recognition but not surprise on his face. "Ah, Radnok, I was wondering when you would arrive."

Radnok narrowed his eyes, his smile banished in favour of a tight-lipped frown. What was the king playing at? The seeker looked around, making sure this wasn't an ambush, before he met the king's gaze again. "So calm, Orlon? Not many are as brave as you."

Orlon smiled. "My wife has beaten me to the other side. I would do it myself, but I haven't the strength. If you wouldn't mind hurrying it up, I'm missing her."

Confusion roiled within Radnok. How dare Orlon ruin the pleasure of his victory with utter apathy? "How can you be so calm? You've lost your kingdom."

The king's serene tone grated on every nerve Radnok possessed, setting the seeker's eye to twitching. "Have I, traitor? My son, the true king of Treloah, has only just begun on his path, and he will return to reclaim that which was so falsely taken. Make no mistake, seeker, your time here is but temporary. Even had I no son, I never would have chosen you. Your heart is malformed, shaped by malignant desires. I regret that it took me so long to realise. By the time your depravity was obvious, I feared confronting you would start a war. How right I was. I'm paying in the blood of my people for that misstep. Now, hurry up, *seeker*, I have somewhere to be."

Orlon tilted his head back, apparently waiting for Radnok's knife.

Radnok pulled a shiny object from his pocket. *Seeker?* "I'll teach you, you pathetic excuse for a king. I'll send you on your way, but not until we've had a little fun." Radnok slid the ridged steel ring over the fingers of his right hand, where its coldness settled comfortably over his knuckles. He flexed his fingers, admiring the one-inch spikes protruding from each of the high points atop his knuckles.

"I think I'll start here," Radnok said as he drew his arm back and punched Orlon's cheek.

The king cried out, and Radnok punched him again, breaking the king's nose, blood spattering on the sheets. Orlon's laboured wheezing breaths sent a spurt of joy through Radnok. *This is more like it.* When he was done, the king's brain would be joining the blood on the bedding.

Drawing his arm back again, Radnok's smile returned, and this time, his smile was there to stay.

Chapter Twenty-seven

Naked, her long legs lazily stretched out in front of her, Lilliana reclined on her temporary bed, smoking cranak while awaiting her husband. She drew smoke deep into her lungs. Drug-induced serenity and happiness unfurled eager tentacles, seducing Lilliana with irresistible oblivion.

She blew out and watched the smoke rise, up, up, up until it reached the ornate ceiling, dark timber beams intersecting, the straight lines framing exquisite artwork of deer grazing, birds singing, and nymphs playing naked in fields. Lilliana looked at herself and giggled. *Maybe I'm a nymph.* She stood on the bed and took another drag of the barunt — the dried paper holding cranak within its rolled-up form.

Euphoria shut her eyes and made her smile. She danced and swivelled her head from side to side, her long hair loose and swinging into her face. Stretching one arm into the air, she swayed, imagining herself to be a willow tree, a heartsick willow tree. Why was the tree sad? Because it had lost its children.

Lilliana stopped swaying and bent from the hips, dangling her head and arms towards the bed. Then she dropped to the mattress, collapsing and curling into a ball. Her barunt had fallen from her fingers. Crying, she rocked back and forth.

A detached part of her mind, a part that had escaped the effects of the cranak, asked, *Are you crying because you lost the cranak, or because you lost your children?*

My children. My beautiful, precious children. They're gone. I failed. I'm a sick whore. I deserve to die. I want to die. Please....

Lilliana wept so hard she shook, her face wet with tears, mucus from her nose running into her mouth.

Why don't you find them? the voice asked.

I can't. My husband would never let me. One is dead anyway. He killed him, my baby boy. He tore him from my womb, and now I'm barren. Please, please let me die. Ephrestine, if you can hear me, please take my pain away. I don't have the strength to do this by myself. Lilliana grabbed a handful of her own hair, trying to tear it from her head.

She screamed.

Lilliana's screams lasted until exhaustion claimed her, and she fell into the blessed oblivion of sleep. She woke to the sound of the bedroom door closing. She opened crusty eyes and rubbed them to clear out the grit of sleep.

"Keeping busy, I see." Radnok stood next to the bed, gazing down at her. "You look like a common whore, not the queen I deserve." He knelt one knee on the bed and slapped her across the face then grabbed her arm and yanked her to her feet. "The castle's safe now. Go and bathe, clean the whore away. Make yourself presentable."

He had pulled her so close their noses were almost touching. His dark eyes flickered with madness and brutality. He blinked, and Lillian saw his temper cool to lust. He licked his lips. "One thing, before you go." He slammed his lips onto hers, invaded her mouth with his tongue while one hand grabbed her breast. He squeezed hard, and Lilliana tried not to flinch. She whimpered from the pain.

He turned her around and bent her over, pushing her head towards the bed. His clothes rustled as he removed his pants, and then he grabbed her hair and entered her from behind.

Lilliana bit her lip and grabbed the bed sheets, tears streaming down her face. The chant of *no, no, no, no* inside her head would never be voiced aloud. She had done it once and suffered a broken arm for her troubles. *This is no way to live. If your mother could see you now.... Radnok's right; you are a whore.*

When this is done, I'm going to the top of the tower. It's time to end your miserable life.

No, Lilliana, you are not a whore, and it is not time to end your life. You have lost your way, my child. A soft, loving voice had entered her mind, and pink light suffused the room.

Cranak didn't last that long, so why was she hallucinating?

You are not imagining this, my child. Your daughter needs you.

Lilliana shook her head. *No. She hates me. She's better off without me.*

Go to her, if you want to live.

My life is not worth holding onto. I want to die.

If you abandon your child again, Adrastine will fail. Become the shelon you were born to be. Know that I love you, Lilliana. You are special, but this man has made you forget who you are. Find yourself again, my child. Love asks us to walk the precarious paths we fear, but those paths are the ones that lead to happiness and fulfilment. You cannot appreciate how deep the ocean is until you have sunk to the bottom of its depths. And you cannot savour the panorama of the valley until you have scaled the mountain.

The rosy haze lifted from the room, and Lilliana felt alone. Ephrestine was gone, if indeed it had been her. The sound of skin slapping together and an occasional grunted sigh from Radnok punctuated Lilliana's loud breaths. She wanted to block her ears. Lilliana desperately needed to escape his foul, invading presence and the pain every thrust caused as he embedded himself deep within her.

Radnok held her hips tightly, keeping her still and close for a moment before pulling out. He dragged Lilliana up by her hair. "Now go clean yourself up, whore."

Lilliana didn't bother to wipe the tears from her face as she grabbed her robe from a chair. Radnok's semen ran uncomfortably down the inside of her legs. She would have a bath and put her robe back on, she decided, and then she would walk to the top of the tower. It was high enough. Maybe she would hold a dagger to her stomach to make sure.

Her fantasy visit from Ephrestine had almost persuaded her to live, to change her life; maybe it was the old Lilliana trying one last time to do something right. But she wasn't strong enough, wasn't good enough.

She would throw herself off, be done with it. At least Radnok wouldn't have the satisfaction of killing her himself — she could take that from him.

Lilliana neared the door, and a knock sounded.

Radnok, tying his belt in place, called out, "Enter."

One of Lord Tensony's men entered, his red-and-black vest marred with dark stains, and his hair carelessly coming loose from its braid. He hurriedly averted his gaze from Lilliana to look at Radnok.

Radnok tucked in his shirt. "Speak."

"Your Highness, we have found something of interest. We think we've found where Orlon's son and his friends escaped. There's a secret passageway in the study near King— Your bedchambers." The soldier blushed.

Lilliana held her breath waiting for Radnok to explode at the unintentional slight. Relief washed through her that her little girl was alive. But, Adrastine was outside in the snow. What if she froze to death? What if Radnok's men caught up with her?

Radnok pursed his lips and snorted out a breath. "Is anyone going after them?"

"Not yet. We wanted to obtain your orders first."

Radnok stalked over to the man and grabbed his ear, twisting it. "You morons are about as smart as pig intestines. Get after them now! Do whatever it takes. I want them caught. You can kill Kerwyn, but bring the girl back alive. If anyone harms her, they won't live to see another rotation of Venturan. Now go!"

Lilliana hastily followed the soldier out and shut the door, not wanting to watch the spectacular anger Radnok would exhibit when he lost his temper.

Her hand itched as she traversed the hallway. She turned her hand around to scratch her palm. And stopped in the middle of the hallway, nervousness fluttering in her belly.

What in Ephrestine's name?

In the middle of her left palm was the image of a dark pink rose, stem, thorns and all. Blood dripped from the bottom of the closed bud, clinging to the green stem to drip off the bottom. Lilliana furrowed her brow and raised her head to look at the ceiling. *Had Ephrestine's visitation been real?*

Certainty settled firm hands about her shoulders. The rose must represent Adrastine, and the tears.... Were they Ephrestine's tears or her daughter's? Her goddess must have been desperate to reach out to Lilliana — goddesses didn't communicate with mere humans. But she had.

The swirl of nervousness in Lilliana's belly quickened into a whirlpool that swelled within her until she thought she would vomit.

Adrastine needed Lilliana; her goddess needed her too. She was shelon; she wasn't some pathetic nobody who would be driven to take her own life by a narcissistic monster. Her beautiful, scared daughter was on the run, right now, out in the perilous weather.

Lilliana's heart pounded with fear and pain. What had she done to her daughter?

For the first time in many years, Lilliana saw clearly and knew what she must do. It was time to crawl free from her addiction and escape Radnok. It might take more determination and bravery than she had, but she would try. If she was going to die, let it be while trying to help her daughter.

She whispered to the ceiling, "I'm yours, Ephrestine. I did lose my way, but I'm back, and I'm ready."

Her trip to the baths had more purpose now. Her steps were sure, her back straight, and her head held high. She was nobody's whore, and she would gladly show Radnok how wrong he'd been. A plan was already forming. The first thing was to escape, and she already knew how. She was ready to climb that mountain … one step at a time.

And she had already taken the first one. Lilliana smiled and kissed the rose on her palm. *Baby girl, hang in there. Your mother is finally coming.*

Humid air tinged with sulphur enveloped Lilliana when she entered the baths and removed her robe. She stepped down into one of two large round pools, the steaming water embracing her as she slid all the way in and submerged her head.

The frozen cage that had trapped her emotions thawed. Drip by drip, the bars melted, freeing agony, regret, self-loathing and fear. Lilliana embraced them, let the torturous sensations fill her mind and her heart. Her sobbing echoed off the walls and turned into wailing as she faced the horror of who she had become, what she had done.

Every cuddle she had withheld from Adrastine, every desperate plea of her daughter's she had ignored, every time she had closed her eyes to Radnok's abuse of her daughter — she opened her arms to all of it. She invited her dark secrets into the light of her admission. Those secrets scratched and tore at the fabric of her being, destroying the barriers she protected herself with.

No longer suffocated by who she had been, but carrying the weight of regret and the desire for redemption, Lilliana leant her head back onto the mosaic-tiled wall of the pool, breathed out and savoured the caress of her last tear as it fell into the tepid water.

Lilliana splashed water onto her face, emerged from the pool and wrapped her robe around her wet body. Her mother had always said there was never as good a time as now. Lilliana nodded to herself and looked at the rose once more.

As she exited the baths and stepped into the cool hallway, she knew she would never take another drug again. Radnok had kept her from herself for far too long. It was time to reclaim her shelon powers.

It was time to go home.

Glossary of Names

Addy — Adrastine. The Rose of Nerine. Daughter of High Lady Lilliana and Radnok.

Archid — Var's chief representative on Venturan.

Baccus — Addy's foster father.

Captain Rondessy — captain of Orlon's army.

Comlyn — King Orlon's advisor.

Conran — Smarnus's advisor and lover.

Courbel — capital city of Treloah.

Dubreat — north western port city of Treloah.

Druce — the finicky god of luck.

Enyak — first advisor and friend to Queen Valtice of Nerine.

Ephrestine — the one goddess of Nerine.

High Lady Lilliana - Addy's mother, wife of Radnok.

High Mistress Sara — Valtice's sister, runs shelon academy in Nerine.

High Priest Tudos — friend of King Orlon and rival of Radnok.

Jacob — spy from Nerine and shelon magic user.

Jarmantin — western seaside town in Nerine where Queen Valtice first sees the damage of drained power.

Jorgan — eleven years old, and eldest son of Kerwyn.

King Felson — former king of Lachmond.

King Orlon — King of Treloah.

Lachmond — where Smarnus lives. The southern-most country of Venturan.

Lord Bronstein — Radnok's rival and friend to King Orlon.

Lord Panover — King Orlon's foolish cousin.

Lord Tensony — simpleton, cousin of King Orlon, ally of Radnok.

Marcern – North eastern port city in Treloah.

Marny — Addy's foster mother.

Mayna — Kerwyn's wife.

Meline — six-year-old daughter of Kerwyn.

Mistress Hannover — head of servants in King Orlon's castle.

Pyren — large town in the middle of Treloah, where Addy first tried to kill Radnok.

Queen Verella — Orlon's wife and queen of Treloah.

Querse — southern port city of Treloah.

Saken — eight-year-old son of Kerwyn.

Smarnus — Radnok's brother and new king of Lachmond.

Radnok's two rivals — Lord Bronstein and High Priest Tudos.

Telouse — the god Treloahns believe in.

Var – the universal god of the underworld. Considered to be evil.

Thank you, dear reader, for taking the time to read my book. I hope you enjoyed it. If you have the time and the inclination, would you be able to leave a review at the retailer where you purchased this book? Honest reviews help other readers choose their next book, and it helps authors find awesome readers. Thanks in advance!

Acknowledgements

Here I am again. It doesn't matter how many books you write, you never write a perfect first or second draft (or final draft for that matter), and you can never keep those pesky doubts from gnawing at your ankles. That's why there are always a few people to acknowledge.

To Ciara Ballintyne for walking alongside me and beating those doubts off with a sizable mallet. You always have wise feedback and helpful suggestions when I come crying to you. Your patience is noted, and I'll always be here to do the same if you need.

To my beta reader, Karina, thank you so much for your honest and insightful feedback. Your feedback helped me make Addy more of a woman and less of a whiny teenager. You can beta read for me any time you like (and, in fact, I'm counting on it).

My first content editor, Nerine, savaged my manuscript in a good way, and for that I am grateful.

To my cover artist, Robert Baird, you have outdone yourself. You've brought Addy to life in just the way I'd hoped. She has wagonloads of sass and attitude, so thanks.

Last, but not least (yes, Becky, I know that's a cliché), thank you to Becky for content edits and those wonderful line edits (you can never have too much editing). Your support and eagle eye have made this book something I can be proud of. I also appreciate the comments that had me laughing — I strongly believe that editors should have chocolate in one hand and a paddle in the other. You were liberal with both, so

I didn't feel overly tortured. Although my bottom was a bit sore by the end, the chocolate in my mouth soothed the sting.